BET YOU DON'T KNOW WHERE LORNA IS!

JACK JUDGE

WATTLE RUN PUBLISHING
PORTLAND, OREGON

BOOKS BY JACK JUDGE

FICTION

DEATH RIDES THE CAROUSEL
THE DEAD LIE RESTLESS IN PEDRO CREEK
BUGLER, PLEASE PLAY "TAPS" FOR BOBO
CROSETTI'S CURSE
I BET YOU DON'T KNOW WHERE LORNA IS!

NON-FICTION

MOJAC'S MEGAN
ANOTHER TIME, ANOTHER PLACE

CHILDREN'S

MIXED NUTS!

Judge, Jack
Bet You Don't Know Where Lorna Is!
Mystery: Fiction, Oregon locale, students, teachers, pets, seaports

Wattle Run Publishing
Portland, Oregon

Bet You Don't Know Where Lorna Is! Is a work of fiction. Any resemblance to actual persons living or dead is coincidental. All rights are reserved. No part of this book may be reproduced in any form by electronic or mechanical means unless permission is given by author or publisher.

Copyright © 2006, by Jack Judge
Publishing Date 2011
ISBN 978-1-4507-2112-7
First Edition

This one is for Steve Holloway, a friend who appreciates literature and still allows time to wade through my works!

This is also for the Monday Night gang: Dee, Don, Dwayne, Colette, Bob, Judy H., Susan, Sam, Judy W., Betty, Irwin, and my Mollie-O. Obviously, they haven't been punished enough!

Prologue:

"Class, as you know finals are a little over a week away. On each of your desks you will find a copy of the article I am about to read to you. It is similar to what will be coming your way on the final. Your assignment is to study the article and then write an essay comparing it to our current system of civic works here in the city of Salem. I want no less than one thousand words and you will have two days in which to complete it. Have it on my desk no later than Thursday. Thank you kindly for keeping the cheering down to a mild roar."

* * *

"An elderly Chinese woman had two large pots; each hung on the ends of a pole which she carried across her neck. One of the pots had a crack in it while the other one was perfect and always delivered a full portion of water. At the end of her long walk from the stream to the house, the cracked pot arrived only half full."

"For a full two years this was a daily event, with the woman bringing home only one and a half pots of water. Of course, the perfect pot was quite proud of its accomplishments, but the poor cracked one was ashamed of its imperfections, truly miserable that it could only do half of what it had been created to do. One day, after once again what it perceived as its duty had been a bitter failure, it spoke to the old woman gathering her daily amount of water from the stream:"

"'I am ashamed of myself because this crack in my side causes water to leak out all the way back to your house.'"

The old woman smiled. "Have you noticed that there are flowers on your side of the path, but not on the other pot's side? That's because I have always known about your flaw, so I planted flower seeds on your side of the path, and every day while we walk back, you water them. For two years I have been able to pick these beautiful flowers to decorate my table. Without you being just the way you are, there would not be this beauty to grace the house."

1

"Each of us has our own unique flaw, but it's the cracks and flaws we each have that makes our lives together so very interesting and rewarding. We must take each person for what they are and look for the good in them; you will find it is there."

* * *

I hear sounds, even though they are distant, so I know I'm awake, but I'm afraid to open my eyes. What is wrong with me? I don't remember what happened. I haven't been this frightened since I was a little girl and that Rottweiler chased me off the sidewalk into oncoming traffic! My Uncle Harry was there and saved me then. I still remember the feel of his strong arms as he yanked me to safety and kicked that vicious dog in the head. But, Uncle Harry is dead now.

Why is it so quiet in here? Is anybody there?

Why can't I remember? I am so terribly confused. I know we talked about her. When they told me she was suicidal and would only listen to me, I knew I had to help. They were very kind after we entered the house and offered me tea while we waited for her arrival. I don't remember talking to her though, or where I am now. Why can't I remember? Why is it so dark in here? Why can't I get off this bed? I feel weak and awfully woozy. Why doesn't anyone answer when I call? Frank, I need you! Please come and get me? I'm really frightened. Oh, why can't I remember?

* * *

II

1

My name is Danny Doyle and in the Detective world I'd be considered small potatoes by those Pinkerton boys. My case files only show numbers for the important ones. Take runaways for example, they usually require three or four hours of driving time and ten minutes to resolve. It isn't brain taxing to gather up and then throw a teenager on a bus. Same for chasing down the alimony ducking sleaze or doing a little skip tracing. So I only reserve numbers for the long, tough cases such as kidnapping, larceny or murder. Lorna D., number twenty-two, was one of the tough ones. Clues refused to surface. Witnesses failed to come forward. Cops and the FBI, with all their resources, kept coming up empty, too. For a while there, I wasn't even sure I had the smarts to solve it.

Seems like I've been a PI forever; you might want to compare me to that PI in San Francisco, except that he's a lot smarter. You know the one. He isn't slim and he isn't fat. He isn't young and he isn't old; at least, not real old. He doesn't give out with his name. Well, I can understand that. Once your name headlines a warrant it's much easier to run down good old Flimflam Fred than John Doe! We both hate to carry a gun, me and the guy in San Francisco. I can't hit much of anything with the damn things anyway. Fortunately, I have the support of two able partners. Maggie is the petite one. Usually immaculate on the job, her every hair will be in place. She is one female who never requires makeup and when she sashays up to a

JACK JUDGE

pickpocket, temptingly swinging her little behind, he'll never realize he's been had until she sets her teeth in an ankle. Maggie has well earned her badge and perpetrators had best hop a bus when she hoves into view.

Mandy's the gorgeous one: long, luxuriant black hair down to here, legs that go on forever and a magnificent chest. Her eyes, brown, limpid, and oh so expressive, make one consider that drowning would be a pleasure. Her inquisitive nose literally twitches when she's hot on the trail of a sleaze. Don't misunderstand, neither of my girls is a tease. But what the hell, what Ma Nature endows, she do endow. Who am I to argue with the old broad! Regardless, my colleagues do a great job watching out for me so who needs to carry a lethal weapon?

Maggie is the Jack Russell terrier. Mandy is the Border collie.

You may as well know I harbor a penchant for the running of the ponies. The Sport of Kings it's called. Well now, a fine Irish broth of a lad like myself certainly isn't into any of that blue-blood royalty crap, so I call it the Sport for All. Besides, until it's exposed to light, blood has no color and then it views red, not blue. So spare me Duke this, Duchess that, Sir this, and Dame that. Call me Dan, Daniel, Danny, or as my old man used to say, "Call me what you will, just don't call me late for dinner."

Outdoors, I'll bet you've had the good fortune to watch Mother Nature happily applying paint to one of her masterpieces. Directly the canvas is dry do you often eyeball your area for sign of anyone else likewise enthralled? Unobserved, do you quickly slip that painting behind your eyes? Not to steal, just to house it away for later viewing enjoyment during a wet winter. I do that with the Bangtails. Truly, a majestic painting to enjoy is when one is viewing the running of the blood horse. Ideally, there will be blue sky and

Bet You Don't Know Where Lorna Is!

a warm sun. A raked and graded track pictures elegant. Standing at the rail, entranced, one's eyes capture huge muscles as they bunch and flex. They delight in foaming mouths and free flowing tails. Horses swoosh by, hooves thundering. Saddle leather groans and jockeys yell, "Go, go, go!" An excited crowd roars. Ears back, nostrils flaring, the longshot desperately strives to make it a photo finish. Who dares deny the beauty of another Seabiscuit as, again, he wins going away? Beats a Van Gogh painting all to hell! Of course, money also changes hands at the same time and therein reposes the rub. The vaunted speedsters I usually choose, members in good standing of the "Equine Tuckered Club", are not seriously into running. In perfect contentment, while brothers and sisters happily run rapidly around the track, they settle for a leisurely stroll!

Additionally, if I spend too much time studying my track bible instead of tending to business the bank account never shows a bulge. Still, if not having to settle for just grits, we three usually manage the occasional dish of hash browns and eggs. That constant look of anguish on my kisser also took a short hike lately. It now rests—hopefully permanently—on the face of 'Beat the Odds' Clyde, my bookie. Last month, a winner at the track, I latched onto steaks for all and I even snagged a brew or two for me.

* * *

So okay my friend, we had that Kinkel kid offing his parents, two classmates, and wounding twenty-five more in May, 1998 at Thurston High in Springfield, Oregon. Include the Harris and Klebold kids knocking off thirteen and wounding twenty-four more in April, 1999 at the Columbine High School in Colorado; recently along comes another yo-yo, that Cho kid from South Korea, wasting thirty-two and wounding twenty-nine more, back

JACK JUDGE

on April 16, 2007 at Virginia Tech in Blacksburg. Why? How the hell do I know? The perps were and are all bona fide space cadets, and they surely qualify for retroactive birth control! But those with a mess of letters after their names will have to figure out the kids reasons. The only letters after my name read PI. I don't try to get into idiots heads or judge them. After they're convicted and given a lethal injection as a reward I don't shed any tears either; my job is to collar and bring 'em to justice. Occasionally I do.

I've heard a famous celebrity, now dead, once claimed he'd never met a man he didn't like. For a plain out fact he couldn't have been a detective. If you care to ask me I'll tell you about scumbags, con men, muggers, pimps, pushers and politicians that I meet every day. I don't like any of them!

I mostly operate right here in Oregon, the prettiest state in the Union when the sun is out which sometimes occurs for a month or two. I'm often called a private eye, a shamus, a peeper or a tin cop. I prefer the term, Private Detective. I'm willing to wallow in most capers but nothing illegal. I don't do divorce work, not since an over-painted blonde job jabbed a finger in my eye as I was snapping a color photo of her making whoopee with a young bozo. Her old man was out hustling for the weekly beans at the time.

You already know I work closely with my two canine pals Mandy and Maggie. Don't laugh. They work cheap, are a lot smarter than most people, I don't have to contend with pantyhose hanging in the shower, and they don't take up much room in my apartment. Maggie has learned to use a pencil to take notes. Her nose is so good she can follow a pair of dirty socks from one end of town to the other. Mandy is even smarter. I could use her to read a sleaze his rights if I was still on the force. There are no flies on either dog. Maggie weighs but a scant seventeen pounds, but it is all muscle. More than

Bet You Don't Know Where Lorna Is!

one fool's discovered she is quick and can jump five feet straight up. Many a torn nose proves it. Mandy once figured out in advance which four blocks a creep we were chasing was gonna run; by the time I caught up wheezing and staggering like Fat Willy, her teeth were halfway through the wrist that had held the gun and Maggie was sitting on his head nibbling on an ear! See what I mean about back-up and why I seldom need to carry a gun?

I bunk in Salem in a small apartment cum office on High Street, just off State. It isn't much, two rooms plus bathroom. Leaky faucets and rust from the shower. Doors lean, windows are warped and linoleum's cracked. I also have the first refrigerator to hit the market after the icebox. An old hot plate, a Braun coffee maker (I like good coffee and grind my own beans), Salvation Army dishes and GI silverware. If somebody taps the joint, they get nothing. The shower runs Hades hot or Arctic cold, no in between. I spared no expense and bought the best Motel Six towels and bedding. The bed is a vintage Mayflower bunk complete with rope for springs. Neither dog is allowed to bunk on it so one sleeps on the queasy chair, the other on my shoes. I say queasy because it has suffered over the years and starts to sag and roll even before rear ends aim for it. To sum up, a kitchen table that leans and two chairs with cracked seats complete the decor. What the hell, I only rent and the roof doesn't leak. At least it didn't last winter. Of course we only got around fifty-eight inches of splash during that wet period!

Everything in the office room sags including me. You want to know what I look like. I've allowed but one mirror in the joint and I close my eyes while shaving. Want more? Some say I am fat. They lie! You could say, I'm a wee touch robust. My hair started a disappearing act twenty-five years ago and now even gentle raindrops hurt. Wearing glasses I can usually spot

JACK JUDGE

the difference between red and green at intersections. I can run like a greyhound for at least thirty-five feet and bench press forty pounds without too much strain. I'm not married. I do have a friend though. We met in a bagel joint on State Street. Naturally it was raining and I figured coffee, cream cheese, and a bagel would help dispel incessant damp. She sat by herself looking wan and worried. One thing led to another and pretty soon we shared her table along with conversation. Seemed like the wan and worry was because she was single and being stalked in a frightening way; Middle of the night phone calls including heavy breathing but no voice; notes in her mail. "... You are mine; no one else will ever have you." It goes on and on, enough garbage to make you throw up, footsteps on pavement in the dark, but no one there. You know the routine. I told her what I did for a living and that I'd look into it. At that, she smiled for the first time. That smile definitely put cheer into a gray morning. Her hair, auburn, full and flowing to her waist, framed a pixie face which also read of strong character. Her legs were slim and like Mandy's went on forever. She was a find. I had to ask. "So how come you're not married?"

I got another slow smile and a shrug. "It's a long story, some day when I know you better, okay?"

For a week after that I kept an eye on her, especially her apartment which was in a cul-de-sac on Rural, just off South Commercial. Sure enough, on another Oregon drizzler, I spotted a guy creeping through the shadows toward her door. It was him. Maggie left her impression on his ankle. Mandy left her impression on his arse. I left my impression where he'd need dental work. I've since heard that once the scabs healed he moved to San Diego.

Bet You Don't Know Where Lorna Is!

Sandra Lee and I became good friends after that. We visit when we get lonely because, among other things, we also enjoy one another's company. After just one night on my rope springs she's opted to spend our special times at her place, or else! My pals are all for that as they grab the bed on my nights out. Maggie always hogs the pillow! Sandy's a great cook. Besides her terrific coffee, there's no rust in the shower, her bed has proper springs, and I don't trip over the linoleum. We get along fine and she baby-sits my pals for me when, chasing scuzz, I sometimes have to catch red-eyes. Maybe I should drop you a little background on me and what I do. Who knows, it may explain why I fumbled with the case for so long. All the mistakes kids usually make when growing up? I made 'em, too. I joined the Air Force after high school and met enough sleaze balls there to convince me justice only occurs when folks take time to care. I opted to become a cop upon discharge. Some of the good guys also turned out to be bad guys! That settled it for me, I needed a job where the responsibility for my actions and honesty were mine alone. I became a PI.

Let's face it, the way I make a living can be hazardous in the extreme. As you know, I have an aversion to guns and unless absolutely-save-my-life-necessity I refuse to carry one. Diplomacy is the tool I use the most and Mandy's bared teeth. As I'm my own boss, can pick and choose the jobs I want, and make enough to sustain the three of us comfortably, I usually enjoy my work. I did that is until I tied into that one particular bummer. Ya wanna hear about the puzzler, case number twenty-two? Okay, help yourself to a beer. As soon as I feed the mutts and make me a belt, I'll tell you more about it. Get comfy in that chair over there, don't interrupt, and listen carefully.

7

Lorna D. was a doozy of a case. I say it was a puzzler because I couldn't latch onto the motive. There is always a motive: greed, revenge, power, jealousy, divorce, fear of discovery. Believe me, it's gonna be there and once uncovered you're halfway home to nailing the perps. But this lady was a school teacher and appeared to have no enemies. Murder had to be a definite possibility but where was the corpus delicti? Adding to my flaming enjoyment, for days nary a flaming clue floated my way.

I gotta credit my teacher pal, Bernie. His take on the crime and knowledge about adolescents truly helped bring down real nasties. So, who is Bernie? Correct title reads Bernard. He is a retired academic. Being a schoolteacher, he is enamored of lectures, his! Hell of it is he knows what he is talking about. Most of us talk like we are tryin' to get around a mouth full of marbles, not Bernard. With him, vowels and consonants receive their proper due. He isn't a smarmy talker; it's only that when he speaks, if your own vocabulary is up to it, his pronunciation and choice of words will be spot on. Having recently worked with kids he is also fully versed in modern slang. Example: "all up in my grill." The act of being in someone's face: "Yo, you don't need to be all up in my grill unless you want me to flex you like a skeeze"; betty; a school term for a girl/lady; "Man, look at that fine lookin' Betty." Bernie knows 'em all and most of 'em I never heard of! In my line of work he's a handy guy to have around. Many a puzzlement as to how kids of today act and think has been a piece of cake to solve, for him.

So, who is Bernie? Why, he's a valued friend and budding amateur detective, one I'm most fortunate to have.

* * *

This case began as most of mine do with my office door squalling open.

2

It all started out so innocently. Remember in the movie *Double Indemnity* a wounded Walter Neff (Fred MacMurray), using a dictaphone in the insurance office, is confessing murder to Barton Keyes (Edward G. Robinson); how for him it had also started out so innocently? Mind, I haven't committed murder but the caper I was involved in started out the same way poor old Fred's did.

It was early spring in Oregon. Field burning, as yet, hadn't destroyed the balance of coming summer with smoke and stink. Chasing down a runaway for rent money, the three of us had limped my old 85 Ford wagon over to the coast and the metropolis of Depoe Bay. Kids today mystify me. Sure we got the head-bangers, perverts and molesters, but seems to me the way too many of our future taxpayers are just plain petulant. A parental "No" is a declaration of war. "You can't say that to me, I've got rights. I'll sue you!"

I had been hired to find a fourteen year old female who was shacking up with a friend and three other losers, three more prime candidates for retroactive birth control, in a bug-ridden-dive up on the hill above the Spouting Horm. Tell you the truth I think the little dope was glad to see me. Toe-dipping in beach tar, smoking pot, an excess of one syllable words, constant scratch, along with the stink of her body, had to be wearing thin. I separated the kid from the other unwashed and, while Maggie and Mandy kept the other slobs stationary, whispered Pop's message into her grimy ear. The gist was for Lovey to quit diddling around, take a bath, pack her dirty underwear pocket Dad's bus ticket and get her butt on the first diesel belcher leaving Lincoln City. One of the unwashed grew a tad mouthy and restless during the sermon from the mount. Mandy chewed another hole in his pants and the complainer decided praying would be considerably more appropriate.

Leaving Depoe Bay, heading north for Lincoln City, I had to laugh at all the tourists clustering around and by the Spouting Horn. I never could figure where they got that name. She should really be called the Wailing Widow as every time she sprays the congregation gets one holy drenching. Purely beats the hell out of baptism. I bet there's not one visitor in twenty, upon returning home, with sense enough to wash her salty tears off their car before corrosion turns it into a rust-bucket before its time.

After I phoned the client to pick Popsey up at the station, I pushed her on the bus and told the driver not to stop for anything, including a forest fire. Dark was settling in so I grabbed burgers for three from the local Wendy's, climbed aboard our flivver, and we, too, hit the road. Lincoln City at one time was a small beach town with nothing but ocean to brag about. The locals called it the Twenty Miracle Miles. There being only one politician with any vision at the time, he called it the Twenty Miserable Miles. A succession of grubby little souvenir shops painted by puddin' heads and a series of ptomaine taverns painted by their cousins. One day the dear city fathers, probably mothers too, got together and consolidated all the little hamlets in those twenty miles and named the whole shebang Lincoln City. Now, you got your Indian Casino, a shopping mall, a mess of loan shark joints, and almost as many fast-food establishments as on Lancaster Street in

Bet You Don't Know Where Lorna Is!

Salem. Shoot, none of the above has improved the city a damn bit but the ocean is still pretty much in control. They also have a new city hall. What can I say, Government is! Lincoln City does have one thing she can brag of: located on the second floor of the city hall is the local library. Along the Coast it is the finest one between Portland and the California border. For a permanent population of some seven thousand live ones it does the city proud. While I'm on trivia, I've been told Lincoln City gets seventy-six inches of rain per year. I seriously doubt that, but I'll buy fifty plus!

Driving northeast on Highway 18 out of the city it isn't long before the flivver noses into the Van Duzer Corridor. Entering the VDC is akin to playing Russian roulette! Deer, elk, bear and small stuff like to roam at will. The most dangerous animal is man and he's usually driving a car or truck! The scenery is gorgeous and hasn't changed in the more than thirty-five years I've been able to enjoy it. However, for the most part she's a two-lane highway now running to seed. During heavy bucket-down time the road is always sliding off on its own. Instead of fixing it properly, the highway department uses a Band-Aid approach. Naturally, a few weeks later another landslide takes a long walk across pavement. It doesn't make sense. When I first settled in Oregon, after strangling on California smog for the last time, this state had the finest highway system in the country. No brag, just fact. It cannot claim that any longer; this in spite of quadruple taxes today and quadruple homesteading folks stuck to pay them. We have a beautiful State; it's a shame to see those fine roads and rest areas going to hell.

The dogs are great company, but not much on conversation. On long drives I enjoy listening to music. The Corridor gives mostly Country wail or

JACK JUDGE

Hoo-bop-de-be-bop, Rock. Whatever happened to Easy Listening? Lacking what I call music to help pass the time and keep me awake, I then play a little mental game. I call it, 'Which idiot from which state just raced by?'

Most cars and trucks passing through the Corridor will be from Washington, California, Oregon, or British Columbia. British Columbians are easy to spot, they usually show white knuckles on the wheel, stare straight ahead, always obey the speed limits, and only start breathing again after they've escaped that two-lane horror. Washingtonians are mostly arrogant, pass everything in sight and never heard of fifty-five miles an hour. The Californians all have a death wish! You can always tell the Oregonians, they're crazy. They tailgate, pass on hills, and veer over the double line on curves. Very few places along 18 allow for passing. When they do the lanes revert back to two in short distances. There are always caution signs: "Right lane ends ahead, form left." Or, "Left lane ends ahead, merge to the right." Inevitably Oregonians, cruising along behind a person such as me, wait until the lane ends before the sumbitches decide to pass! Cousin, that sure as hell leaves the innocent no place to go. You either swap bumpers or fenders, slam on the brakes, or abandon macadam for trees and brush! If you survive, you'll spend at least twenty minutes on the passing fool's pedigree and never repeat an epithet. I'm a graduated expert at it!

On this particular balmy evening I had the window down enjoying forest smells. I'd no sooner mind-named my game players when one of those clowns zipped by me going like a goosed mule. Oh, yeah, over the double line and on a curve. For the next five miles I discoursed about his family tree at length with my two pals. Just past the newer rest area, where the road

Bet You Don't Know Where Lorna Is!

narrows into two-lane again, I glimpsed lights off to the side in the brush where no houses were. Slowing down, I saw a lump in the road kick once and then lie still. A local resident, it was a deer. Stopping for a closer look I saw, unsurprisingly, that the lights belonged to Speedy Alka-Seltzer's car which was now halfway up a stout fir. He was still breathing although I suspected some head bones were badly bent. Luckily he was alone. I walked back to my car and used the cell phone to give the location to the State police. A sweet sounding voice asked if an ambulance was needed.

"Naw," I said, "the deer's dead!"

Callous! Bad behavior! Cynical! Maybe all three. After all, who gives a rip if a lousy deer gets snuffed? I do! I've absolutely no time for arrogant or blatant stupidity. If the bum is lucky—and we aren't—he'll be back on the road again. Next time what'll you bet an innocent party, probably a family, will be unfortunate enough to get it in the way of Mr. Lethal. I didn't catch his license plate, by that time I didn't give a damn anyway.

Highway 22 forms a junction with 18 at the Hebo cutoff. On the northeast side of two-lane 18 sits another Indian casino. They've recently added their own, up to date complete with sundries, gas station. Why not? We're out in the middle of nowhere here. The losers, most of them leaving sans their cash, can still max out the credit card for enough gas to get home. And, three miles back at Grand Ronde, you also got Fast Cash Johnny if credit's good. Whatever will they think of next to aid stumbling mankind?

Highway 22 breaks away from 18 just shy of Willamina and ribbons east toward Dallas and the state capital. Fairly straight, except where passing lanes end and more fools can cut you off, it normally rides safely. Of course

13

JACK JUDGE

an errant cow wandering across smack in front of you can also ruin your day, but hey you're cruisin' out in the boonies for cryin' in the beer.

Mandy and Maggie always perk up about ten miles out of Salem. Just past the intersection of 99 West and 22 there is a dairy which sports a truly lovely slurry pond. On good days one gets to enjoy that lovely stink all the rest of the drive on into our fair Capitol city. M and M always bark their appreciation of nature's Chanel # Phew. I try not to stir the air in passing.

I parked the wagon on the street in front of home sweet home around nine. It was almost full dark and the girls were growing restless for their chow. A burger each doesn't go far with those two. I stopped in the office first to check the answering gizmo. Nothing earth shaking: The proverbial, "Let us repair your house weather-stripping." Another pestered: "Isn't it time for remodeling?" I look around and laugh at that one. Razing the whole joint would be a definite improvement. And leave us not forget: "Let Us consolidate your credit card debt, we can save you money!" Oh, sure. A wise old bird once told me, "It isn't how much money you make, it's how much you don't spend." As a consequence, I stay as far away from credit cards as I can. One message was important though. 'Beat the Odds' Clyde, my favorite bookie, was complaining bitterly.

"How do you do it, Danny? The ten-spot you laid on that long shot, Sarava, to win in the Belmont, cashed in big. The fool beat Medaglia d'Oro by little more than a nose. At 70-1, he paid $142.50 for a two dollar bet."

Dearie me, the Doyle family's picked up $712.00 clams for the wagered tenner. Steaks are in the offing. Still moaning, Clyde added,

"How come ya dint grab the trifecta? Sarava, Medaglia d'oro and Sunday

Bet You Don't Know Where Lorna Is!

Break and a big $25,209.00 would now add a heavy list to your right hip. Tell me how a bum like you does it?" Never, Clyde me old son, never!

I often gab and coffee in a bagel bar with Bernie. He once informed me he had taught school for twenty-five years, over twenty-three of it right here in Salem, before he retired. Standing in front of a room full of jabberers, tryin' to get them to shut up long enough for some teaching to take place, and doin' it for twenty-five years is just naturally gonna make anybody a little strange, so I make allowances. Nevertheless, old dad does have a system for betting on the ponies which he swears by. He claimed he laid ten bucks on Sherluck in the Belmont in 1961. Crossing the wire first, the sucker beat Carry Back out of the Triple Crown, and paid $132.10 for a deuce. Up to Sarava, that was the biggest bet ever paid at the Belmont. That kinda dough was a bundle in '61. Folks sure are different. You'd think a retired teacher would bore hell outa you only talkin' Literature, but Bernie talks horses and kids as well. He knows both like you wouldn't believe. Don't ask, I'm not gonna tell you the system he uses for betting on the broomtails. You'd probably run out and put the rent money down. No way will I contribute to your sinful ways!

Mandy and Maggie continued buggin' me for chow so I quit dreaming about our windfall and filled their plates. My Mandy is a touch peculiar. Trust me when I say it is a proven fact that Border collies are the smartest dogs in the world, with Jack Russell's bein' second. I know the collie is smart, she proved that when she brought all those lost sheep down Deadfall Gulch and safely over the Santiam Highway just below where 20 and 22 merge. If not for her sniffing out and then running that one-eyed clown over

15

Long Way Down Gorge, I'd be dead and we never would have nailed the killer in, *Murder is a Sheepish Business.*

But, there I go getting sidetracked again. I mentioned a peculiarity. It has to do with food. Born and bred to protect and herd sheep, which she better not harm, what's her favorite dish? Lamb Stew! According to Sandy mine is a killer stew. If I do say so myself; she's right. Want the recipe? The secret is in flouring and sautéing chunks of lamb, minus the fat, first. Add garlic, then a can of chicken or beef stock, toss in celery and onions, both chopped; cook carrots, turnip, lots of pearl onions, green beans, (no peas, I hate peas!), and chunked potatoes separately. I don't like my veggies "mooshy," as my Pop used to say. Cook meat slow and low. Don't forget to throw in a bottle of good white or red wine—never use shlock—add the vegetables half an hour before serving. Slice and warm *fresh* French bread, I suggest spreading it liberally with garlic. Then go sit and pig out. Mandy always drools when I cook. But, a Border collie that's nuts about lamb stew? Give me a break.

* * *

Right, I'm supposed to be tellin' you about Lorna's case. Here goes. Mull it over for yourself. Likely you'll figure out who-did-it way before I did.

June 10. The day started like most others here in Oregon: rain, just bills and junk mail to read, nothing on the infernal machine; then the office door, griping about the damp, squawked open. It was early for my office security alarm to sound off. I never oil the hinges so they will squall like a cat got its tail plugged into a hot wall outlet. A skinny little guy, wearing a clean but well-worn suit, brown oxfords, and a cap like Don Knotts wears on Matlock,

Bet You Don't Know Where Lorna Is!

enters. His eyes were blue and kind. He really did look a lot like Barney Fife. Thank God his voice didn't squeak. He'd age out at a hard used forty. Remember the, 'It started innocently' bit? Tune in good from here on out.

He inquires hesitantly, "Mr. Doyle, the detective?"

Her slumbers disturbed the collie stretched on the sofa and then yawned. She sports a lovely set of molars and looking down her throat I could see where she might have made the little guy a scosh nervous.

"I am Danny Doyle, what can I do for you Mr. . . . ?"

"Frank Diddens is my name. I'm the sales manager at the Carrows Ford Agency up on Lancaster. I believe I'm in need of your services. My wife, Lorna, has been missing for three days. I'm afraid something serious has happened. She never stays away this long without telling me where she'll be. I've had no word at all. I've called friends, hospitals, and been to the police. No accidents have been reported, but no one has seen her since close of school on Friday. She teaches High School English at Sagen High School in south Salem. The police have made inquiries but so far they've discovered nothing. Lorna is always tired at the end of the school year but she's also seemed a little upset lately. My daughters and I are very worried. Will you investigate for us? What do you charge? Can you begin now?"

"I charge $160.00 a day plus expenses Mr. Diddens. And yes, I am free to take your case. Give me more particulars: Do you have a picture of your wife? How long has she been teaching at Sagen? Does she often go away by herself? Are things copacetic between you? How long have you been married? Any other kids? How about money troubles? Any women in your life you'd just as soon she not know about? Any guys in hers? Has she ever stayed away on her own before? You mentioned she's been upset, any trouble at school? What's with her health? School kids causing bad vibes? She gets along with the faculty? Do you have any idea where best to start?"

"I'll answer as many of your questions as I can, Mr. Doyle: I believe our marriage is fine. I have no outside female interests nor does she have men friends I don't know about. Charlene and Elizabeth, our two daughters, are ages fourteen and twelve. We are Catholic and attend Mass regularly. We've been married fifteen years. Teaching is hard work and most stressful at times, but I know of no trouble. She gets along fine with her co-workers and is much respected throughout the school where she's been teaching for twelve years. In 1994 Lorna was voted 'teacher of the year' by her Salem peers. Her students love her. Occasionally she will spend a weekend at the beach to sort of "recharge her batteries" as she would say. When that happens and I cannot make the trip with her she always tells me where she'll be and when I can expect her home. Lorna will also frequently call to talk to our daughters and to reassure me. Nothing like this has ever happened before! Here is a fairly recent picture. To me, she looks happy. I have no idea where to tell you to begin. Only, please hurry up and find her, my daughters are distraught and I'm quite frantic myself!"

Maggie chose that moment to wander in to check out the action. She took one look at Frank and immediately jumped into his lap. A good sign that, my Maggie will never cozy up to people she doesn't trust. My little voices were not urging caution either and Mandy slowly began to wag her tail. I guessed we were going to do our damnedest to find Lorna. Judging by the photo she was a good looking dish, with long, brunette hair and a nice

Bet You Don't Know Where Lorna Is!

smile. Maybe a touch on the skinny side but then again I don't ever remember running into many fat teachers; must have something to do with the job. Even Judge, while a scosh stout, wasn't fat, and he was retired. Lorna would ticket out at about thirty-nine. I was beginning to work up a touch of envy. On the surface this looked like a nice happy family. Time would tell.

Diddens left me a five hundred dollar retainer and took himself off for further checking of his own. At the end of that week I knew the schools would turn the kiddies loose to bug their parents for the rest of the summer. Didn't leave me much time for investigation so I decided to start with Sagen. It is a fairly new school. I'd done a little research before tossing the dogs into the wagon. The school locates south on Madrone just off Liberty Street. It houses some 2000 students, one principal, three assistant principals, five counselors, and about 115 front line troops called *teachers*. Lorna Diddens pushes advanced Literature to Juniors and Seniors. I figured my best bet would be to check into the office first—they're damn fussy about insisting folks doing that for which I say, amen—inform of the reason for my visit, get an identity tag, take a quick peek at Mrs. Diddens' class, if permitted, and then hie me off to a counselor for a little pumping action.

On the way to the school, I reflected on a story Bernie had told about an incident in his school which could have turned out bad. It occurred some twenty years ago. He had been the five-six grades team leader for seven large classes of eleven and twelve year olds in one of the fairly ancient elementary schools on the north side of town. Their classrooms located on the third floor; they were leading about two hundred kids down stairs to their basement cafeteria for lunch. Suddenly, the outside doors on the second floor landing opened and a scuzzball grabbed one of the girls and tried to yank her out the door. Two men teachers spotted him and, like warts on a toad, got all over his bod! He lit out running and they chased him halfway to Lancaster Blvd. before the sleaze got away. You know as well as I do creeps have been around forever; unfortunately, there are just more of them today. I say the tougher the security in the schools the better. Hell, they can even pat me down if it will make them feel safer.

I found a spot in the shade for my pals. While it isn't normal in Salem, June can get hot. Dogs cooped up in a hot car rates as a no-no with me. Even if the walk is further, I park them where a breeze is blowing and the sun cannot get at them.

I checked in with a nice, somewhat chubby, middle-aged broad who warmed my day with a great smile. But I bet if I had given trouble she could have shot-putted me with one hand. I signed up, got an identity card to pin to the lapel, an okay to visit Lorna's class with admonitions not to stampede or worry the kids, and directions even Mortimer Snerd could have followed. Counted an adult now, I truly like schools and the people who run them. The office lady had reminded me a substitute teacher had Lorna's class. She was a cute little trick and had no idea why I was there. I really only wanted to take a quick gander at the kids to see if anyone got nervous, so I lied and told her I was a parent and my kid could be attending Mrs. Diddens' class in the fall. I was only trying to get the lay of the land and I promised I'd be so quiet even the mice wouldn't know I was there. I got a sour look for the mice crack, but she bought the rest of the baloney.

Bet You Don't Know Where Lorna Is!

I swear the kids of today are better looking than in my day, at least the ones interested in an education are. The boys are well-built, clean and pretty much away from the long, greasy, hair-down-to-sit-down-land of not so long ago. Middle schoolers, not these kids, are the ones wearing the pants five sizes too large for them. When they walk they wobble like they've had a serious accident. The girls are cute, smiley and bright; although with those short skirts, pantyhose or no, I don't for the life of me see how they can sit comfortably and not suffer horribly from drafts.

No one gave me the fish-eye; so, after a long but casual look-see, I tip-toed out to go hunt up a counselor. Why had Lorna looked worried? That little tidbit still gnawed at me. Naturally, I had to hike to the far side of the school to locate a counselor's office. No wonder everyone checked out thin; if I trod those hallowed halls everyday I'd skinny down, too. I toyed with the idea of ringing the fire alarm to check how fast two thousand kids and one hundred twenty faculty members could bail outa there, but that would lead to my expulsion; I manfully desisted, settling for an inward chuckle.

Mrs. Langer was a pleasant-faced, pleasant-appearing, pleasant-talking, pleasant person and, "oh my, wasn't it a pleasant day?" And how could she help me? I had to play it cool here. These people were not stupid. If I gave out with the real reason I was there a safe bet shouts it would be all over the school by lunch time. I didn't want to spook anyone. On the other hand, I had to get information and that would require expressing a little of Frank's concern. I decided to inquire if maybe the 'year end blues' might be responsible for Mrs. Diddens worried state. Showing all my teeth in what I hoped was a confiding smile, rather than a leer, I opined I was a friend of the family, a sort of confidant, and as Lorna hadn't laid any info out for Pop, he felt that maybe the school might have a few clues.

"I don't have any pertinent information that would help, Mr. Doyle. Of course there are always rumors and a little gossip in large schools. And the last five school days comprised finals week which is always stressful for students and faculty alike. So much depends on grade point average for the seniors hoping to gain entrance to prestigious colleges. All test results had to be in by last Friday and that added more pressure on the staff."

She leaned forward in her chair lowering her voice as though I was going to get some real gossip, a little dirt you might say.

"I did hear a rumor, I'm sure there was nothing to it, about Lorna and one of our male teachers perhaps being a bit involved last fall. They'd been seen having coffee together a few times off campus, and several times he walked her to her car after school where they were observed in close conversation. I had heard they were holding hands and standing close to one another, rather intimately. As I said, I'm sure there was nothing to it."

Quote the raven smiling like a barracuda that had just speared a juicy morsel on the wing. Is that what they call a mixed metaphor or just screwed up word grouping? If Mrs. Langer was any example, I would just bet there would be only a *teeny smidge* of gossip cruising the hallways!

"Might it be possible for me to get a copy of the current yearbook and her class lists? Maybe Mr. Diddens could identify some of the students closest to her. They might be able to shed a little light on things. If it's not much trouble I'd like the address of that male teacher. He may be able to help."

"Oh, Mr. Harding is no longer with us, he left at the first of the year and I

Bet You Don't Know Where Lorna Is!

understand is teaching a mathematics course in Bend now. His class, always popular, was also very difficult. Sagen only accepts the best teachers."

Still clueless, I collected the yearbook and class lists; also the address of the puzzling Mr. Harding. By nature of size alone Sagen would be better rated than schools in Bend. Why did he leave, being so popular and all?

I'm good at remembering faces. On the way over to chat up the barracuda I'd noticed six guys and two cuties talking and laughing together by the gym doors. They all looked just like the kids next door, the kinds who make Mom and Pop proud and this country great. I had no suspicions. Hell, so far I hadn't a clue as to what to even have for lunch. I just have a habit of looking people over. In my business they are sometimes holding objects they plan on hitting you with! Thinking of taking a look for those folks in the yearbook I exercised my myopic eyes, thank God for glasses, and cataloged them all for future reference, then placed them in my noggin memory file. No bells were ringing an alert. The dogs were not beside me signaling "on guard" which they do very well. Quite often, I've shown both my buddies photos of suspects, heard 'em whine, and watched their fur stand up. Of course, the fact that the pics showed faces uglier than dirt might have contributed a tad to their actions!

* * *

Returning to the wagon, I was informed by energetic tongues to let Mandy and Maggie out for a romp in Bush Park. Back at No Frills Detective Agency I checked for calls; none, so I hit the library and cranked out a little research on Bend High Schools. They have two: both good but no better than Sagen and smaller enrollments as well as faculties. Harding was indeed teaching at the newest fount for wisdom in that city. During the school year their buildings incarcerated fifteen hundred plus students, seventy full and part time staff, one principal, two assistant principals and four counselors. Not a big comedown for Harding. Maybe he'd fallen in love with the scenery. God knows, there's enough over there to knock your eyes out.

Sandy has her own business as a dress maker and designer. After eyeing her creations—some on, some off—once my eyeballs quit caging and un-caging, I told her she was terrific. Sure I gathered points, but it happens to be true, she is a flaming artist! Her time is pretty much her own so I conned her into fixing a picnic lunch for four and also into coming with me on the morrow. I had no leads and decided to check out Harding in Bend. For the next three school days nobody ever does much of anything, except maybe conduct field sports on bailout day. I felt obligated to Diddens to do something. Besides, no other clients were trying out my security system!

Early next day I gassed up in Salem and let the wagon hit the road. We had a good one hundred and thirty miles of driving through some of the most beautiful scenery in the country, if not the world. My aging eyes are never able to grab enough of the grandeur as the flivver rolls along. It is so gorgeous it brings a lump to my gullet. Hey, if you don't believe me, go look for yourself and then apologize. Take Highway 22 out of Salem and head east. Lyons, Mill City, and Detroit Lake call for a gradual climb. Beaucoup snow fell last year; the lake was full—with water and vacationers. Most of the vacationers were still on top of the water. The day was clear, the sky near, and Sandy dear; good to be alive. Mount Jefferson, majestic, still sported lots of snow. She doesn't shrink down to her shorts until late August.

3

While munching a bagel and slurping coffee one day, Bernie told me how when he was in his late fifties, and as foolish then as now, he and the wife, along with friends, climbed Old Jeff. The old geezer likes his comforts so he carried two camp stools and a toaster along. He also put a lovely full plastic bottle of brandy in his pack, just in case of a chill! He carried all the frozen chicken for the group. Add pots, pans, tent, sleeping bag, socks, shorts, necessary paper, matches, and probably half of Safeway. About halfway up he began to poop out a tad as the damn pack kept getting heavier. By the time they all reached the campsite he was almost on his knees. When the others saw the two stools and toaster they all hooted at the tenderfoot. The guy who makes the climb all the time hefted Bern's pack and damn near got a hernia. He figured it weighed at least eighty pounds!

Continuing to thrill me, the old geezer had prattled on how they had no sooner erected and staked their tents when in blew acres of overcast and it grew cold enough to SNOW! They were a starving group but nobody had the slightest desire for food so they all crawled into their sleeping bags, still fully clothed, and shivered and shook like ancient skeletons dancing in the morgue while the summer weather tried for twenty below!

Come morning, barely minutes from presenting as frozen cadavers, they gathered gratefully around a big roaring fire the real camper had built. Yeah, it was still dark! By and by, when all had scoffed pancakes, gulped down mugs of hot coffee, and spread jam on toast, things began to look up. The lovely sun rose with a smile and presented a perfect day.

One of the group's members didn't arrive until that morning. He earned his living as a chef and, as a surprise, he contributed fresh strawberries, cakes, and whipped cream. The chicken, defrosting in Bernie's pack on the climb, had deposited its juice all down his back but it stayed cold and fresh after they threw it in a snow bank by their camp. Everyone had a ball. Stumps don't make the greatest of chairs. Mollie-O, Bernie's wife, sat on her ever-so-comfy stool, which by this time was being enviously eyed by the other stalwarts, while she sketched. Oh, I forgot to tell you, everybody but everybody had lined up to use the tenderfoot's toaster!

A good time was had by all. The hike down the mountain was uneventful except, at the bottom the group unanimously wanted to kill Bernie! All the way up and all the way down that lovely bottle of brandy had enjoyed a comfortable ride. When they were freezing the first night and could surely have used a slug; forgotten, it had remained secure in his pack. He remembered it at the foot of the mountain, just after he slipped his gear off his shoulders and tossed it into the back of their patiently waiting wagon. Correct, he is definitely shy the olives demanded for a good martini!

Highway 20, heading out from Springfield, joins 22 not too far below the summit. At the top, looking back and to the left, Mount Jefferson portrays in all its glory. Lean over and look back to the right to also enjoy the view of Mount Washington. Start down a long straightaway and on the passenger side Blue and Suttle Lakes come into view; the hundred and thirty mile drive is pretty well short on conversation. Too many lovely vistas, capturing your attention, will vie. There is but one thing that mars the enjoyment of all that incredible beauty. INCESSANT TRAFFIC! It is two-lane most of the way from Salem and quite curvy in spots. Remember how I described the zany drivers in the Van Duzer Corridor? Well, when they get through scaring hell out of you over there, they drive to Bend and do it all over again! The population of Bend was 18,450 in 1985; it has leapt way past 60,000 today. A large percentage would be ex-Californians. When they moved north, they still wanted sunshine. Bend boasts of over 300 days of the boring fellow. What's a day without a little rain, a little fog, a little blow, a lot of damp? Most of those pampered folks bellow, "Lousy!" Pah to them. Webbed of the feet they're not.

Chirping like a well-fed canary the wagon cruised into Sisters. The locals have decided to turn her into a frontier style town. Like all of Oregon, she's growing. You got your Llama ranch on the outskirts, a small mall, gift shops up the dump stump, and snack food enticements. I like Sisters; the air is pure on either side of the highway and her humidity is low. The Metolius River is not too far back down the highway; great fly fishing. The tab at the eleven cabin resort, per night double occupancy, is 180 clams plus 6% tax and $15.00 more for each extra person. At first glance that seems like a lot and it's damn sure too much for my pocketbook, but it is a beautiful spot. Each cabin comes with kitchen: including pots, pans, dishes, linen, warm blankets, firewood, you name it. Today, I guess, the tab is not exorbitant as the joint abounds in butterflies in the spring. Bad news! No pets allowed, even if you leave 'em in the car. Mandy and Maggie sneered as we passed.

On the way to Sisters we had already passed Black Butte Ranch with their golf courses and their posh homes. Folks who live there or rent homes at the ranch had a hell of a scare from a forest fire this year. I believe some houses were lost. Fortunately, Ma Nature rejuvenates herself although I hear she's not much on rebuilding castles for the well-to-do.

We pulled over for a pit stop for all at a nice little wayside on the far edge of town. Sandy hauled sodas out of the picnic box and water for the mutts. From Sisters, the road leads pretty straight and level on into Bend. Gawking out the windows we admired mountains: Three Sisters looking benevolently over their domain and Three Finger Jack never stops waving to them. I was sure they'd have been christened Winkin', Blinkin' and Nod. Not so; the locals named them Faith, Hope and Charity. Not very flaming original!

Now on Highway 97, having made good time, we rolled into Bend about 10.30 A.M. I headed straight for Mountain View High School located out on 27th. While Sandy took the dogs for a leisurely walk I hurried to the office to check in. If possible, I wanted to collar Harding before lunch and between classes. I timed it right and caught him in his class just after second period. After one look, I knew there had been no hanky-panky between Lady Lorna and himself. His face resembled a miniature bloodhound and his deportment shrieked of a shy, Mr. Peepers. His handshake, flapping like a fresh caught trout, left my own flipper dripping. As soon as he opened his mouth I could tell he was an intellectual, definitely not a Mr. Macho. Likely he had never read of or seen the term before, unless it was on a stove. I opened the proceedings:

"Mr. Harding, I've just driven over from Salem; my name's Danny Doyle.

Bet You Don't Know Where Lorna Is!

I'm a private detective making inquiries about Lorna Diddens who seems to have gone missing. Have you seen her recently? What can you tell me about your relationship? Other than as her co-worker, have you ever been involved in any patty-cake parties? Are we slanting toward a divorce for her here or just an occasional roll in the hay?"

I figured, shove him into a thorn bush and watch what springs back! Mr. Shelby Harding gasped, his jaw dropped, and his yawp began to open and close like the trout I've just mentioned.

". . . why, who, where, did you get such an idea?" he spluttered. Mrs. Diddens and I've never been more than professional educators together . . . why, why, the very thought is repugnant . . . we, we, we've shared no social relationship. Whatever gave you the idea we had?"

"A little birdy at your last school hinted you two might have been playing footsy and got carried away. You had been seen having coffee together after school and quite often you walked her to her car. If there is nothing to it, why did you leave Sagen High?"

"Mr. Detective, you have my assurance there is nothing to tell; either to add to, or relieve, gossip. I was concerned about one of my students. He also attended her English class. We simply shared notes in an attempt to formulate a plan which would help him. He's bright and ambitious but some subjects are more difficult to grasp than others. Teachers always want to help students succeed; it's why we chose the profession in the first place."

"Believe me, Mr. Doyle, that's all there was to it and whoever filled your head with that malicious gossip is a cruel creature to say the least! My move to Bend is my business and is of no concern to others. I bid you good-day."

"Uh, just one more question, chum. What say you lay the name of the student on me?"

"Sir, I am a teacher and conscience bound to protect any and all my students. Nothing would be gained by giving you his name. A great many pupils have difficulty with their classes. Would you expect me to divulge all their names and problems to you? I am certainly not going to add to any further gossip. Once again, I bid you good-day!" And he left the room.

Well now, old Shelby had just displayed a tad bit of backbone there and risen in my estimation. Could he have been protesting a wee touch too much though? One thing I was sure of, while Frank Diddens was no Errol Flynn he didn't look like Pluto either, there had been no hanky-panky!

With no point in hanging around Bend, knowing I'd get no more from Harding, I hied me off to collect Sandy and my girls. I'd planned to take us to the Inn at Seventh Mountain for lunch. 'Beat the Odds' Clyde had ponied up my winnings and I was flush. Unfortunately, the inn was undergoing renovations and the dining room wouldn't open until later on in the fall.

There's a scenic drive which makes a loop out of either Sunriver or Lapine, one eager to show off more of Oregon's breathtaking wonders: Ponderosa Pine forests, lakes and rivers, deer, elk, bear, marmots, chipmunks, birds, butterflies; choose your own, it will probably be there. I told the girls we'd the time now to enjoy it. I'd take the turn out of Lapine, we'd picnic along the way, then wend our way leisurely back to Bend along Century Drive. I'd spring for dinner at the Riverhouse; they put out a prime rib that will put hair on your chest. Maggie and Mandy already had enough on their chests and Sandy wasn't into growing any on hers; they got the idea though. Regretfully, we'd have to head back to Salem after chow. I'd gotten nowhere and had a hunch time was running out for Lorna. Before leaving, I cancelled our motel digs and long-distanced the Salem police. There was nothing new. I figured I better do a little checking over at the Coast next. Diddens had said Lorna often went there to stoke up on Nature's freebies.

My wallet was shy a hundred and fifty bucks when we left Bend. Well hell, I got stuck for four steaks and what's a steak without a dollop of booze? The sky looked soft and drowsy as we rolled. Halfway to Sisters, dusk began to slip into dark. By the time we eased through that old frontier town it was night. That heavenly scenery by day had became but a memory and our lights only picked up a yellow line heading into nowhere. Deer, you blamed well best keep yourselves to the forest and out of my way! The dark now made room for conversation and pretty soon Sandy asked how Bernie and I had become acquainted?

"His full name is John B. Judge; he goes by Jack, only I call him Bernie."

"Whatever for?" queried the curious.

"I don't know. I suspect it bugs him a little when I do. Why did people call Louis Armstrong, Satchmo? Or Mel Torme, the Velvet Fog? When males become friends they do that, it's a guy thing. Besides, his middle name is Bernard. Our initial gabbing began because of mutual friends, like dogs. He had a Border collie, name of Megan, for sixteen years. He and the wife both taught and operated a sheep ranch at the same time. Those who teach do not make big bucks even though they're expected to perform miracles like they do. They were trying to increase their income. Old Bern knew Border collies had been proven to be the smartest dogs in the world; in fact, after he retired, he wrote and had published a book about that dog, along with their life on the farm. It's entitled, *Mojac's Megan*. I will loan it to you if you like, it's a good story, illustrated, and full of humor."

"His second has just come out, too. This one is in bookstores as, *Another Time, Another Place*. It is really pretty much an autobiography of his early life, service in the United States Air Force with a rescue squadron, breeding and raising birds, collecting wild animals in the jungles of South America, selling monkeys dressed in doll's clothes, taking birds and monkeys to the Southern California State Fair at Pomona, and how he met his wife. Also fully illustrated, the adventures he's had will really crack you up."

"I'm going to pump him more about teaching kids and what makes them tick. He only taught as high as sixth grade, but kids are kids. True, high schoolers are older and bigger but you still have to establish rapport and they all need support. Anyway, I'm stuck without a lead. I've nothing to lose by enlisting his help even if he does lean a tad bit over the other side of nuts!"

"You definitely have a sadistic streak, Danny Boy. From what you've related to me he sounds quite nice. I think you just love to bug him."

No question, she had me there.

The trip home was uneventful except that the dogs snored. Oregon's deer population also remained stable during our passing. We were all bushed. I dropped Sandy off at her digs, headed to mine, and then took my buddies for a walk. My brain kept running the oval track. While it enjoyed the exercise it always started and stopped at the same dead place. Where could Lorna be? And why not let hubby know? Flang it, I decided to give it a rest and hit the sack. Tomorrow I'd head for the beach and nose around there.

4

The drive to the coast remains unchanged. How I reveled in it. I can only take so much progress coming in the form of tract houses, fast food joints, gas stations and trucks towing triple trailers. Ever try to pass one of those road-hoggers during a driving rainstorm? It's akin to trying to swim the length of the pool underwater! Progress brings crowds, traffic, and litter: on the road, beside the road, tossed off, fallen off, and blown off.

"Excuse us, you local people, our weekend travel garbage accidentally escaped from the car's trunk, ha-ha. You mind picking it up?"

Fortunately, trekking along 22 from Salem then on to 18 and forward to the big waves Mother Nature still presented her face, clean and scrubbed, as she has for well over thirty years of my life. Thank you, Lord!

Speedy Alka-Seltzer and his dented car were long gone as we drove past. "Very best of good luck, pal, surely do hope your car wasn't totaled." And reader friend, if you believe I sincerely mean that, how about you applying to the city government for a job shoveling fog off the bay?

I stopped off at the Lincoln City Police Station first; best to check for bad news right away: Nothing re unknowns, strangers admitted to the hospital, or newly discovered bodies. That at least brightened my mood. Next step, flash Lorna's picture at motels, B&B's, rentals and the casino. You have any idea how many places there are where one can lodge in Lincoln City? Mandy and Maggie finally barked, "Enough." "Same here," wailed my own ouching feet. Our circulation needed priming. I took them for a long walk on the beach. Well behaved, I knew they'd come when I called so I turned them loose to run. Oh yeah, and good God-a-mighty away they flew after gulls, sandpipers, kites, other dogs, ducks and, for all I knew, rum-runners! I found a handy, damp, sand-laden log, parked my fanny and watched my family run. Their tongues hung out a mile but they had a royal ball.

About half an hour later I stirred my stumps, whistled two, sand-coated, lolling canine tongues, followed by their bodies, to me and we continued the search. It was almost time to watch the sun take a header into the ocean before I got a break. I showed Lorna's picture at a cute little motel on SW 10th Street. It had a great ocean view and the rates were reasonable for the times. Of course, I remember when you could get a swell room with a double bed, kitchen, fireplace—and an ocean view—for fifteen bucks. I know, I dwell in the flaming past, those value days are gone forever!

The desk jockey recognized Lorna right away. "She and her husband often stay here on weekends. They are a truly nice couple and quite neat. There is never a question of trash left, loud arguing, or noisy parties. I've been in this business a long time, mister. Those two are welcome to stay with me, anytime."

Double checking, I flashed a picture of Frank at him.

"This guy the one she stays with?"

"That's him, that's her husband. I'd know him anywhere. Neither one has been here for a while though, I'd say at least three months. I can look it up if you like. We are a small motel and request reservations quite some time ahead. Whenever the Diddens left they usually would book well in advance for their next time. They paid by credit card and once in a while by check. I have never had a problem. Is there some trouble Mr. . . . ?"

"My name is Danny Doyle, and there is no trouble that I'm aware of. I'm a friend of the family just over to the Coast for a visit. Frank told me this was a nice place to stay. As school is winding down for the year he surmised Lorna might be coming over for a few days. I just thought I might run into her. By the way, do you take pets?"

"Yes, we do, at extra cost. I'm sorry though, we don't have a vacancy. At this time of year and on through September we are booked solid, I couldn't even squeeze the Diddens in this month."

I hadn't bothered to show ID and I hoped by asking about pets I might have sidetracked him. He was a nice old geezer but I suspected was also the local gabber in good standing. No point in flushing quail out of the field prior to hunting season. I thanked him for his courtesy and split.

Back in the wagon the girls reminded the boss of chow. A quick look at my watch showed it was more than time and explained why I, too, was peckish. At least I'd learned two things: Lorna and hubby were the only together-two bedding at the beach and she hadn't been over for quite a spell, certainly not last weekend. Damn it all, without sign one to guide me my mind was back circling that bloody oval track!

I treated my pals to steaks at the Dory Cove, mine inside in a booth, theirs in the wagon. Even a glass of Riesling did nothing to assuage rising anger and frustration. Back on the road, I called Diddens from my blabber machine and brought him up to date. He'd nothing to report either. Lorna had now been missing for almost six days. Bad vibes began pummeling my aging frame. I put the pedal to the metal, as I now had no recourse I'd have to take another look around Sagen. I also planned to sound out Sandy prior to her hitting the sack. In addition, I needed to call Bernie and arrange for bagels and java in the morning before I headed out to the school. He was going to fill me in on what makes school kids act the way they do, or else!

I dropped M and M off at 'home sweet home' and laughed as Mandy almost beat Maggie to the bed's only pillow. Sandy, looking scrumptious and fresh from the shower, smelled good enough to drown in. I filled her in on the day's lousy results and requested her take on the situation. Curling up on her sofa with her feet under her, she sipped from the glass of Gewürztraminer I had just poured, cleared her throat and said:

"Danny, my treasure, I have absolutely nothing to offer, simply questions: Do we know anything about her background? How about her teen boyfriends? Any troubles come her way while growing up? What about family life? Does she get along with brothers, sisters? Do we have any criminal backgrounds to consider? How about junkets away from Mom and Pop involving toe-tickling? For that matter, what do we know about Hubby's background? Is he as pure as we think? Seems like pedigree searching can't do any harm my sweet Irish squeezer; speaking of which, how about scooting over here beside me now and getting in two or three hours practice?"

I managed, briefly, to set Lorna on the back burner during that pleasant interlude. Yet, Sandy had posed good questions, so I requested she punch up the computer early and start digging for dirt while I finished with Sagen. Thursday's dawn, the last day of classes for students, arrived dry. I knew the quiet halls would cater to staff only on Friday, as they finished up records. Report cards would be handed out later in the afternoon to the parolees.

Bernie, at 7 A.M., chewing happily on an onion and cheese deluxe, was his usual unflappable self. Totally oblivious of the big blob of cheese displaying all over his chin, he also remained sublimely unaware of my subtle hints to remove it. Exasperated, I grabbed his napkin and did it for him. Yeah, I can see where sometimes murder could be a definite option!

"Are you going to educate me about school kids or are you just going to sit there and smear cheese all over your fat face?" I snarled.

"Patience, friend sleuth," he mumbled, tearing off another hunk of bagel. "I am supposed to imbue you with twenty-five years of teaching experience for but two cups of mud and one lonely bagel?" How about springing for another? An Asiago with cream cheese and lox would be nice, don't forget another cup of friend Bascomb's hot Joe, two sugars and a dollop of cream."

Replenished, and after smearing another blob of cheese from his fresh bagel all over his Roman nose, sounding like a rusty capstan hauling up an anchor, he cleared his throat and began:

"I suppose I'll start with Child Growth and Development 1-A. Not to worry, I'll skip the terrible two's, three's, and 'Quick, let's send them back,' five, six and seven's. Most of my days spent with the little monsters began at age ten and stretched to twelve. I started off in Salem at a large school working with fourth graders for three years and then became a five-six Team Leader at the same school for another ten. I next moved to a rural school for a fun-filled decade, plus six months. Having received time off for good behavior, I then retired. In yon large school we had one of the top, if not the top, five-six grade teams in the city. No brag—fact; credit for that must go to the teachers on the team plus our strong emphasis on responsibility and citizenship. Incidentally, more than one Salem school copied our program. Children will accept responsibility, but only when they are taught to do so. We worked hard and long to develop and strengthen those traits in our students and it paid off. Discipline problems were few and far between and never for major infractions. Parents supported all our programs and as a matter of course most reinforced them at home. No school or teaching staff can ever do it alone, nor should non-educators ever expect them to."

"I have been facetious with some of my remarks re kids, as you've no doubt noticed. I hasten to say they are not to be taken literally. I am most thankful that I chose a career in teaching. It has been my great good fortune to work with many of the most delightful little people on earth. I have also had the good fortune to attend their weddings, observe them in action as adults, and visit with them after a span of many years. Do not be misled. While the crud of the world get far more attention than they deserve, thanks to the Media which feeds on litanies of misery. That same crud does not control it and they never will. That, my investigator friend, you can take to the bank. Never forget the true heroes of September 11 who bravely and unhesitatingly accepted their final responsibility. Those people, for the most part, were products of American Schools."

Old Bernie did go on and I began to grow restless. Although what he spouted was interesting and true, so far it had offered me no help.

"Judge, honorable sir, will you get to the nitty-gritty. I'm flat spinning my wheels here."

Bet You Don't Know Where Lorna Is!

"Hist, my impatient one, I'm getting to it. You cannot build a boat without completing the hull! I see a need to lay a little history on you. Think 1776. The population of the thirteen colonies at that time was right around three million. The *percentage* of no-good folk was the same then as it is now. When a miscreant was sentenced to the stocks in Salem, Massachusetts, exposing him/her to public derision, the folks in Concord were not aware of it, regardless of the crime, until the stage driver from Salem shared the news with the Concordians. This also applied to hangings. Throughout the colonies news of criminal behavior was passed in the same way. You've heard the old chestnut, 'How do you pass gossip? Telegraph, telephone, tell a woman!' "

"To continue, we are long past the days of the pillory and yet we still relish public derision. Ever listen to some of the late night talk show clowns? Are not their comments often tasteless, hurtful, and cruel?"

"It's true, as a nation, we do tend to give up rather quickly on the tried and true; however, it wouldn't cost much to build new stocks in the town square, and I know where I can lay my hands on two dozen rotten eggs. I would dearly love to exercise my pitching arm throwing at the CEO's of WorldCom.Corp, Enron and Tyco, and all those other thieving corporate bums!"

"Danny, me old son, what would you estimate is the population of the United States today? Give up? We now count over three hundred million. Certainly the number of no-goods has increased dramatically, but the *percentage* has still remained the same. Thus today, while we surely do have more scumbags, sleazes, pimps, pushers, muggers, killers, and just miserable trash, they are never gonna outnumber the good guys."

"Patience me lad, patience, I'm trying to get there. This is taxing work. I don't suppose you'd pony up for another lox-loaded bagel? I was afraid of that. Very well, I shall continue: Is there an abundance of bad kids in our schools? There definitely is not! Regardless of Kipland Kinkel and his rampage at Thurston High in Springfield, Oregon; those at Jonesboro, Arkansas; West Paducah, Kentucky; Pearl, Mississippi; and Edinboro, Pennsylvania during 1997-98; those events are atypical. By the way, did you know they were sloppy in searching that rotten little monster Kinkel at the police station and he lunged at a cop with a knife he'd had taped to his leg? Try these statistics: Data on the specific threat of school-associated violent deaths reveals that children in this country face a one in a million chance of being killed at school; so why all the fear, political speeches, and hype? The difference between how news traveled in 1776 and the Media frenzy of today explains it. How is the public informed in our day? Try telegraph, telephone, newspapers and TELEVISION. Communication is now *instant*! Concord, Massachusetts knew about Springfield, Oregon at the same time we did. They were kept up to date for days and days. It was a veritable feast on misery. Although much of what was uncovered was surely misinterpreted and the public, nationwide, misinformed, no stone was left unturned. I truly hate the constant, never-ending emphasis placed on crime by the Media! Yeah, I know Dan, solving some of it is how you make a living, but do you take out full page ads day after day discussing the sordid details? You are, of course, familiar with Pavlov's Dogs?"

I damn near answered, "Yeah, he turns them into that gourmet Portuguese linguica," but the subject was too important for flippancy so I gave him:

"He was the guy known for classical conditioning. Didn't those mutts of his, offered the same stimulus every day, respond to it? He discovered all animals, I presume that includes man, could be trained or conditioned to expect a consequence on results of previous experience. In other words, present the same thing every day and folks will not only expect it, they'll look forward to it, like those loads of horse puckey political speeches!"

"Keerect, me old son. The Pavlov of today is easily recognized by the disreputable name of, *Media*!"

"Okay, perhaps we know a few of the reasons for the abundance of misery we hear and read about. Should we expect more of the same in the classroom? Let's take a look at the make-up of a typical one. According to the experts each group of students will include twenty percent of the bright to very bright, sixty percent of average to high average and twenty percent of low to quite low. If you break that down in numbers for a class of thirty, six make the teacher dance for joy, eighteen make him work but keep him happy, four bring on headaches, and two bring on migraines. Why the mixture? Many factors: intelligence, stable environment (mom and pop elect to stay together), inherited genes, language barriers, itinerants (in agricultural areas these would usually be the children of harvesters) constantly on the move following crops and growing seasons their kids never stay in one place long enough to form firm friendships or pick up needed knowledge; often lacking skills in English compounds their problems; finally, consider poor to totally miserable environments."

"Unhappily, those six on the bottom will no doubt rate below grade level.

Reading, writing and math skills won't sufffice for the class in which they've been placed. Remember, Public Schools must accept all children regardless of abilities, or social attitudes. Are you with me so far? Naturally, the 20-60-20 rule only applies if the class hasn't been stacked. What's stacked? At the end of the school year Principals seldom assign students to their next teacher for the forthcoming fall. Thus it falls to the teachers to perform that little chore. I have no quarrel with that. In fact, the kids should only be assigned by an instructor who knows how well they perform, which teacher would likely work best with the kid, and how well the little guy will work and get along with those others also assigned to his new class. Social aspects as well as the academics matter a great deal when planning for classroom harmony. Let's suppose though, this group of teachers show a touch of wear around the edges. Better believe it is all too common. One can only face so many classes over the years without becoming a touch stir crazy. Don't tell me it doesn't happen in your miserable excuse for a vocation, too! Oh happy day, a brand new teacher's been assigned to the next grade above theirs this Fall, one just out of college and raring to go! Given the liberty, meaning not closely watched, those teachers may assign all their pills to the tenderfoot. That is exactly why, when I team-taught, I assigned all the students to their next teachers. I knew and trusted my people and I also knew the kids. If I had placement doubts, I would check with the teacher who'd just sent the little darling home to bug Mother for the summer. I would indicate where I planned to place him, and ask for their recommendation. It is not difficult to do it right and it is also why I think all principals should get to know, and *work*, with every kid throughout the damn school year. Many of their useless meetings could be ditched in order to find the time! Stacking doesn't happen often but it only takes one to make the newcomer's classroom experience hell on earth! Even in a normal situation the teacher can expect from two to four discipline problems. We are not talking murder and mayhem here. Just a little, 'I'm gonna bug the teacher because learning is so hard and the other kids laugh at me.' "

"Danny, classroom teachers—at all levels—have to watch out for pitfalls on a daily basis; a large number of those being social and having nothing to do with academics. In the first place teachers were hired to instill important academic skills into young heads; nowhere does it say they are to solve all their social problems as well. The public is quick to forget that. Children can be terribly hurt by peers: the callous, the indifferent, the uncaring. The smart teacher, always on the alert for such situations, had better nip them in the bud. You better believe that the troops in *front* of the class definitely need eyes in the backs of their heads!"

"Consider this: A classroom lesson in a fifth grade is progressing quite nicely. Suddenly, a girl in the front row bursts into sobs! The teacher immediately thinks, 'What the hell did I just say to cause that? We are studying geography. The damn skills test for the state is tomorrow and we have to be ready.' Regardless, that fine lesson of his just came to a screeching halt. Nothing academic was going to penetrate juvenile heads until they found out why Janey was bawling her head off! It didn't take long. The little girl was terrified her Grandmother, in hospital being operated on, was going to die. She loves her Granny very much!"

"What does the teacher do? The only thing he can, he flicks the lesson in and then talks to Janey and the class about death and how to cope with it."

"A bonehead politician demands the teacher be held accountable for those kids flunking the geography test. What the hell do you think, Danny?"

I knew if this old boy didn't wind down soon, Mandy and Maggie would each have a serious accident at a time and in a place they hadn't planned. I cleared my throat warningly.

"Gotcha, my old bean, a tad bit more and I'll send you on your way. By the by, are you now ready to forsake your deplorable vocation and apply for a teaching credential? Here's the last, me old lad, and this one is not based on statistics as far as I know. Although I've discussed it with other teachers and some agree, it's strictly my own theory. Naturally, I believe I'm right!"

"The biggest mistake school boards made in the twentieth century, I presume on the advice of administrators, was to accept the formation of Middle Schools! Hear me out. Quite some time back, before we had kindergartens, there were but two levels of schools: First grade through eighth, called Elementary, or just plain Public School; graduate from there and advance to the level of nine through twelve which was called High School. There were usually two classes per grade in public school. To my mind this was a distinct advantage. Seventh and eighth graders, being the eldest, were looked up to by first, second third, fourth, fifth and sixth graders. The vast majority of those in the upper grades took the responsibility seriously and looked out for the smaller tots. As a result hero worship was the order of the day. Too busy watching over and even working with the little ones in lower grade classes, discipline was rarely called upon to raise its sleepy head in the seventh and eighth. Considering that 20-60-20 rule to be accurate, teachers in the two upper grades where serious discipline could be required would figure on only two smoking guns per class. Thus, adding the seventh and eighth grades together, the total would be but eight sweethearts you'd prefer to see transfer! School boards have since compounded the problem by adding the sixth graders to the middle school mélange! Now, I'm playing with numbers as you well know. Nothing is locked in an IRS file here. Occasionally a third, fourth, or fifth grader could ruin the day, but threatening to flush them down the john would usually bring 'em back into the fold mighty quick."

"Take Salem's Middle Schools which now most unfortunately do include those sixth graders and the average number of classes per school—ball park—runs to about thirty, ten classes for each grade. Multiply, and hopefully the multiplier will likely be low here, 2 x 30; employing the 20-60-20 rule and you'll come up with 60. Odds are each school is contending with a minimum of sixty tough cookies. Better believe they exert much influence on the good students, and it seldom proves to be beneficial!"

"You've noticed I bemoan placing sixth graders in middle schools. Why? Because they are still terribly young and *vulnerable*; they really need the security of a homeroom with but one teacher. Support and comfort from that teacher as well as establishing that all important rapport is a must at that level. Moving them from class to class every fifty minutes doesn't do much for their stability. We do not need to run an academic assembly line for children from the age of late eleven on up to fourteen. Those years are invasive and the most emotional and difficult period of their lives. Their bodies are undergoing frightening changes. Include this, they also fear; they fear failing, fear embarrassment, fear not being accepted by the 'all important' group, they fear damn near everything! This is the time when those kids are in most need of understanding. So why does society holler, 'Hurry and grow up, kid, it's time for dating, make-up, beer, pantyhose, socializing, and peer approval. Without that group approval, kid, yuh got nothin'.' Add to that the pontificating of those who have never spent *day one* teaching yet know how to cure all the ills. 'Let's load the little laggards up with homework.' So, every night the strugglers trudge home with two to three hours of busy work which the teacher will promptly trash can the next day. Who the hell has time for correcting busy work and still have enough left over to do a proper job of planning and teaching lessons of *meaning*?"

"I'm getting my dander up, it's time to get off my soapbox. Besides, you should have some idea where to look now. I truly hope nothing has happened to the wife of your client. If it has, and you think it is school related, I suggest a careful perusal of school records, maybe even rap sheets. Look for the ones on the low end, those for which school is an agonizing ordeal. Try to determine where growth in learning is not taking place and anger is. Do not overlook those on the high end. The ones who plan on entering colleges of prestige: MIT, Harvard, Yale, Military Academies, Stanford, Princeton. Grade point average will be of vital concern for those students, for without a high rating there will be no hope of acceptance. Watch for those getting D's, C's, or B's—not A's from Lorna. Academic colleges stressing high grades make no exceptions. Of further note Danny, when the young put their smarts departments to work the elders better look out! Check out the following example."

Bet You Don't Know Where Lorna Is!

The corners of Bernie's mouth always turn up when he sets me up for one of his jokes from a never empty bag. They were quirking then and I knew he had one cooking on the front burner:

A fireman, working on the fire engine outside the station noticed a little girl slowly passing by in a little red wagon. Tiny ladders hung off the sides. In the middle of the wagon's bed a garden hose lay coiled. The youngster was wearing a child's fireman's helmet. Her wagon was being pulled by her dog and a limping, woebegone cat.

The fireman walked over to take a closer look at her rig. "That sure is a nice fire truck," he said admiringly.

"Thanks," replied the little doll, "I fixed it up all by myself."

The fireman looked a tad closer and noticed the little girl had tied one of the wagon's ropes to her dog's collar but had fastened the other one to the cat's testicles.

"Little Partner," the fireman said, "I don't want to tell you how to operate your rig, but if you were to tie that rope around the cat's collar, I think you would be able to move a lot faster."

The little girl thought about that for a moment and then replied, "You're probably right mister, but then I wouldn't have a siren."

* * *

"Danny, unless we work with kids all the time we tend to forget that they imitate us. We set the example. Like who the hell else should it be? Of course, a lot also comes from their peers. But, in the main, it is the ones closest to us that we follow. While researching, take a look at parental backgrounds as well. Finally, follow Sandy's suggestion and jump into your clients histories. Start with the doctor's careful snip of the umbilical cord and the first slap on their tender pink butts. And now I must away. You're not going to fetch more bagels and I have to go cut my prize winning lawn anyway. Smile, maybe your Lorna is away simply having a wart removed!"

* * *

Stationed outside in the wagon, parked in the shade of the bank lot adjacent to the Oyster Bar, Maggie was eyeing an old Calico cat saucily flicking its tail at the world, while Mandy's attention was on a fairly new Porsche also taking up residence in their shade. The two people sitting in it were busy observing Bernie and Danny as they exited the restaurant.

"Is that the foo?"

"Yeah, not the baldheaded one with the glasses, the one could be a po-po. He's the one all up in the kool aid. He chills out there a lot."

"I've got him. I'll remember his ugly grill, too. Okay, we're up, let's roll, we've got to get back before we're missed."

Backing up, a purr of contentment throating from the engine, careful not to peel out of the lot and draw attention, the driver eased the Porsche through the light and cruised east on State Street.

5

Bernie had given me a lot to think about, but nothing that hinted at where and what Lorna was doing. Returned to the wagon, I let the dogs out for their breaks for which they were truly grateful. It was just bonging ten on the city hall clock so I headed us for Sagen. I figured to waylay another counselor and quiz 'em about problem kids in the school and which classes had the most. How I hate to grope when I don't know what I'm groping for. Rattling south down Commercial I got on the horn to Sandy and asked her to fire up her computer and dig deeper into the Giddens. Maybe something would surface. I also called the sheriff, the city police, and Frank. No news.

Sagen was enjoying a lazy day. What's to study on the last day of school? Right away I tied into another counselor, Harry Putter by name. With all the hoopla on the latest craze in kids' books he probably came in for more than his share of ribbing. Come to think of it, he did look a little like golf's money stick. A long drink of water, about six-three, he'd scale out at around one hundred and thirty-five pounds. The lump, protrusion, you name it, on the back of his head stuck out much like the back end of my ancient putter. His schnoz, long and pointed, forming what we love to call an 'eagle beak,' identified quite well with the front of my same putter. I quickly dispensed with internal levity as soon as he opened his mouth. No buffoon, I could tell right away this guy knew his kids, knew his colleagues, knew his onions, an' had a whole lot of what today is called 'street smarts.'

"It's nice to meet you, Mr. Doyle, how may I help you?"

On the way to the school I'd been trying to figure how to play it. Do I cozy my way in a side door like I'd done with Mrs. Langer or march in through the front? Flang it, time was of the essence here, I flat stomped in the front!

"Mr. Putter, I'm a private detective. Lorna Diddens has been missing for seven and one-half days. Her husband is quite concerned. It's most unlike her not to keep him apprised of her whereabouts. I've been hired to find her. Do you possess any information which would be of help in locating the lady? Has she been experiencing difficulty with students, staff, curriculum, or school in general? I've been informed she's seemed a bit depressed lately. Are you aware of any health problems? Anything at all could be of help. Is administration making unwelcome changes for next year, such as assignments, class loads, course levels, or change of subject?"

"Mr. Doyle, that's quite a generous list. Suppose I try to take it in order."

Without missing a flaming beat, he worked his way through my questions like reading from a script. Unfortunately, he also answered "No" to all of them, except one!

"Rumors, as you know Mr. Doyle, run rampant in public institutions. This one is vague, but it seems to me I heard of a possible involvement with one of her students two years ago. I understand he also enrolled in her advanced English literature class for this year."

Consulting his records, he continued. "His name is Ernesto Luis Escobar and the young man has been no discipline problem for the school; in fact it's quite the opposite. He is well-liked by his peers and is a highly rated basketball player. We won the championship this year, you know. No little thanks must go to Ernesto. It is my understanding he would like to attend Stanford; admittance there would require a scholarship as well as a high grade-point average. Naturally, English has been his second language but I don't know how successful he's been with Mrs. Diddens this year. Her class is difficult. We do not have her final grades as yet. The young man shows great promise, Mr. Doyle. I should be most surprised to find him failing in any of his subjects. Perhaps you would like to interview him? I believe most classes have been dispensed for today, the last day of school. Undoubtedly, he'll be mingling with classmates in the halls, they all love to swap addresses and exchange hugs. I do believe they call it 'Parole Day.' Do you remember back to the exhilaration of those golden days?"

Golden days my sainted grandmother! I worked my butt off just to keep from failing. What I remember of high school is drudgery, endless hours of study, and nervous sweats on exam days; I don't know how I escaped a damn ulcer or, at the very least, a flaming twitch!

I thanked the 'Putter' for his help, wished him a hole in one, and stepped through the door into hallway bedlam. A mass of students: laughing, talking, hugging, crying, bragging and signing yearbooks! I figured girls would sure be able to point out Ernesto, so I collared a little cutie and asked her to finger him. Lifting a tear-blotched face, she pointed to the far end of the hall where a six-foot-six troop was holding court. Weaving through noisy wail and woe, then immediately getting a crick in my neck, I stepped up to the guy who was busy peeling a clinging blonde off his tall frame.

"Ernesto Escobar?"

Looking puzzled he nodded courteously and answered, "Yes," then waited for me to continue.

"Son, my name is Danny Doyle. I wonder if we could talk for a few minutes in private, how about the empty classroom behind you?"

He looked even more puzzled but I also think he was glad for the reprieve. Out of the corner of my eye I could see the blonde was getting ready to launch herself at him again. He caught the impending action as well and hastily opened the door for me. We both stepped into a room filled with quiet. Sheesh, I'm getting too damned old for the young!

For an eighteen year old, he displayed a lot of dignity and politeness. I liked that. With way too much impunity today far too many kids smart-mouth adults whenever the mood strikes. In my day, those same adults would have bounced them around a while until some manners found their way back to remind of respect. On a hunch, like I'd done with Putter, I also flew this one straight, level, and right at him.

"Ernesto, I am a private detective hired to look for a teacher. Mrs. Giddens has been missing for almost eight days. Do you have any idea of her whereabouts?"

It has been said that Mexican people don't turn white. Ha! That young lad turned as close as damn it into a fair-skinned gringo. His jaw dropped to the basement and for a moment I thought he was going to pass out on me.

"Muh . . . muh . . . is missing! Mrs. Giddens is missing? We had heard she was sick. Some form of female trouble. I was sure she'd come today to wish us all well. May the good God protect her! How may I be of help?"

Bet You Don't Know Where Lorna Is!

His English was excellent. Score one for Lorna. I have been poking around in this business for quite some time and have also conducted more than my share of interrogations. If this kid was lying I looked like Troy Donahue; the bathroom mirror, always truthful, tells me otherwise. Ernesto was genuinely upset. He cared for her, of that I had no doubt. No way was he mixed up in anything harmful to that lady.

"Mrs. Giddens has been missing since last Friday afternoon. Her husband has no idea where she might have gone. Who told you she was sick? I also have to tell you I have it on good authority that you've spent extra time after school with her. What was that all about?"

"Mr. Doyle, Mrs. Giddens is one of the nicest people on earth. I would never harm nor cause her trouble. If it were not for her I wouldn't be able to pursue my dream. I have the wish to attend Stanford on a scholarship. She has spent many extra hours tutoring me since my sophomore year. Thanks to her my grade-point average is now high enough to apply for that college. I do not, as yet, have my final grades. Our teachers usually present them on their workday, the final day of the school year. That is tomorrow."

"I believe you, son, but once again who told you she was sick? While I'm asking here, has Mrs. Giddens had any trouble that you know of with any of the students in your class this semester? For that matter, has she had difficulties with any of the students in the whole school?"

"I know of no trouble, sir. She is a friend to all. Her course is hard but with concentrated study her exams can be conquered; I know, I've done it. As to her sickness, I don't personally know who told us. Perhaps one of my other teachers mentioned it, or somebody in class told it to someone else and

I heard it from them. I am sorry I cannot remember a face for you Mr. Doyle. Sir, if you find out anything, or if I can be of any help whatsoever, please contact me. I truly revere that lady. I will be working in the garden section at the Wal-Mart store on south Commercial over the summer."

"Okay, Ernesto, I'll take you up on your offer. Here's my card. Call me anytime. You, in the meantime, might query your classmates. Use caution. You know them, I don't. It's a long shot but maybe one of them can shed a little light here. Until I find Mrs. Diddens I won't know if there's any danger; still, most people find being careful avoids acquiring those nasty scars one receives from a prowling cougar, comprende amigo?"

Back outside in Frenzy Hall, I wove my way through the huggers and weepers by sliding over a floor wet with tears and escaped to the sunny, the blue, and the quiet; except for traffic noise of course. Oregonians have to suffer Nature's tears in the winter. I say "nuts" to them in the flaming summer! I needed to sit and think somewhere calm, and I knew Mandy and Maggie were ready to split. The collie had that 'long time no lamb stew' look on her kisser. I've informed that Maggie will eat anything so I headed for the Original Pancake house on Commercial for a waffle, for *me*. Time enough for their stew, even though a certain party had gone into her drooling act. Unfortunately, I had gathered no new information to aid the thinking I wanted to do. Did that sentence confuse you? It sure as hell did me!

My waffle slid down nicely. So did a side of ham out for each of my pals. I then drove to the office to check calls, including threats and pleas from bill collectors; nothing new on Lorna. The larder showed signs of neglect so I headed to Fred Myer on Commercial to stock up on fruit, spuds,

Bet You Don't Know Where Lorna Is!

veggies and pet food; then over to WinCo for English muffins and coffee beans. I'm nothing without hot Java in the morning and you know I grind my own beans. WinCo, for well over two years, has been selling coffee for two to three clams less a pound than any of the other chains. They've done the same thing with bananas; thirty-nine cents a pound for seems like eons. Wanna tell me why the other guys don't care to compete? I love Safeway! Their ripe Cantaloupe displays this week at a mere nineteen cents a pound. Fork over fifty-nine cents a pound next week. Same supply of cantaloupe!

For some reason I kind of enjoy shopping. Must be I like to check out the food, especially the meat department. Mandy isn't the only one who likes lamb. A prime loin lamb chop cooked medium rare, with mushrooms and baked potato, is to die for. Yeah, I stocked up on lamb stew, too.

It was coming on for four when I finished all my chores which included a trip to the laundry and the dry cleaners. Sometimes I envy dogs; except for the occasional unwanted shower from the garden hose, they are never stuck with raiment to launder or clean; also nada on the shopping, cooking or dish washing. Desire a hot date? Stand on the sidewalk and bark and no flaming regrets later. If it weren't that I'd have to wear a collar I'd opt to be a dog.

Having struck out once again at Sagen, I decided to head for Sandy's. Hopefully, by surfing about on the internet, she'd found some background info from the class list I'd given her. One thing I had learned, there would be no bottom students to worry about. Lorna's class was advanced and far too tough for those experiencing academic woes. If any student had caused her serious problems it would have to be one with lofty aspirations or a very big compelling ambition. For later, I picked up yo Domino's giant 'everything' pizza, the kind you bake yourself; then the dogs and I surprised Miss Sandra. While M and M wrestled for position on her sofa I fixed us a couple of libations, rum and coke for me, gin and tonic for her. Then, arranging computer printouts of the day's findings on her coffee table, we got comfy.

Most of the information was extraneous: Lucy T., a blonde, had been born in Salem, attended Englewood Elementary, Parrish Junior High, and then moved south to attend Sagen High School. Excellent record; broke left arm falling off her bicycle at ten; chipped a tooth on the monkey bars at twelve; staunch Catholic; homecoming queen her Junior year; liked boys but seldom dated, studies came first. She desired to attend U of O at Eugene where she would aim for ophthalmology: Grade point average 3.9 overall. No drugs; didn't booze at parties; didn't smoke. She made friends easily but could not be led. Good kid. Dull? Not, by God, likely! Dolls like her make up the backbone of this country. Line up a bunch more so I can hug 'em all!

Bill J., football star: Born in Silverton; moved to Salem in time to start at McKinley Elementary; Judson Junior High next, then Sagen. Knocks people down, but only on the football field. Partied while a sophomore; got pie-eyed, falling-down drunk. Discovered there was no charge for the killer hangover but still stayed in bed for three days; hasn't touched a drop of booze since; aiming for Annapolis and a Navy career. Good student, Captain of team; grade point average 3.8 overall. His father, a Navy flyer, is a First Lieutenant with a fine record. Mother is a lawyer. Ten years with Jacob, Gordon, Bloom and Judy. Neither parent has had so much as a traffic ticket; religion, Presbyterian; solid folks.

Bootsy D., musician: Born in Corvallis; folks took up residence in Salem

Bet You Don't Know Where Lorna Is!

in time for her to enter Whiteaker Junior High; moved across town her freshman year of high school. She is very capricious and well-liked; aiming for scholarship to Julliard; grade point average 3.7 overall; occasionally dates Boom-Boom, a tackle on the football team. Her father is a banker, Mother is a nurse; two sisters, ages fifteen and six; another stable family; good neighbors; dog named Boodle! Send us more, Lord!

Janowitz, D. Born in Ogden, Utah; moved to Salem in time to start fifth grade at Hoover Elementary; checked into Judson Junior High in eighth grade; enrolled at Sagen as freshman; good student; grade point average 3.8 overall; he's aiming for electrical engineer. Family is not affluent and a scholarship would help. Father works in meat department at IGA out on Vista. Mother's a clothing clerk at Macy's, in Salem; has three brothers, two sisters; stable family. No religious preference. The kid is very popular with classmates. Good sense of humor. No problems with authority figures. Plays drums in school band.

It went on like that. Mrs. Diddens' class enrollment equaled twenty-four, none of them below 3.0 grade point average. Three more want to be lawyers; one is opting for MIT in Massachusetts; two are looking at medical school. Four desire to teach: in Elementary, Junior or Senior High. One has a Gung-Ho Marine father and that kid is hoping for West Point. Eight are aiming for college with no major chosen as yet; the balance plan to decide over the summer. None of them have been in any serious trouble. Two of them had difficulty with grades in sophomore year but apparently worked their way out of it. As it looks now, all of Lorna's class should graduate with some form of honors. The school valedictorian will come from her class. If

I'd been in her class I bet I'd have amounted to something, too. For sure, I'd have spent more time with her than visiting with the principal!

Friday would be the last day of school for staff. Students, except for those who'd asked to have their final grades mailed, would wander in around noon for their report cards which brought a thought to mind, I had better check tomorrow to see if Mrs. Giddens had sent in her final grades. Sheesh Louise, with nothing to go on, the puzzle still remained. Where the hell was Lorna? What the hell, if any, was a motive for her disappearance?

Deciding to take a break, Sandy popped the pizza in the oven; I made a salad while Mandy and Maggie drooled on one another in anticipation of chow. ESPN listed Thursday night fights. TNT was in the fourth inning of a Chicago-LA baseball game, TBS pictured Atlanta's Braves clobbering her latest foe. I don't care for the fights, reminds of how often I've been belted. Belting hurts! Atlanta is now the current dynasty of the National league and she wearies me. Besides, I don't care what sport you watch, the announcers all have what I call, IMOM. Incessant movement of mouth! Channel on to golf, football, horse-racing, hockey, baseball, basketball—any sport—and if they aren't banging your ears with commercials, the motor-mouths are off and running. Of course, it isn't only sports. Tune in the nine o'clock movie on ABC, CBS, NBC, TNT, TBS, A&E, you name it. The film starts and you get to watch it for an uninterrupted fifteen minutes before the first commercial. It goes downhill from there. Most of the ads are inane, vulgar, silly, insulting or stupid. I do like the AFLAC one. That crazy duck is especially appealing. Have you seen the one with Yogi Berra? I feel a kinship with him, probably because my friends say we think and talk alike.

Bet You Don't Know where Lorna Is!

By the start of the second hour all the stations have the effrontery to interrupt a steady stream of commercials for an oh-so-thin slice of the movie. Uh-huh, I'm supposed to get heavy into an ad for hemorrhoids, the one where either he or she, grimacing and squirming in a seat at the opera, has to stomp on toes while jumping up to head to the john for relief. Yep, they have to go and interrupt a serious drama like that to flashback for another three minutes of the swell movie. Four minutes later, like clockwork, we see and hear why the girls are all wearing jockey shorts or getting stuck in their Maidenform bras. I say to hell with it! All that malarkey makes me want to toss. I can live just fine without all that bilge.

If I grow desperate I'll even play checkers, chess, pinochle or poker with Sandy, except she always beats me. Even that damn Mandy, holding a pair of treys, can bluff me! Maggie is not into poker, she'd rather eat the cards. Besides, after dinner I will usually opt for a game of 'slap and tickle'. That one is mostly okay with Sandy and it's a hell of a lot more fun.

Anon, after two or three fast games under the sheets, a sleepy Sandra informs she will start checking the Giddens out tomorrow and she sends me home. I gather my sleepy pals, squeeze my hostess a few more times and head out to the wagon. Home, after a quiet walk around the block, we three call it a night.

I'd been bushed after the pizza bash and hadn't bothered to check my messages until Friday morning. Probably a good thing because one of them made me so mad I wouldn't have been able to sleep anyway. After wading through the usual trash I got to it:

* * *

"Peepah, youse is stickin' yer lousy PI nose inta 'tings what ain't any a yer bizznez. Considá dis a friendly warnin' from us, ya ain't gonna ged anudda. Gid ta hell away outa it. Ya ain't gonna find no profit init fer youse!"

* * *

Well, well, seemed like I'd struck a nerve. If so, where and why? The accent had a definite touch of New York, but I wondered if it hadn't been just a touch overdone? I had met and bunked with a ton of New Yorkers in the Air Force. While it's true they mostly talk funny, occasionally they'll string whole sentences together long enough so that Masters in English, such as myself, are able to understand them. Something most foul here was beginning to stink in the woodshed. And who might I inquire is *us*?

Lorna had now been missing a full week and still nothing led to why? Remembering my thought of the previous evening, I called Departmental Records at Sagen and asked if Mrs. Giddens had delivered her final grades as yet? I was told, "Yes," but they had been E-mailed not hand delivered.

"Isn't that a tad unusual?" I asked. "I thought all teachers were required to deliver their grades personally."

"Once upon a merry time they surely did, sir. However, as we all happily splash around in the computer age now, it is becoming more commonplace to use that devilish machine as has Mrs. Diddens in this case."

"Were there any unusual changes in the final grades over, say, the midterm results?"

"I'm afraid that information is not available to the general public, Mr. Doyle. You'll need a dispensation from higher authority to gain access to a teacher's grades or grading system."

Bet You Don't Know Where Lorna Is!

"Look, Pal, I presume you are aware that Mrs. Diddens is missing. I am a private detective and have been hired by her husband to locate her. Anything that the school can make available may help me to accomplish that. Suppose you call Carrows Ford out on Lancaster; ask for Frank Diddens. If he gives his permission to share that information call me at 353-4402 and I'll come out to the school and pick it up. That way nobody will get on your case. What do you say?"

"Mrs. Diddens is special at this school Mr. Detective. I'll be happy to comply with your request. I have some students waiting to see me now. Once I am free, I will call the agency and get back to you. I shouldn't be more than an hour."

True to his word James Fleury, from Records, called forty-five minutes later and said the information I'd requested would be available in fifteen minutes. I held the door of the wagon open like a bleeding chauffeur for my two M's, and then we smoked and rattled our way back to Sagen.

James was a surprise! A husky lad, he was built like Johnny Weismuller; he was also considerably younger and in much better shape seeing as Tarzan was dead! I do not know about Cheetah. Fleury had a nice smile, good teeth and a strong grip. I liked him from the git-go. Apologizing, he requested I study the information in his presence as it could not leave his department. He then handed me a folder which contained the midterm results as well as those all important final test scores.

Nostalgia pinched my pear-shaped bod as I tried to fit into one of the student desks. Hey, when you reach my age I'll bet it will be squeeze time for you, too! I gave her grades a quick eye, then slowed down and followed up with a more thorough scan. Nothing earth-shaking showed, with perhaps one puzzler. Everyone at midterm had scored B+ or higher. The final grade showed A- to A for all students but two. Ernesto Escobar and Bill J. each received an F. Now wouldn't that lock a balky ram in the sheep squeezer! True, kids that shine in sports, adding prestige to the school, sometimes ease off a tad when battling the academics. But football is a fall sport and basketball slam dunks in the winter, so what the hell was going on here?

Ernesto hadn't indicated trouble with studies. In fact, if memory serves, he'd seemed confident of the results on the final. I'd yet to run Bill J. to ground but, as the kangaroo said to the Aborigine, I'm gonna hop right to it. Something smelled. Wanta bet one of those hundred year old Chinese eggs hadn't fallen off the top shelf, pranged itself on a lower one, and decorated those two kids with broken shell and rotten contents?

Lorna's class being English Lit, the test would have been of the essay kind. God, how I'd hated blue books! Unless teachers were lazy and just putting in their time, they never gave multiple choice exams in English classes. Having spent the whole semester trying to teach their captives how to write it was only natural an essay would be the proper way for them to achieve parole. To this day, Thomas Hardy and his Tess of the D'Urbervilles can go get stuffed. I wasn't that enchanted with Edith Wharton's Ethan Frome, either! Come to think of it, all those old geezers put me to sleep. I'll take Dick Francis or Lawrence Block any day.

6

"Jim, me stalwart lad, do you have the blue books from Lorna's class? I'm more than a little puzzled over two of these grades, they don't add up with the information I've been given. Neither of the students should have failed her last test."

"No, Danny, we don't get to see those, they remain with the teacher. The books will probably be found either in her classroom or at her home. Given time, I believe Mrs. Giddens often goes over test results with each of her students. She feels that they deserve explanations for the grades they receive. You will have to search diligently and far to find a better teacher."

"Isn't it a little unusual for a teacher to not show up at school on the final day, Jim? I understand she also hasn't called in to explain the reason for her absence to the principal."

"That is puzzling, but most of us believe Lorna is away conducting private business; if so, it explains why she E-mailed her grades rather than delivering them. Other than straightening out classrooms the principal feels nothing more is required of teachers this semester. Classes for next term will be assigned in late August. Lorna will be back long before then."

"I'd really like to take a gander at those blue books, Jim. Suppose you and I wander down to her room and toss it. I promise to take nothing and it will save time if we look together."

While walking to Lorna's room I posed another puzzler, "Jim, how do we know it was Lorna who E-mailed those grades to the school? Could anyone else have done it?"

"I really doubt that, Danny. In this fun-filled computer age all the teachers use passwords and they guard them very carefully."

Perhaps, thinks the famous detective, but are there not those delightfully mischievous folks, called hackers, running around loose in the woods? How tough could it be for one of those weasels to snag a password?

We tossed and we tossed. There were no flaming blue books in teacher Diddens' classroom. Be damned to that noise! Something was definitely not kosher and Danny Doyle was bloody well going to find out why! My next stop would be the Diddens' residence where I planned to do a lot more tossing. I located Frank at work and he agreed to meet me at their home in twenty minutes. Mandy and Maggie reluctantly hurried to take care of the necessaries and then I burned rubber to meet with Diddens.

We did not toss their house, we bloody well ransacked it; upstairs, downstairs, in my lady's chamber. I even looked behind the water heater and in the water chamber of the toilet. Nada, zip. We didn't find so much as a broken pencil let alone any blue books. Curiouser and curiouser!

Either Lorna had discovered a need, planned on her temporary absence, and taken the test booklets with her, or . . . ? There were still no clues to help us, but I felt sure there was something more than sour in the sauerkraut and it was definitely going to spoil somebody's summer vacation.

While I had Frank corralled, I took advantage of the opportunity and asked for further family history. He and Lorna had hailed from where, meaning their bailiwick? How about numbers, names, and locations of both

Bet You Don't Know Where Lorna Is! 65

sets of family members? What and where did schooling and or training take place? Had there been any serious health problems for either? How about rapport with neighbors? Ever make the lovable tax man mad? Could a colleague be angry with him, at work, at play? Anything, like damned anything, which might give one tiny clue? I hauled out pad and pen for what I hoped would soon be enough info to keep Mandy, Maggie, and me checking for a week.

Frank was born February 21, 1962: Had grown up in Santa Fe, New Mexico. Roman Catholic. Youngest of four brothers. Mother and father died in train wreck ten years ago. Completed high school and started work in Shell gas station in Las Cruces. Saved money, took some business and auto mechanic courses at U of NM. Was hired at local garage and in a couple of years progressed to Auto agency and into sales. One brother, the eldest, lives in Seattle, married and with two kids. Next in line lives in Portland; single, works in advertising. The one up from Frank lives in San Diego, married and divorced twice. Works in Penny's shoe department. Now lives in swinging single's condo. He was into Mary Jane but not heavy. None of the brothers has ever been in trouble with the law. Ask him, the family is pretty stable. While none are presidential material (who is?) they, including Frank, are pretty average fellas and no problem to anyone.

Lorna was born in Las Vegas, New Mexico, July 24, 1963: Also Roman Catholic, two older sisters; Mother and father are living. Folks now reside in Santa Fe. Good student. Grades qualified her for entrance to U of NM at Las Cruces in 1982; met Frank in Student Union. Dated on and off for four years before marrying. School had to come first. She always wanted to be a teacher. No fooling around with booze, smoking, drugs or wild parties; does like a gin and tonic or a martoonie from time to time. Likes to socialize but keeps self in control. Hey, if Frank took her to Las Vegas, Nevada, for a good time, that lady would sit down in the middle of the Mirage Casino and read a book! Her eye is on raising kids—hers and the ones she teaches. Gets along well with neighbors and colleagues; no enemies they are aware of. Simply trying to do best for her family while working to help pay off the mortgage. Student taught, then instructed for three years in Santa Fe High School. After promotion for Frank, they moved to Salem in July of 1990.

Salem was eager to hire her and Sagen High got lucky. I was really beginning to like this lady a lot. Promising to continue the search, I took my leave of Frank and headed back to the office.

* * *

A little work had begun to trickle in: A bond jumper had been traced to Eugene. Another kid, all of thirteen, had taken to the road and been spotted in San Diego. In my work I also double as a process server. A sleazy book publisher was definitely not going to appreciate the ringing of his front doorbell. He and his partner were blaming their failure on one another. One of them figured to duck responsibility by latching on to the old ploy, "Help! Save me! I'm claiming bankruptcy." The courts allow it. Guys like that need to be tarred and feathered and tossed in an iced-over Willamette River!

The courts were on short weeks due to budget cuts, so I decided to await the pleasure of serving the lawsuit papers for a few more days and opted to talk Sandy into driving with me to Eugene to pick up the jumper. I've an ex-Marine, ex-cop, friend. Retired, he lives on Coronado Island in California. I

Bet You Don't Know Where Lorna Is! 67

knew he could check on the runaway. In his prime, this guy'd been hooked on running himself. He even ran to work. I can see running from, not to! Because his feet were always shredding Nikes his buddies labeled him "Scooter." One time, a loser ripped off a newspaper stand then legged it up the street like a cheetah after a gazelle. The bum had a one block head start but Scooter hops outa the police car and starts after him anyway. Soon, not even breathing hard, he's running side by side with the gonif. This is what he says to the klutz:

"Pardon me, sir, but you have broken one of the laws of this fair city and I have to arrest you. Please stop immediately before I have to knock you down which, unfortunately, may do you something of an injury."

Well, as only one of his lungs was now working, the guy stops. Scooter hadn't even broken a sweat. Another time, after our hero gets tired of chasing yahoos and transfers to LA traffic detail, he's at Third and Figueroa directing gas burners driven by idiots when the world's worst jam-up occurs. My pal blows his whistle, waves his arms, does a little tap-dance, looks up to Heaven, and blows his whistle again. Nobody bothers to listen to his directions, so Scooter says, "Hell with it!" He walks to the drugstore on the corner and orders himself a coke. "Let the damn fools sort the mess out for themselves." Scooter is my kind of guy. I was sure, if the old geezer could still find his way downtown, he'd collar the runaway and put her on a bus heading for Salem. My rates for collaring runaways are one hundred clams a day plus expenses, unless they've left the country. I knew I needed to be fair and split my fee right down the middle with the old geezer. I figured to mail him forty of the hundred if he nailed her in one day.

You already know the dogs aren't much for conversation. That's not altogether bad as Sandy talks enough for all of us. I'm not complaining. She has an inquiring mind and likes to discuss puzzlers. For example, early on Saturday as we cruised down I-5 toward Eugene, she asked.

"How do you know that runaways won't be going back into a bad situation, one much worse than they'd experience on the road?"

"Good question, love. Not to worry. Before I'll agree to bring them back I check out the family. If I catch even the slightest whiff of bad family relations I won't accept the contract. I also make it very clear to the client that *I will* be coming around to see how successful the reunion is. I make it plain, if Pop beats the crap out of the kid, he'll have M, M, and me to reckon with. Most runaways have just been denied some juvenile desire and with a good mad on taken a hike. When I show up they are usually tired of their so-called adventure, glad to see me, and mostly a hell of a lot wiser. Lots of hugging, kissing, and crying usually takes place at home, and life goes on."

"That's good to know," says my softy. "How about this bond jumper we're going to bring back, isn't he liable to be desperate and dangerous?"

"Yup, there is always that possibility; however, I will seat him in the back beside Mandy. She will lay her friendly grin on him, constantly! He will be another one to discover that she shows all her teeth when she smiles. Since I've been using new chicken flavor toothpaste on both my girls' choppers their teeth just naturally shine pearly-white. Maggie will sit behind him on the cargo deck. She loves to get up close so she can breathe softly in people's ears. We won't have any trouble with him."

"Okay, Smarty, can you give out with an educated guess as to the missing

Bet You Don't Know Where Lorna Is!

Lorna? Any evidence to point to her location, yet?"

There she had me again. I'd been mind-mulling the *dese, dose* and *us* of the phone message and trying to pin down the *us*? Logic said the note was referring to the Diddens. Certainly they had occupied most of my time over the last nine days. If so, whose flaming toes had I stepped on and what were they afraid I'd find out, that Lorna could be counted among the dead?

Traffic was moving well on I-5 and it was a gorgeous sunny day, the kind Oregon will present when even she is weary of rain. Tired of racking my one brain over the unknown, I obeyed an impulse and cut west off the freeway to take 34 over to Corvallis and thence south on 99W toward Eugene. 99 is only a two-lane highway, but she's a pretty drive and not always crowded during weekdays.

"Sandy, I have a question for you. If you had the choice of going to a baseball game, attending a Mozart concert, playing a round of golf, or visiting an art gallery, which would you choose?"

"I'd take the Mozart concert."

"I see I need to clarify here. I mean, in what order would you be inclined to place those four choices?"

"The Mozart concert first and then the art gallery."

"How about the other two choices?"

"Oh, you're asking me to make four choices!"

"Yeah."

"Okay, well my third and fourth choices would be the Mozart concert and the art gallery."

"God damn it, will you place them all in order of preference or not!"

"Why don't you just tell me what's sizzling in your noggin? The minute you turned off I-5 I knew you were planning something. What is it, golf or baseball?"

Brother, it's downright scary when they can figure you out that fast!

"Okay, Sweets, here it is. There's a nice little wayside not too far down the road will make a lovely pit stop for the dogs. Then, about eight miles from Eugene we can make another short stop. You know I like to play golf from time to time. While I'm no longer young I am not exactly in my dotage either; still, the last three or four times I have played I couldn't hit a cow in the ass with a shovel. I think the trouble is with my driver. I've had 'The Slammer' for well over thirty years and I know he's kinda tired. So happens we're going to be coming up on a place called Fiddlers Green in a few more miles. The place has golf clubs up the dump stump along with all the other equipment that pertains to the game. You pick out what you want, take a walk out to their driving range, and try it on for size. If the fit isn't good go back and reach for something else. I purely have this feeling that my new driver is impatiently waiting there for me. We've plenty of time so I figured you'd like to look the place over; it won't take but a few minutes and then I'll buy lunch at the Electric Station in Eugene.

We stopped briefly at the wayside for the dogs; then, back on the road again I said,

"What do you say, love, wanna give Fiddlers Green a go?"

Just then the wagon turned off 99W all by itself and onto the long drive leading up to golfers' heaven. Sandy grinned and just shook her head. Mandy and Maggie, accustomed to retrieving my golf balls, mostly from yo sand, brush, and rotten water hazards, perked up right away. An hour and a half later, and six hundred bucks shier, we hit 99W again toting my new 'Bazooka' driver, along with a nine wood, and a new putter!

Lunch tickled our palates and was thoroughly enjoyed but I only saved samples for M&M. I didn't dare gripe about the expense. Hey, do you know how much that joint stiffs you for a flaming burger?

* * *

The police department in Eugene is located in the city hall on Pearl St. They had been advised I was coming and the culprit was soon released to me. He was an ugly sucker and had been a long time between baths! He had been nailed for pulling an old con, the one where he generously offers the mark a killer deal as he's got to skip town in a hurry. A buddy has two thousand clams locked away in a suitcase for him. Once retrieved, the guy is willing to split the two grand with the mark. Trouble is, the loot is in storage and will take fifty clams to bail out. He's broke, which is why the offer of the deal in the first place. After the sucker ponies up the dough he is to wait out front so as to not draw any attention. While the dope waits out front the thief pockets the fifty and slips out a side door. In this case though the mark turned out to be a cop and his backup was waiting for Bathless outside that same side door.

Yep, that wool puller's been around almost as long as the Badger Game.

I suspected our guest also had some priors. Coupled now with his latest con the law was probably going to send him away for quite awhile. Crime don't pay, guy! At least it isn't supposed to.

Politely, I held the rear side door of the wagon open for him. Continuing with further politeness I introduced Mandy and Maggie. On cue, they both smiled kindly. Articulating clearly I explained the rules to Bathless. I also informed of the consequences of breaking them and away we rolled heading north. As predicted our passenger was silent and well-behaved all the way to Salem which allowed me the time to concentrate on my driving while also fantasizing about some long, over two hundred yard, drives. Wouldn't you know it though, Sandy kept grinning to herself every time she caught me hunching in my seat as I mentally dispatched a beauty.

I dropped Old Smeller off at the police department on Liberty and headed directly to Payless for some relief for my cringing wagon. Lysol was on sale so I bought a quart! Though no closer to solving Lorna's disappearance, soon to be in double digit days, all in all it had been a lovely respite.

On Sunday in an attempt to discourage a headache I decided to go test my 'Bazooka' at the Evergreen course in Mount Angel. I promised Sandy breakfast if she'd keep her lip buttoned when, and if, I made a bad shot. Tell you the truth I did belt a few good ones but I couldn't concentrate and flicked it in after five holes. The headache remained and I decided if I was going to be stuck with the pain I'd go home and restudy my notes on the Didden's case. Nothing performed a high jump up from smudged pages so I decided on one more flaming trip to Sagen. I wanted to check grades for every one of Lorna's students, from freshman to senior. Ernesto's and Bill J.'s final grades still baffled me.

Bright and early Monday morning I decided to go buy Judge a bagel and test the waters for any bright new ideas of his before heading out to Sagen.

"Focus, dear boy," buzzed the old geezer, his mush full of lox and cheese.

Bet You Don't Know Where Lorna Is!

I hate it when Bernie does that. Focus the hell on what? Not to worry, he was off and running and could hardly wait to pack my ears. Jesus, are all school teachers as bloody windy?

"Danny, it's possible you may be looking in the wrong direction," he chirps, "I take it you've found no indication of hanky-panky, no money troubles at home, no difficulties with staff at school, no problems with her family, her physical or mental health; nothing buried in her past, nothing about family members who may have spent time in Butterfly Village (the Funny Farm to you!), and no threatening mail. There would seem to be but two areas left not thoroughly explored: She took off because teaching was wearing her down and she plain wanted a change of pace; maybe she's opted for a complete career change. Believe me, it happens! Secondly, perhaps a student or students have given her trouble. Why the latter? Could be a connection to grades but why that would cause her to disappear is quite beyond me."

"All this cogitating is enervating, Danny me old son, I don't suppose you could see your way clear to ponying up for a bagel and a cuppa? No! I was afraid of that. Ah well, I'll just add a touch more to your education re the benefit of career changes before I go home and fertilize my lovely lawn."

"Many years ago I was an assistant parts manager in a Chevrolet agency in Southern California. Soon after I married I'd felt a compelling need for a Vocational change myself. I have always enjoyed photography and decided to head in that direction. Freelancing seemed to be the ticket; however, newspapers and magazines will only buy quality work. It seemed to me that such would necessitate the purchase of a good camera. That idea hied me to yon camera shop for advice. The old boy behind the counter babbled of Nikons, Hasselblads and a honey of a German-made 35 millimeter with through the lens viewing; it was called an Exacta. Naturally, my pocketbook dictated a used purchase only. Even used, cameras like those don't come cheap. He showed me an Exacta he had but recently taken in, then hastened to inform me that the lovely camera I was now holding had been manufactured in West Germany, not East. There was a world of difference in quality between the two areas which made his offering an excellent buy, he spouts. At that time, including the case, I believe it was priced at one hundred and ninety clams. Mind, the year was 1958 and that added up to a load of clams. Both our salaries, Mollie-O was teaching, amounted to but a pittance; still, nothing ventured as they say, so I bought the flaming thing. One of the best buys I ever made. Later, upon becoming a teacher myself, as an aid in teaching geography, I put together many a slide show for my students and none of my kids ever nodded off during the showings! I digress a tad, must be my raging thirst, are you sure . . .?"

Pumped up with another bagel and coffee, the old goat continued:

"It wasn't long before I found out that my Exacta, good as it was, wouldn't lead me into the realm of big time photography. For that, a format type camera was needed. Do you subscribe to Arizona Highways, Danny? If not, buy a copy and check it out. I guarantee you'll see some of the most beautiful photos to be found anywhere. Most of them will be the products of format cameras. The very best format camera is a Linhof Technika, also made in West Germany. To buy a new one today, trot out six thousand clams plus! Even used jobs go for four or more. Look it up on the internet."

"Naturally, I whippied off to my favorite vendor for needed photographic equipment—his words, not mine. Even back then, when he told me the price of those sweethearts, I realized I'd have to get a second mortgage. Wouldn't you know though, he'd just taken in a used one which came complete with body, telephoto, standard and wide angle lenses, a top mounting viewer, and a carrying case. It was an absolute dream and only a few of those lovely clams, like a mere nine hundred and fifty of them!"

"Behold a few disadvantages to the formats: they are heavy, bulky, and cumbersome; film comes in packs and is expensive; they take time to set up. Naturally, having now become an artist in the field, you don't just point and shoot with them, one must create. It can take anywhere from fifteen minutes to half an hour just to prepare for the shot. We bought the damn camera!"

"General Motors used to put out a magazine called 'Friends.' It was a nice little creation and often requested unusual quality photographs for which they'd pay. One of my first format camera shots, after I'd spent what seemed like ten years learning how to use the sucker, was of Twin Lakes in the Mammoth Lakes region off Highway 395 in the Sierra Nevada's. A fast narrow stream feeds the lakes via high falls. Mollie-O nearly had a fit because I stepped out into the middle near the drop-off. Balancing myself on a rock, I aimed the camera by sight rather than through the viewer and then took the shot. It turned out rather well and can be viewed today in the July 1960 issue. GM paid me five Lincolns for it, far from a fortune but not too shabby, either. I mounted a copy of the photo on cardboard which I retain to this day. I figured I was on my way to a Pulitzer!"

"Stop squirming, Doyle! Remember, the theme of this refreshing essay is

Focus. Besides, I'm almost to the point of no return anyway."

"Our next freelancing project, to write and photograph the story of the birth of twin colts, came about by accident. Birth and then survival of twins is extremely rare in the horse world. I wrote the story from the viewpoint of their mother. Her name was Ginny Sims and she was terribly proud of her offspring. So okay, it loses something in the translation but that is not the point. Using my format I got some good pictures, typed the story, and then decided to go for broke. Back in the late fifty's Life Magazine liked to feature the unusual in animal behavior. Toward the end of each edition, but before the reader reached the back cover, they would often print a full page photo of man or animal engaged in doing something dumb. I remember one in particular was a shot of a flaming rabbit eating spaghetti!"

"Having trouble breathing, lad? Doesn't pay to choke on a mouthful of coffee, does it? When will you learn every word I utter is true!"

"To continue: I gathered some of the colts' prints and mailed them along with the story to Life. Some six weeks later I received the nicest rejection. Can you believe it, a flaming turndown after they'd already printed a picture of a bloody spaghetti scoffing rabbit! Undaunted, I tried six or seven more publications. No interest. Finally, in a telegram, I offered the story to the Quarter Horse Journal in Amarillo, Texas. Back came a cable right away: 'Send pictures and story soonest, we will print it.' "

"Hallelujah, I cried, "fame and fortune are heading our way!" I wrapped prints and script carefully, ran to the post office, and watched as my stamped creation was placed in the 'out' box. That was my first mistake!"

"Five weeks later, having heard nary a word from Texas, I penned them a line: 'Gee guys, I'm sure you must be awfully busy, but I have heard naught re the progress of my story. Shuckies, you've even forgotten to pay me for my little gem?' "

"One week later I received a check in the mail and a notice telling me the date of publication of my masterpiece. What was the total on the check? *Twelve dollars and fifty cents*! It cost me more than that just for the film and mailing expenses. You see, me old son, I relied on their good faith to pay a generous sum. Thus, I failed to bargain before mailing everything to them. Theirs is a monthly magazine and my story came out in the January, 1958, issue. It sites on page 33 and I still have a copy in my library. Of course the moral is that *some career changes can turn out to be dismal failures.* Fortunately, I had retained my job so bidding sayonara to the freelancing photography biz wasn't too painful. I've taken some pretty good shots with that format but nothing which brought in a bonanza, like say for a Monet."

"As you have been almost patient, I'll spring for our next bagel and coffee and then add but a brief postscript to that almost career of mine."

Bernie hastened to stoke us up and once his bloody coffee had just the right amount of cream and sugar he continued:

"I kept that lovely big camera for many years, long after I'd chosen a teaching career. Film was still expensive and, being selective, my format pics were few and far between. Twenty years after I'd blown my nine hundred plus to purchase the format, I decided to try my hand at making movies. This was about five years before the advent of camcorders. Bell and Howell had just come out with a dandy 8 millimeter job with automatic zoom. Wow, was it ever a smasher! They wanted nine hundred clams for it, on sale! Rite-Aid, in downtown Salem, put on a demonstration and I had to have it. I carried my Linhof to the salesman and suggested a swap plus a little to boot. I failed to notice the gleam in his eye when he spied my treasure. We settled for a three hundred dollar difference—from me!"

"Ah, Danny, sometimes it really hurts to be so damn dumb! That Bell & Howell never did live up to expectations and it soon died in the industry as well. Shortly, out came the Camcorders and you couldn't get rid of an 8 millimeter, even if you threw in your sister and she also modeled for Vogue! I tried every damn camera store in Salem, placed ads in the paper, and pinned notices on bulletin boards. It was like trying to give away the seven year itch! I finally did it. Still in mint condition, including its locking case, I sold it at a garage sale in April of 2001. Though I had handed out over nine hundred dollars for it, I still believe I made out like a bandit. Are you ready? As I bid it a fond adieu, I pocketed a whole *forty-five clams*. The bloody buyer's check bounced!"

"*Focus*, my lad; go back to those class lists. Start checking deeper into family backgrounds from there. It is quite possible some pushy parents are the ones deciding careers for the recalcitrant. Pressure on kids to succeed, from almost all walks of life, is horrendous today. Could be one or two are at the breaking point. Focus and be resourceful, I say."

Bernie's mouth was quirking again!

"*Coping with the world's challenges today requires resourcefulness. Consider our dear Sister Mary Ann who works for a home health agency. Why just last week she was out making her rounds, visiting homebound patients, when her car ran out of gas. As luck would have it, yon Texaco gas* station, a block away, was still open. She walked to the station intent on borrowing a petrol can and buying some gas. The attendant informed the only gas can he owned had just been borrowed by another unfortunate soul but, if desired, she could wait until it was returned."

"Since Sister Mary Ann was on the way to see another patient, she elected not to wait and walked back to her car. Once there, she looked for something in her jalopy that she could fill with gas. Nothing surfaced until she spotted a bedpan that had been requested by a patient."

"Having always been resourceful, even in her childhood, the good Sister Mary Ann walked back to the station carrying the bedpan. The attendant filled it with gasoline for her and smiled as she walked slowly back to her automobile, trying not to spill any. Stepping carefully to the back of her car she gingerly poured the contents of her carrier into the gas tank."

"Two men had been watching her from across the street. When Sister Mary Ann stepped up to her car and emptied the bedpan into the tank, one of the men turned to the other and said,"

"If that sucker starts, I'm gonna go see the Father tomorrow and become a Catholic!"

* * *

"Well for heaven's sake, Dan, I do believe my coffee cup is empty. I guess you . . . ?"

This is probably a good place to mention that during the dull parts—which I hasten to assure you will be few and far between—you will undoubtedly continue to be subjected to more of Bernie's jokes and that is eminently fair as I certainly don't see any good reason why I should be the only one having to suffer!

There is no doubt about it, sessions with old Teach definitely perk up a guy's spirits. Heading for the wagon, I warned Bernie to be careful and not inhale while fertilizing. Why his lousy grass needs the time and care he lavishes on it, beats me, it will only continue to grow! I hate cutting lawns.

I was still laughing over his gas can story on the way to Sagen. The dogs, including yours truly after three cups of coffee, definitely needed pit stops so I stopped off at their favorite watering hole, Bush Park. After we took care of our needs, they also conned me into a run. If Maggie's legs weren't so short I believe she'd beat Mandy to the Frisbee. If that ever happened, I have a hunch Mandy would leave home. Second to snagging sleazes, Frisbee is her life! She is so proud of herself after a great catch that even holding a mouthful of plastic she gives out with a bragging bark! I let them fool around a while longer and then ordered them to climb aboard Burping Bertha (bet you name your vehicles, too). Sagen awaited and it was time we earned our dough. I also reminded my partners that listening to the incessant chirping of Bernie had not, so far, slipped me clue one as to the whereabouts of the fair Lorna.

7

As I turned a corner, a couple of streets away from the school, I spotted a kid checking out mailboxes. He was feigning innocence but his act didn't seem quite kosher to me. I figured he was probably boosting mail. I drove around the block and came back on the other side of the street. Sure enough, he was reaching into another box about four away from the first. I opened the passenger door and sent Mandy and Maggie out to talk to him. Then, parking quickly, I walked back. Both girls, wearing their wide, "Howdy" smiles, were holding him close to a tree. He wasn't smiling at all.

"What's up my man? Do you work for the post office?" I asked.

"No, but I have a perfect right to be here," he whined. "The neighbors are away. I live just down the street and they've asked me to collect their mail for them. I do it all the time, so why don't you just get lost, Gramps!"

Well looky there, along came a compelling urge to find out if his head would fit in one of the mailboxes! But, alas, mature adults should exhibit tolerance toward our youth. Reaching way inward, clear to the bottom of my gizzard, I grabbed a chunk of restraint and then flashed my ID at him.

"As you can see, me bucko, I carry a badge." On a hunch I added, "Now suppose you exhibit some bleeding manners and point out just which house is yours."

I had to admit he was smooth but he was also beginning to sweat. He pointed to the far one of five. There was a fancy just washed Lexus sedan parked in the driveway.

"Tell you what kid, I will bet either Mom or Pop are home. Leave us just go and check to see if you're legit. The dogs will do you no harm as long as you behave. Just walk carefully in front of me."

By now he wasn't far from blubbering. "Kid," I added, "As I see it, there are two items of note here: You don't live in that house. You are not collecting the neighbors' mail you are stealing it. And that, my lad, is known as a federal offense. The Feds will lock you up and throw away the key for boosting mail. So what's it going to be? I take you up the walk here and surprise the owner, I take you downtown, or you tell me the truth right here and now. I may be able to help you."

By now he had turned to jelly and the truth came pouring out. He did not live there. He was stealing and would never do it again! He'd lost his summer job and needed dough to pay off some guys from school who were hustling him. Further inquiry elicited he attended Sagen but was not an honor student. There was a surprise! I made him put all the mail back. Then I sat him in the wagon beside M & M while I drove to the school. I planned for the two of us to have a cozy little chat there.

* * *

Damn him! Damn him to hell! Always pushing. Always pushing his nose into other peoples' business. I've never wanted to kill and now I don't know what to do. And SHE! She had to make a big deal out of nothing. Cribbing is being done all the time, why jump on me? Well, she's taken care of, but what if he finds out? I hate him! I can't figure a way out. That fat detective keeps snooping around and I think the other guy with the glasses is helping him. Nobody cares! Nobody understands us! Those who should are too wrapped up in their own petty problems. Who can I ask for help, Taffy? Oh, yes, good old Taffy never lets me down. God, I'm scared!

* * *

Would you believe good old Sagen looked just the same? Have I only been on this case ten, soon to be eleven, days? If Lorna hasn't been kidnapped why the hell hasn't she called Frank? How come nobody has seen her and reported it to the cops? If she has been snatched, how come there hasn't been a ransom note? How come, how come?

I found a cozy spot in the shade outside the school, parked, and turned to Junior Dillinger:

"Okay kid, for starters, name, rank and serial number? In other words, what's your name, address and phone number?"

Still intimidated by my grinning duo, the kid couldn't get the words out fast enough:

"My name is Greg Billings. I live at 414 Joplin St, South. Our phone number is 363-5372. I am a junior at Sagen. Please mister, the only reason I was stealing mail is because of the guys who are threatening to beat me up. They are seniors at Sagen. I borrowed thirty bucks from one of them. He is one of the school's macho guys, figures on going to a military school. His old man is a biggie in the Marines. He wants fifty percent interest or he and his three buddies are going to break my legs! I don't have a job. I asked my old man for a loan but he doesn't have the thirty bucks to spare. What else could I do?"

"What you could have done is go talk the principal or the cops, kid. Why the need for thirty clams?"

"You ever try to impress a girl, mister? I ain't the best lookin' guy at Sagen and girls don't usually give me the time of day. There's this real cute little trick in my math class who thinks I'm okay. I just wanted to buy her a present. I thought my Ma or the old man would cover me. How did I know of their money troubles? Parents don't tell their kids about stuff like that. I tried to get a job at all the local markets, including Safeway, Albertson's and Fred Myer, but all the other guys beat me out."

How well I remember those puppy love days and the absolute abject misery that went along with 'em. I had to admit the little weasel had a point.

He wasn't much on character and his continual, irritating whining wore at my nerves until I'd had enough.

"Look, kid, we all have troubles. You ever hear that a little beforehand reflection sometimes does wonders? I'll admit I don't like the idea of scruff breaking your legs for a lousy thirty bucks, so I'll make you a deal. I'm going to allow you play junior detective for me. Let me remind you it would also be best if you kept your mouth shut about it. I want you to make a list of all the kids in Mrs. Diddens' junior and senior classes and then star which ones might become troublemakers, or possibly be already in trouble; act discreetly. That means use caution. I don't want to raise any suspicions, you dig? List them all from minor rule breakers on up to major. In return, I'll pay the three Hamilton's you owe and get those bozos off your back. In addition, if you do the job right, I'll drop fifty more in your lap."

"Here is my card. Call anytime when you have the list and I'll arrange a meeting. Remember, detectives keep a low profile; a further piece of advice, your buddies are not the only ones capable of breaking legs, capisce? Now tell me where I can find those four winners and then get lost, Mandy hasn't had lunch yet! "

* * *

Bet You Don't Know Where Lorna Is! 85

Naturally, the kid's nemeses mostly hung out around the basketball court on Sagen's sports field. They weren't hard to spot. Mostly pseudo macho, loud profanity emanating from two of them, they were trying to impress three little miniskirts who, if they ever had to sit down, would expose everything north of Cleveland! The other two guys just grinned sheepishly as the vile language of Dink and Donk polluted the air.

"Hi guys, do you four heroes know a kid named Greg Billings?"

"What's it to ya, Old Pops?" sneered one of the loudmouths.

"I have coin of the realm here from him if such be owed you, my learned young sir. May I have the pleasure of introducing Maggie and Mandy along with my humble self? I am Greg's Uncle Savior. Perhaps he's mentioned me? No, don't jump around like that guys, Mandy gets a mite nervous at sudden moves and she's yet to enjoy her mid-morning snack! I understand Greg owes one of you gentlemen thirty clams. I am here to tender it. Naturally, men of the world like yourselves wouldn't be foolish enough to mention such a shoddy item as unfair interest, would you? Greg can be a little foolish at times. Letting you four bloodsuckers latch on to him is one of those times. Have you all noticed Mandy and Maggie's nice smiles? They are fond of Greg, as is his uncle. Tell you what, take the thirty, knock off the threats, stay away from my nephew, and we'll call it square."

"Old Pops," smirked the other mouth, a long drink of water sporting a lovely case of acne. "What we do is no business of yours, best be careful or we'll bounce you around awhile before sending you on your way!"

"Oh, dearie me guys, I really don't recommend you trying that. Maggie here has Bull Terrier in her. Once she latches onto a big fat nose she never lets go. Mandy, on the other hand, is a slasher. She will have you bleeding from four or five places before you can cough. They always leave some for me, too. It would be my pleasure to arrange for a couple of you to spend your vacation in the hospital! Now, none of you needs to get the least bit bruised or, during these delightful summer days, spend precious free time in traction. Why don't you take the bread and forget all about Greg? I'm quite sure your parents won't want to hear of threats of extortion, let alone pending lawsuits. Am I getting through, guys? Good! Greg and I chat most every day, he'll be sure to keep me posted. Gosh, but it's been peachy keen having this swell little talk fellows, we must do it again sometime."

After a bout of giggling from the mini's, and some more posturing from the macho's, the tall blond kid held out his mitt for the thirty and they swaggered off. Mixing spite with spit, as Mandy air-mailed them one last growl and Maggie farted, I added, "Ya'all stay out of drafts now."

Highly content, we three ambled off in the direction of Sagen's office one more time. At the school door I put the girls on a "Down, stay." If necessary M and M would hold that vigil until the Cubs won the flaming pennant! I'm sure you agree with me, good training is all with children!

8

All school staff would be splitting for the summer layoff in another two days; before that occurred I wanted the home addresses of all Diddens' students. You can often tell quite a lot from home environments, especially those of the four delights we'd just met. It wouldn't do any harm to size up their parents either.

The school office folk, once I'd asked them to check with the Salem police for my bona fides, were obliging and promised to fax the info to Sandy. I told M and M I'd treat them to a burger right after I talked to Ernesto Escobar and Bill J. I was still perplexed why those two were the only ones to turn in such a dismal final exam? I pointed the wagon south on Commercial and we coughed our way to Wal-Mart where friend Ernesto was laboring for the summer. He was busy loading shelves with goods no one should ever be without: crackers, pop, candy, Twinkies, popcorn, peanuts, red and black licorice. You know, all that healthy stuff!

"Ernesto, me old son, we've got to talk. When do you get a break?"

He promised to meet me in a half hour by the snack bar sign: "Come get your burgers and hot-dogs here and please try our great coffee." So I wandered off to check out all the new stuff I certainly couldn't do without.

Later, ever so proud that I wasn't one thin dime poorer, we collared a plastic booth, ordered Java for me, Pepsi for him and I got down to it.

"Ernesto, why did you turn in such a lousy bluebook on the final? Didn't you tell me you were doing well in Mrs. Diddens' class? A crummy F won't help to get you into Stanford."

"Mr. Doyle, I am truly most mortified. I swear to you, my saintly mother, and God, my work was not of the failing kind on that test. I knew how important it would be and I studied long and hard. The night before the exam I placed my head down for but two hours sleep, yet I was alert and ready to do my best in the morning. I know I didn't fail. When I finished the test I was confident of an A, at the very least an A-. Perhaps, because Mrs. Diddens has not returned, there has been a mix-up with the bluebooks. I pray much for her return so I might ask the reason for that shameful F!"

Bloody hell! There purely had to be a maggot in the meatloaf or my name wasn't Danny Doyle! Hopefully, Bill J. will prove to be the answer to my prayer for one desperately needed explanation for his F!

* * *

Bill J. lived on Madrone about a block and a half off Commercial. Nothing pretentious, the home looked comfortable and well cared for. Ernesto had told me Bill J. was well-liked at Sagen. Far as he knew the guy had no enemies. His main trouble was trying to fend off girls. His greatest wish was to make it to Annapolis. I hadn't even met the kid yet and I was already in his corner.

His mother, a tall, leggy brunette with a lovely smile let me in and gestured toward the backyard where Bill was working out with weights. He planned on playing Navy football provided he'd be invited to check in at Pop's alma mater. Once again I jumped right in with the important question.

"Young man, as you probably know your English teacher, Mrs. Diddens, is missing. I am a detective and have been hired to locate her. Do you have

Bet You Don't Know Where Lorna Is!

any information regarding her disappearance which might be pertinent? I also understand your grade point average up to her final exam has been exemplary. Do you mind telling me why you got an F on her final?"

"Sir, I know she's been absent since giving her final exam and she also didn't show up on the last day to wish us well. That has been tradition with her. My final grade is devastating to me as I prepared well for the test. Mrs. Diddens is an excellent teacher and most fair. Sagen needs her."

His mother had come out to the yard in support, a good move on her part I felt and that family continued to earn high marks from me. Bill's mouth turned bitter as he prepared to offer me his answer to the puzzler:

"Sir, I swear I do not know the reason for the F. I want to go to Annapolis and I knew how important that exam would be. I did study hard for it. When I handed my bluebook in I was confident of the result. I needed a B. I'd have bet a touchdown on my next game I was going to get an A or A-. Now I may not be accepted for the Navy. I have worked hard all through school to reach my goal. I can't understand why I failed. If there is anything I can do to help you find Mrs. Diddens, please ask. Not only do I want to know if she is alright, I have to ask her where I went wrong on her final."

With tears in her eyes, the mother spoke, "Mr. Doyle, my son is a good boy and he does not lie. There has to be something wrong with the grading. He has not been eating or sleeping and I know he's going to make himself ill. His father and I are very worried but we have complete confidence in his integrity. Please do what you can to help him."

God damn it to hell, if this kid was fibbing a bum named Hitler was just misunderstood. By all that's holy, I'm going to get to the bottom of this if it takes the rest of my life and you can bloody well take that to the bank!

Promising Bill and his mom I'd keep trying to find Lorna, I stopped off at a Burger King for chow for my girls, and then I aimed the wagon toward Sandy's. I wanted to check the results of 'Operation Parent Study.' I was also badly in need of a soothing neck rub!

After pigging out on a bake at home Galucci's Pizza Supreme, a sublime neck rub, and a careful perusal of the kids' backgrounds in Lorna's classes, I dragged my dog-tired bones home. I'd left my girls, replete with burgers and fries, in the wagon. I know! Potatoes are not good for dogs' right along up there with lettuce and catsup. Yeah, yeah, yeah!

I always scan my surroundings before venturing out. Truly bushed though, I got careless this time and paid for it. Treading Sandy's front walk I headed straight for the wagon. Opening the driver's door just as the girls barked, I heard a scraping noise behind me. Turning, I was just in time to greet a railroad tie with the top of my head! A second before my face assaulted the sidewalk I managed a strangled yell! Half conscious, admiring colors in the Fourth of July fireworks going off in my head, I then heard:

"Yuh wuz warned Peepah. Guys what don't lissen is in fer thumpin's and dat's just what yer gonna ged!"

Almost immediately I also heard, **"Oh, ouch, Jesus, get them off me!"** There followed a snarl, a yelp, another oath, running feet, the slam of a car door, the roar of a powerful motor, and the screech of burning rubber as a vehicle tore off down the street.

Of course my assailants were unaware of a couple of things. I never leave the wagon's doors locked when my girls are incarcerated inside and they also know the difference between a: *"God damn it, you are both in big trouble"* holler, and an *"I need help"* bellow! Both girls can exit through an

Bet You Don't Know Where Lorna Is!

open door before a sleaze can sneeze! Would have behooved the scuzzballs to check the dogs' backgrounds: Mandy and Maggie each rate as graduates of the Excessive Smarts School. I speak truth; their intelligence has been well documented by researchers over the years. Probably the same ones who got bored writing on the sex habits of the Tsetse Fly!

Both girls have extraordinary smellers. Mandy can always find lost sheep: in forest, city, open country or desert. Maggie? Hell, she can find a lost sheep in a perfume factory! When those two open their mouths and expose their Pepsodent smiles at scumbags, ain't nobody gonna be doing anything dumb! No sir, ain't nobody gonna do nuttin'!

I came back to life quickly when their two, soft, wet tongues tried to lick the bristles off my skinned mush. I hate a lickin' dog!

By the by, did you perhaps notice how rapidly the phony accent had taken a hike? I suspect the large chunk of torn and bloodied blue jeans reposing on the ground by Mandy might have had something to do with that. I had learned a couple of things, too. The voice I'd heard crying for help had been young. I'd peg it at around eighteen—nineteen. And the driver of the car, provided it wasn't stolen, came from the well-to-do. The motor in that baby had sounded an awful lot like a Porsche or Jaguar. I guessed I was finally picking up some clues, even if I was collecting same on my face!

Can you explain to me how solid concrete can always imbed bits and pieces of itself into tender tissue? I slowly climbed back up on my feet and, along with my pals, went back and beat on Sandy's door. No way were M & M going to pluck bits of sidewalk out of my scraped jaw. While it had been painful, I had learned another thing. Somebody was growing very nervous concerning my doings. And what had I been doing, besides mainly hanging out around Sagen? I was becoming more and more convinced the answer was there. While Sandy probed, picked, and iodined; I, between "ouches and dammits," took out pad and pen and jotted down a conjecture list:

A. His New York accent is phony just as I'd thought and he'd proved it when Mandy bit a chunk out of his ass!

B. Motive? What could someone lose from a failed test? Try a scholarship, a lifelong dream, prestige, possible loss of face, parental displeasure, rejection from desired college; your turn to pick one.

C. How to correct for failure: Kidnap teacher? Dumb! Change grade? How? Steal and destroy test booklets? Insert false test results via a computer? Almost all kids are computer nuts today. I'd already thought of usage of a hacker. It would not present that difficult a problem to change grades as long the teacher didn't know. Kill teacher? Dumb and dumber! If not kill, then do what with her? There's a tough problem for a desperate kid, already in over his head, to solve. Why the hell F's for Ernesto and Bill J.?

D. Who is or could be the perpetrator(s)? Entirely possible more than one has been caught up in the mess. What could be his/her solution? Oh, yeah, I wasn't about to rule out the female sex. What did the perp have to fear the most? If I knew that, and if Lorna had definitely been kidnapped, maybe I'd be closer to finding her. There had to be a pattern. If only I could think like today's kid. I heard that!

   I thanked Sandy, gave her a lingering kiss, which I enjoyed even though my lips hurt, and took the dogs and my aching bod away home. Nobody was lurking outside the door! Before crashing, I wrote a mental note to myself to check with Bernie in the morning. Perhaps the old goat would be willing to offer something more on kid behavior. A hunch was attempting to penetrate the vacuum in my head. Just suppose some of her students had grabbed her for whatever reason and now, like juggling a hot rock from one set of burning hands to another, were trying desperately to figure a way out. If I considered that, perhaps they hadn't yet been dumb enough to kill her!

Spying Bernie at his usual table next morning, reminded me of a question I'd been meaning to ask him. As usual he was pigging out on a fat bagel and . . . ? What displayed on its two virgin halves looked positively disgusting. Giving my bruised mush a quick scan, he gurgled through a huge mouthful:

"What ho, Dan my man, hast a lowlife miscreant had the audacity to tell you to shut up and instead, being one of the truly valiant, you stood up?"

"Me first, Bern, What the hell are you eating?"

"The darlin' manager of this establishment has adopted a new policy, boyo. It's called bring your own fixin's, then buy one of our bagels and knock yourself out. I've spread mine with peanut butter and over that layered some lovely New Brunswick sardines. Wanna try a bite?"

"Jesus, you've got a death wish Bernie, I don't even want to smell it! By the way, why's Barney's classy joint here called Bad Bascomb's, Bagels?"

"The old beaver owner is a movie buff, especially for those early ones. He is extra fond of Wallace Beery whom, you should know, was big before the cameras back in the thirties. Wally played the part of Bad Bascomb in a Hollywood Western shoot-'em-up filmed in 1946. The bum actually was a meanie and kept stealing Margaret O'Brien's lunch when they were on the set. He always spoke like he was gargling on a load of gravel. Noah Beery, Junior, of *The Rockford Files* was his nephew."

"Never heard of him. He ever accomplish anything noteworthy, like marry Greta Garbo, or Janet Gaynor?"

"C'mon Dan, you never heard of *The Champ*? Beery won an Academy Award for it. Little Jackie Cooper caused floods in theaters with his crying scenes. It was the only time in Oscar history that two actors tied for the honor. The other guy was Fredric March, so the Academy honored each of them with a statue for the year 31/32. Fred got his for *Dr. Jekyll and Mr. Hyde*. Danny me lad, I truly worry about your lack of knowledge of worldly happenings. I offer lessons in ancient and modern history for a reasonable fee. You really should sign up."

"I don't go all the way back to the thirties, Bern, even watching movies. How about you stuff your lessons and finish eating that vile looking mess insulting an innocent plate. I have some information on the Diddens' case which may finally start us looking in the right direction."

After wiping a blob of peanut butter off his right ear Bernie paid heed while I informed of the mail booster, the four losers, the phony New Yorker, my scarred face, and thoughts as to why the whole mess with Lorna had come about in the first place. I further ventured the belief that if it had been a spur of the moment act of desperation, by a kid or kids, perhaps Lorna might still be alive; yeah, but for how long was the bloody question?

"So, okay Teach, what is the driving force or fear behind this irrational act? What can the perp, he or she, hope to gain here, Bern my man?"

Right away he looked at the bagel counter and tapped his coffee mug suggestively on the table. He could damn well look for a year before I'd bring him one loaded down with more of the same garbage I had just seen desecrating the one he'd just scoffed!

Slurping a Java refill and contentedly destroying a plain, he then cleared his throat, like a preacher unloading brimstone on sinners, and began:

"I do believe you're on the right track Danny Boy. What drives people to commit crimes? Bad genes, greed, ambition, fear of failure or incarceration, love—misguided though it may be—anger, displeasure from the group; witness the Mafia hood failing to 'make his bones' for the tuti-fruiti-conshootie; psychotic behavior; the list extends. With a kid, I lean more toward ambition and fear of failure. We all abhor failure, but not enough to kill or kidnap for it. That leaves us with parental push which would have to be excessively heavy; look for the macho parent, military, professional, or executive, who is always on the kid's back to achieve and for which only the top rung will do, regardless of the child's desires. I believe I would talk to mothers first, and then take the measure of fathers. Try to have the kids present when you talk to the men and watch them carefully, but unobtrusively. If you are subtle and clever something may shine forth from the murk. I am cognizant that every once in awhile your brain throws off its lethargy, so I'm sure you've thought of checking out who owns the sporty job, possibly a Corvette or a Jag, which roared off just as the sidewalk changed your face for the better. You actually display a slightly quizzical look now, almost like a man of letters, it's rather becoming."

"That is not a quizzical look, Bernie, the miserable scab is pulling on my flaming cheek and it damn well hurts!"

"Testy are we? Well, I'll leave you with another suggestion you've also no doubt thought of; delve deeply into the backgrounds of the four losers. I've a hunch that some members of that winsome group have been tossing barn manure in the punch bowl!"

"Bless you, dear Doctor Whiz-bang. Where would this dullard be sans those wise and toothsome little smidgets of yours prying open oysters, which display wondrous pearls before my awestruck eyes?"

"No need for sarcasm, Dan, my lad, I but offer succor to the needy. I fear you need to spend some learning time with Shirley Goodness."

"Bern, have you been trying to shovel fog off the bay again? Need I remind you that I'm already keeping company with Sandy. One broad at a time, thank you very much. Besides, who the hell is Shirley Goodness?"

"Not too late to sign up for some lessons Mr. Doyle. I suspect I'd better introduce you two via a wee story. It won't take long so sit back down and finish your coffee. I'll wait if you'd like to replenish our cups. No . . . !"

* * *

"Not terribly long ago a young mother was most pleased because her young son was about to attend first grade; no kindergarten back then. She dressed him in his finery, packed a lunch, took his hand, and they then set off for the school some five blocks away. Knowing he'd certainly be safe when she did this, mother decided to make it a habit and escort him daily. After the fourth day Junior begged her to desist. 'None of the other kids' moms bring them to school and the other guys are making fun of me, I'm going to belt Roger Bumble if he doesn't stop! C'mon Mom, I can walk to school all by myself now.' "

"Junior's mom, no fool, catching sight of brewing storm clouds agreed to let the little squirt travel to school on his own. However, she had an ace up her sleeve. Shirley Goodness, the lady next door, escorted her own young daughter, Mercy, to Daycare at the same time each day. Daycare situated one block farther than Junior's incarceration site and was also on the same side of the street. Thus it went. Junior was constantly observed, one might say even protected, while wending the way toward his daily learning tasks."

Bet You Don't Know Where Lorna Is! 97

During those groping toward knowledge days, as kids are wont to do, he soon made friends with schoolmates. Those new friends, likewise living in the neighborhood, began to walk with him on a daily basis to Englewood School. After a week of this one of Junior's buddies whispered to him that he was being followed and maybe they had all best be careful. Junior snuck a nervous peek behind him and then relaxed."

"There is nothing to worry about guys. Why, that's only proof of what I have been learning in Sunday school about being good."

"Being good!" cried Robert, the studious one in the group, "what has that got to do with that lady who follows you every day?"

"You guys know anything? The bible states, 'If you will only but behave, surely goodness and mercy shall follow you all the days of your life.' "

* * *

"Are you alright Dan, you had a real choking fit there. Be doggoned if your face isn't awfully red, too!"

"Your day of reckoning is nigh, Bernie!" Having been led down the garden path again, I offered a fervent wish his damn lawnmower would cut his foot off and I left to allow the dogs' potty breaks and collect Sandy, along with addresses of Lorna's students. The four losers would definitely be checked out first. I also wanted to get Sandy's take on the mothers. A female's version of other females is usually accurate, or so I've been told.

Names of the innocent, until proven guilty, have to be protected, right? So I'm going to call those four, Bo, Bart, Biff and Burt. They all lived in close proximity to Sagen. Their homes were not posh but definitely far from fixer-uppers. These were the circular drives kind with beaucoup manicured lawns and pillared entrances. Bo was the blonde and we had discovered that his father was the Marine colonel. I pressed the button on Bo's front door. Chimes sounded. I was waiting for '... *the halls of Montezuma*', but nope, what we got was a pleasant musical tinkling immediately followed by the bark of Rin-Tin-Tin! Mom herself opened the door. She was a tall willowy blonde, heavily made-up and with the look of one who spent too much time in the direct rays of the sun. She wasn't hard, neither was she soft; more the type like, "Yeah? No, we're not interested in buying, shove off!"

Holding on to the collar of a huge German Shepherd, which made me glad I'd left the girls in the wagon, she just looked at us. I quickly introduced us to cover the awkward pause and asked if her son Bo was home. In the nature of my investigation I should like to ask him a few questions, in her presence of course. She seemed surprised that Lorna was missing. Guess Bo wasn't in the habit of talking shop. Colonel Pop was unavailable. He was away off in the boonies doing whatever Marine colonel's do. They were both real proud of Junior and did I know he was going to follow in his father's footsteps and attend Annapolis. Why, he'd be the next Norman Schwartzkoff for sure!

Mom seemed just a touch evasive as she fed us all that jazz, almost like it wasn't all Beef Wellington in that household. She kept pushing her hair back and turning her eyes away from us. Naturally good old Bo wasn't there, probably out ripping off wrinkled little grannies for their Social Security checks. Damn, I'd wanted to get his reaction while we talked to Mom. I wrote myself a mental note to be sure to schedule another trip for when they were all home practicing family bonding, and then Sandy and I took a hike.

9

Bart was "Acne Face" and he lived two blocks away; same kind of drive, lawn, and chimes. Their dog was a miniature poodle, thank God! Mom leaned a touch toward plump but she had a nice face and a pleasant smile. Pop was a lawyer. We lucked out as they were all home; again, both parents were unaware that Lorna was missing. Pop checked out smooth. Tall, silver at the temples, slim, he obviously kept in shape by working out; he was also a tad bit condescending. Private Eyes were, to say the least, of the ruffian types. One spent as little time as possible with them and then immediately washed one's hands; I presume in Clorox.

Our Bart was heading for Harvard and law school. They'd better try to do something about that acne in the next four years or he would never make it as Perry Mason. He also needed to do a whole lot about his attitude. While conversing with Mater and Pater it was interesting to notice how, every time the kid opened his mouth, Pop would torpedo him with a look. Could it be that Father Dear knew more than he'd let on? Mom continued pleasant. Pop was in a hurry to get rid of us. Another mental note was also promptly etched in my memory bank to definitely schedule a return visit to Bart and his loving family.

I'd asked Sandy to casually check out both garages for a sports car while I kept the parents occupied. How did they think Sagen's academic rating stacked up re the balance of high schools in Salem? Were the teachers' high or low caliber? Everybody is an expert on teacher shortcomings today so I figured both parents would be good for at least twenty minutes on that subject alone. They didn't disappoint. Absolutely amazing what is expected of the teacher riding herd on approximately twenty-five learners per period, which adds up to one hundred and fifty students a day in high school, and thirty to thirty-five in the same all day class in elementary. Sheez, even the joker we are stuck with in the White House now would think twice before trying to get elected to tackle that load for four years! Sandy discovered no fancy fuel guzzlers designed for snazz and built for speed in either garage.

True to form, Biff lived in a fairly luxurious home on the next block over from Bart, another large two-car garage; a framed two-story with a medium hip roof wearing shakes. The lower level sported a brick facade, large picture windows, and a fireplace. It also came complete with circular drive, musical door chimes, spacious lawn, and Ma and Pa.

Pa had a face like a rock slide. He was built like one, too. Weighing in at around two-eighty, most of it muscle, he stood six-four in his socks and I'd have bet each thigh would out-measure my whole flabby waist! I promptly stepped back so that Sandy could stand interference in front of me! His voice sounded like it was rumbling up from a mine shaft. Surprisingly, his blue eyes were kind. Expressing curiosity they showed no alarm and he made us feel genuinely welcome. Damned if I didn't like him! Ma was just the opposite; she'd stand four-foot-seven in her socks and weigh ninety-five in her shorts. A brunette with warm brown eyes, curly hair and a lovely smile, she pictured elfin. Drooling just a little, I elbowed Sandy aside when Mom stepped out on the porch to greet us. As we followed them indoors my lady, doing her best with a rigid index finger, happily sunk my floating rib; it

Bet You Don't Know Where Lorna Is!

felt like a railroad spike! I stifled a yelp and accepted my punishment gracefully, though it hurt like hell. The loving smile never left my honey's lips but her eyes could've melted yesterday's cheese and crisped cold cuts!

Biff was playing couch potato and watching TV on a screen big enough to float Star Trek reruns over a crowded ballroom. Interestingly, he was watching the History channel. As I remembered, he'd been quiet and civil when I'd run into the four of them before. He looked a lot like his Pa. In time he would probably be able to wrist lock Pater and then win at 'thumping the opponent's arm on the table in three.' I was pretty damn sure he could take me right now. Damned if it ain't hell to get old!

Contrary to pals Bo and Bart, Biff had informed his folks of Lorna's disappearance and they showed proper concern. While their son was no Einstein, he was more than holding his own in studies and certainly qualified for the U of O where he figured on acquiring a degree in Business Administration. He planned on going into Real Estate, Pop's field, where he'd have a good chance at giving ol' Dad a run for his money. My instincts are usually pretty good and I couldn't see this kid giving Lorna trouble regardless of any influence from Bo and Bart. Actually, I only hung around awhile longer because I was subtly trying to convince the parents to pry Biff completely away from the other two losers though I had no hard evidence to use as a pry bar. No one in the group was stupid. I could but hope. Knowing I had pushed that boulder up the hill as far as I flat out could, I caught Sandy's eye and we split. My girl was of like mind; for sure we could take that kid off the list, *maybe*.

Surprisingly, Burt's digs were not as plush as those of the other three. He lived about a mile away, on Roebuck. No circular drive. Garage attached to house and one drove straight in on the driveway; frame and single story, two bedrooms, a one and a half bath, Franklin stove, composition roof, small lawn and backyard. These folks worked hard, paid their bills and the bank account would never dent the national debt. Loans would be required to take care of emergencies. As my old pappy used to say, "They're married to the friendly Equitable Savings and Loan and never the twain shall part!"

Folks like these were the salt of the earth. They worked as cashiers at Safeway or Wal-Mart and pumped gas at the local Towne Pump, Texaco, or Eddie's Discount Gas. Fast on the gab they responded well to teasing, if not done in a mean way, and would give back as good as they got. Clothes: Off the rack from JC Penny's or Sears, overalls and jeans worn during the week. Pop's suit, donned on Sunday for church, would be shiny in the seat and his shoes were probably working on their third resole. Little they had, little they'd ever get, but, one thing for sure, you could always count on them. When it comes to fighting our wars they always answer the call, shedding their blood in the process. I'd go on but you've got the picture. Dear Lord, how I love these people. If Burt was into anything nasty by God, I was going to take him out to the garage and personally kick his ass!

We'd managed to visit and gab our way up to six p.m. with the other families and so caught Burt, along with his folks, at home. Dad pumped the gas. He was thin, wiry, and balding; a six footer, he sported a mouthful of teeth needing attention; for all of that, he had a ready grin, a strong grip and a friendly nature. Mom pictured a fading redhead. Not yet stout she was still packing a few too many pounds, she also needed dental work. Some of that was probably diet. Most of it because service jobs are grudging when it comes to medical insurance and very few, if any, will offer dental coverage.

Bet You Don't Know Where Lorna Is!

You checked what teeth cleaning and a set of x-rays run today? Yeah, it damn sure is that much. Don't you dare mention a need for root canal work!

The good news from Burt's folks, he had earned a scholarship to Willamette U which meant he could live at home all his college years. If he worked summers and those faculty layoff times—most citizens are quick to call them vacations, teachers don't get paid for them though so I'm sticking with layoff—young Burt would make out fine. He'd his heart set on becoming a lawyer and Willamette rates high in that field. Obviously, this kid had no academic problems and surely had no bone to pick with Lorna.

"Burt, do you know of any problems your buddies have had, in or out of class, with Mrs. Diddens?" I queried, "How about Ernesto and Bill J.? Are they good students? What about any other students either in your class or her others? I know it's none of my business but why do you hang out with Bo and Bart? Biff I can understand, but the other two seem way off-center compared to the two of you. Help me out here, what's the big appeal of those two losers for you? While I think of it, do any of those guys own a sporty car, like a Porsche or Jaguar? Do you know how they get spending money? Burt, I realize you may be a tad reluctant to answer some of these questions. If it will ease your conscience, I've already asked them of Biff so you wouldn't be opening a bag of popcorn and spilling it all over the floor here. I sincerely hope you are as concerned about Mrs. Diddens as we are and willing to go the extra mile to help us find her."

I'd been interested to catch the reaction of the four when they recognized me from our previous meeting at Sagen. Acne Face had been evasive and sullen; Bo, I had yet to interview; Biff had been forthcoming as was Burt and neither of them was afraid to look me in the eye. Unfortunately, for me,

their answers didn't help. "Don't know," was prominent throughout, with the exception of the duo's appeal. Burt felt the same as Biff: Bo and Bart were groovy guys, always ready to rock and roll and neither one was ever shy of loot. They talked wise-ass but had never done anything dumb while he was around. Bo had a beat-up Toyota Camry so they always had wheels. None of their other buddies had cars. Cruising 'the gut' on Lancaster was fun and the girls were out in force at this time of year, but only for fun not for wrestling in the back seat. Bo was always bragging about a dish who was putting out for him, he wouldn't give out with her name though.

Once again we had very little more to go on. After wishing the family luck, I decided, after taking the dogs for a romp, to take Sandy to dinner at the Oyster Bar. Located on both State and Liberty Streets, it is one of my favorite restaurants for several reasons: Number one, the food is great and the service is excellent; ambiance is of the sea: meaning ships lights, buoys, nets, booths, old time signs, and an old gas pump including globe, the kind in use back in the thirties; best of all, *no smoking* in the State St. section. Puffing yourself to death is allowed on the Liberty St. side. Both sections are completely separate as they're divided by fully enclosed walls. I've never been in the Liberty St. part so I don't know if they both use the same kitchen. I do know when I eat there what I smell is food not the stink of coffin nails. They put out a roast pork dinner you can cut with a fork. You want a sandwich for lunch? Their clubhouse is the best in town and the clam chowder is to die for. We both opted for the roast pork accompanied by a truly lovely Johannisberg Riesling from the Bookwalter Winery located in Washington State.

California, Oregon, and Washington all have dandy wineries now. And I

Bet You Don't Know Where Lorna Is!

plan to visit each of them before I'm reduced to gumming my food and sipping liquids through a straw.

Have you ever noticed that a reformed smoker is a pain in the ass? I mean, they curl their lip at the smell and move away from people who reek of Chesterfields or Luckies. They ask if the restaurant is non-smoking and when informed one side is, one side isn't, sneer disdainfully at the proprietor and inform him that smoke is a slave to no master; therefore, what is busily stinking up *the smokers' side* will soon float over and stink up *the other side.* In a high old dudgeon they hasten themselves out the door to go raise hell in another restaurant. Yeah, those troops are real pains in the gluteus maximus all right. I oughta know, *I am one of those reformed smoker*s!

I got hooked on the weed at the ripe old age of seventeen. Back then it was a culture thing. You ever watch Perry Mason? He never went anywhere without lighting up. John Wayne, Dean Martin, Nat King Cole, William Talman (when lung cancer from coffin nails was killing him, he got on TV and begged people to quit) all died from using the noxious weed. We, the dumb but innocent, didn't know those bloody gaspers would kill us, and the tobacco companies kept lying their heads off about the dangers. I smoked for almost thirty years before a tiny but persistent cough told me I'd better pay attention to the warnings from the Surgeon General. I quit the intelligent way, *the first time,* via Pall Mall! Why Pall Mall? They were the longest unfiltered cigarette. A smoker is in constant need of a fix. Once my eyes cracked open in the morning I would light up my brand then cough my way through two packs a day. The Pall Mall way, I'd wait until putting away my first cuppa Joe then I'd take two healthy puffs and carefully butt it. Arrived at work prepared to face that day's challenges, I would fire that butt up once more for a couple more puffs and then gently grind it out. I figured one gasper would last the whole day, easy. Granted, I was forced to use a toothpick to hold that last little bit because my lips always ended up in extreme danger of cremation. This brilliant method worked for two days until I pranged into a crisis from too many creditors bugging me in one day. The hell with it, I smoked *two* Pall Mall's that day. One day later I realized it was a no-go. I smoked the whole damn pack and decided to deep-six intelligent method number one. A month later, cough growing worse, I told myself, again intelligently, to just quit cold turkey.

The following is a surefire way to stop that filthy, noxious habit. Because I like you, I'm not even going to charge one dime extra for sharing it: You don't need Nicoderm, patches, gum, or Smoke Away. Use corn nuts! What you do is empty all the ashtrays in the house, then go out and buy a pack of your favorite brand. Stash that pack in a bureau drawer among your undies so you'll know it's there in time of dire need. I tried cold turkey one way and spent hours sifting through ashtrays looking for a long enough butt to light. Not good. Ashtrays empty and sparkling, reserve pack stashed, you want to resort to those corn nuts. Whenever craving jumps around in your gizzard slip a handful of those nuts in your mouth and chew. Of course, you will sound like Chester the Chipmunk as you masticate. Naturally, the salt from the nuts will also retain water. In fact, your body will balloon. So okay, ladies will need to let their skirts out and probably have to buy new corsets or, as I've often heard them called, hinder-binders. Men, too, will need to spend the monthly allowance on larger-sized slacks.

By using the corn nut way, if a whole gang of you become dedicated simultaneously, and vow to kick yo puffin' habit together, during say that all

Bet You Don't Know Where Lorna Is!

important Super Bowl. Everyone decorating the same living room at the same time, volume on the flaming TV will soon be turned up high. So what! One needs to look at the scenic view here. Just think, in no time you'll be back to enjoying the lovely aroma of flowers. In no time, you'll not only be back enjoying cooking aromas, your mouth will savor the taste of food as well. In no time, perhaps as little as a year, you'll enter a restaurant that allows smoking. Then, in no time, you'll turn out to be just as obnoxious about the stink as the guy presenting this lecture, me!

Over coffee, Sandy and I compared notes. Item: Bo had a girlfriend but wouldn't cough up a name. Item: Acne Face was a weasel, was good with computers and had bragged he knew a hacker. Item: Biff and Burt could safely be eliminated as suspects; we'd both had the same take on them. Item: Bo had a car, always had money and definitely needed to be questioned. Item: Bo and Bart were 'groovy,' liked to cruise and test the waters for trouble, maybe minor but trouble all the same. Item: None of what we'd learned gave a hint as to the whereabouts of Lorna.

After dropping Sandy off, I decided to check in with Greg and then take another gander at Bo's digs; maybe the little snot was home by now. Mandy and Maggie, too young for wine but content with their helpings of the roast pork I'd conned the cook into supplying for an additional ten clams on the bill, were happily catching up on some zee's in the back of the wagon. I stopped at a Dunkin' Donuts on South Commercial to load up on a container of coffee and, prepared for a long night, headed for the Billings home and friend Greg. Previously, when I'd been questioning them, I'd asked Bart, Biff, and Burt for the names of the girls the four of them were hustling on Sagen's playground. True to bloody form, Bart had been noncommittal; Biff and Burt did not know the girls, although they recollected seeing them from time to time in the corridors at school.

Greg had little to pass on to me, he had heard Bo refer to the name Sally B. from time to time but had never seen or met her. He'd also heard that one of the girls in the senior class desired to attend the Air Force Academy but he couldn't put a face, address, or name to her. Checking my copies of Lorna's class lists revealed no Sally B. However, there was a Sara P. in one of Lorna's Juniors classes; worth investigating, especially as she lived but a scant three blocks away on Thistle Ave. I filed the info away, drove to Bo's, and parked three houses down and across the street. There were no cars in the driveway, although lights were on upstairs and down in the house. Biff had given a good description of Bo's car and as it was still early I figured to wait him out. Stakeouts are a royal pain in the arse! Usually nobody shows, the bladder swells, the neck cramps, the hours march by an eon at a time, and a numb butt goes to sleep! I passed the time by trying to dredge from memory the names of all the states plus their capitals. Yeah, I know, Mandy and Maggie didn't know them either! Do you? What the hell, it kept us occupied and anyway, I don't have to take that damn test anymore.

Two hours into sitting and waiting and Bo's Camry showed up. I took M and M for quick pee breaks and then ambled over to see if I could spook the adolescent S.O.B. into carelessness. Hopefully, he'd drop some pertinent information re Lorna's whereabouts. Grudgingly, Bo's dad admitted me and dear Bo was just as surly as our prior meeting. Why not? Crud is! He added nothing to what I already knew, would not vouchsafe his girlfriend's name and, of course, knew nothing of Mrs. Diddens. I watched his eyes carefully during his recital and the little bastard was lying through his teeth!

I observed he blanched at the name Sally B. but declared no knowledge of same. He'd heard of Sara P. but declared she was but a casual acquaintance. During the past week he had been over to the Coast visiting friends, nameless to me, and was terribly sorry he couldn't be of more help. All my questions were fielded quite deftly for a high schooler. I could feel in my bones the telling of whoppers was a practiced art with this kid. Gritting my teeth, I thanked him for his sincere cooperation and, barely restraining myself from slamming the front door, took my leave. Fired up as I was, if either one of my sweet doggies had so much as barked I'd have decked them! Tomorrow morning I was going to hunt up a small stick of my own and poke it in that kid's shifty eye or down his damn throat!

Early in the A. M., not long after the sun started to wilt the flowers, I began to sharpen that stick. Okay, kid, you like to play 'Snakes and Ladders' let's see if you like to frolic in the bushes with my version. Just happened I had a friend in the telephone company. Just happened she owed me a favor. Just happened she was over-fond of See's candy. Just happened I bought a two pound box—nuts and chews—as soon as the shop opened. Just happened they have raised the living hell out of the price of but a single pound of those bloody cavity pills! Ah, well, it was all in the interests of justice, right? Besides, a dinner and booze would have cost me more and it would have been a hell of a lot harder to deposit her on her front stoop later without complications. My sweets-lover friend was not keen on printing unlawful information and then passing it on to a pal. I dangled a large piece of pecan roll in front of a twitching nose and it was a done deal. I had the phone records for Bo's family for the past six weeks and was exiting out her office door before she'd swallowed the last creamy piece.

I needed time for perusal so I headed for Bagel Heaven. Would Bernie be in attendance? Does it rain in Oregon? He was there slurping his coffee and contemplating another disgusting concoction in front of him.

"Daniel! *Salaam aliekum*, infidel. Hast thee been aware of the sirocco airing from the Middle East? Hast it not been busy packing your schnoz with dire portents of a belligerent nature? Hast not Allah, the merciful and good, sent benevolent greetings? May he but smite thee gently between the eyes with a ripe fig! May Scheherazade visit thy tent and tantalize with the dance of the Seven Veils. May your ancient camel, afflicted with an eye-watering case of thirty-day halitosis, expectorate to leeward rather than to windward where you gracefully recline on a bed of sable fur; such rudeness from the dromedary would require an immediate change of clothing for your regal self and turn thy face scarlet in hue. Dost thou crusade to rid the world of evil-doers and scumbags proceed apace, oh valiant one?"

No question about it, retirement was beginning to affect Bernie's sanity! He took a bite of whatever was dead in his hand and I had to ask:

"Okay, so what do you call that mess of glop today?"

"Danny my lad, this is an asiago bagel liberally laden with cream cheese, avocado, peach jam, and topped with sautéed mushrooms. Wanna bite?"

"Jesus, Bernie that looks like something found in a prehistoric cave! It's way too early in the morning to inflict that kind of punishment on my eyes. What say you toss it under the table or cover it with your hat? I'll go get us two fresh, with lox, and freshen your coffee. We gotta talk."

10

I told Bernie about Acne Face and his skill with computers, his acquaintance with a hacker and his loyalty to Bo. I told about Bo's Camry and his snotty attitude. I mentioned Sally B. and Sara P. I also told how Sandy and I had crossed Biff and Burt off the list. I told how Greg, Biff and Burt stated that Bo would not divulge the name of his girlfriend and none of them could recollect ever seeing her. That remained a real puzzler to me. How could Biff and Burt go through a year of school together in the same class with the other two without catching a glimpse of the cutie? And who was the kid who had her eye on the Air Force Academy, and for that matter what the hell did that signify? If we could pin down the hacker and put the fear of God in him we might find out how many grades had been changed and why Ernesto and Bill J. had been singled out for F's.

All that, along with studying the phone lists, grabbed time and cost me two more bagels and coffee. I swear I don't know where that old boy puts it. If the only exercise he gets is cropping his damn lawn, he ought to be as big as Dom Deluise! Fortunately, I'd managed to slip the remnants of Bernie's first disaster into a handy trash can while wending my way up to replenish with something a body could enjoy with the eyes, and then eat without the stomach rebelling.

The phone records showed four numbers that had been called repeatedly from Bo's house. One was to the Colonel's office. That one had been dialed the most. Another repeat was to the wife's analyst. Mom talked to him a lot! The third often called was to the Salem Golf Club. Pop liked to play and had a low handicap. That figured! Number four was to good old Bart and I presumed the calls were made by Bo. There were lots of random calls. A Newport number at the Coast had been called twice. Later, I planned on ringing those singles from home, maybe a girl would answer and I'd finally get lucky. I told Bernie to go visit a mosque and brush up on his Arabic, then I split. I'd a pal in the State Finance office who had acquaintance with a few hackers in our lovely State Capital city, and isn't that tickety-boo?

If there is one thing Oregon does not lack, it is an under-abundance of state buildings. Sean O'Leary's office took up space in the Finance edifice. He was one of the best at what he does, although I'd die before I ever told him that. His head is too large for his hat now!

"Salutations to one who digs into offal and carrion searching for truth, justice, and the American Way." he cried. "Shamus, what brings you outdoors today sloshing around in the State of Eternal Downpour?"

"Yeah, yeah, a bucket of wet clams to you, too. If it makes you happy, I just spotted Brother Noah sailing down Liberty St. on the back of a huge bloody whale. First off, I thought he was waving and bestowing greetings of the paternal kind on deadbeat bureaucrats like you. Turned out he was shaking a mighty big fist and swearing! At the risk of disturbing your lethargy feather merchant, leave us drop the chit-chat, I am in serious need of your dubious services which, undoubtedly, they purely are."

I filled Sean in on the Diddens case and asked for his knowledge of local hackers. I also asked him to compile a list of computer whizzes, those most likely to be attending the local high schools or colleges. Some could even be

Bet You Don't Know Where Lorna Is! 113

recent dropouts.

"Trouble yourself no further, Danny. I, in all due modesty, have some reputation in that field myself. Where sits the computer needing the skilled attention of one who excels in taskbar, menu, font, byte, mouse, and all such other modern electronic lingo?"

Uh-huh, another one who's been spending too many of his lunch hours listening to the prattle of a certain bagel scoffer I know. I told him about the case I was involved in and Sean suggested I bring Lorna's computer, along with her floppy discs, to his digs. There, he informed, would be found all the tools and gadgets he'd need to pry secrets from the hard drives of any of those modern electronic marvels. Personally, I've never even turned one of the little beasts on and I don't intend to. Whatever happened to the good old Remington typewriters? Hunt, peck and whiteout!

It had stopped bucketing when I ventured out into the slop again. The weatherman had predicted cloudless skies and balmy sun. I'm not going to comment. Should the climate be any different from all the other good news?

I'd promised to collect Lorna's computer and discs from her husband and take them over to O'Leary that evening. I was thinking maybe a break could finally be coming for Diddens. He was quite amenable to loaning out the computer so after taking the dogs to lunch I ran over and collected it. Of course I allowed for their usual needs first. Next, I decided to check both my office and the police station for any current info on Lorna. Two calls to install siding on my rented apartment, one on another runaway, and a try at selling me steaks. Angus beef from Omaha and only twelve clams a pound, plus shipping. They'd come in carton loads of twenty-five pounds each. Care to do the math? Try three C notes plus the postal tab. Now you people from UPS be sure to honk your horn when you come to deliver!

The cops had been getting ready to call me. *Lorna had been spotted in Newport!* A witness, an off duty cop, had spotted her running from the Yaquina Bay Recreation Site toward Elizabeth St. this morning. She was barefoot, her clothes were dirty, and her hair was in wild disarray. The cop was not sure but thought he saw her either getting into a dark blue van or being forced in. He also thought he heard her cry for help. By the time he got there, the van had pulled out and was last seen heading under the bridge toward the bay front. Information was sketchy and he could have been wrong as he'd only seen her picture once at the station. He called it in and a small force of Newport police checked out the area. No dark blue van was spotted and no one they spoke to remembered seeing her. The cop cannot swear it was her, but he is pretty sure it was. It would take a thorough search of the bay front before anything might be uncovered and the Newport Police, lacking positive identification, don't have enough men to do that.

So the ball was in my court. With no time to waste, as it was just coming up to high noon, I called Sandy and told her to ring Greg, Ernesto, Bill J., Biff and Burt, tell them to pack a toothbrush and meet me at my office. I phoned Diddens and told him to gather as many friends and relatives as possible and meet me in front of the Canyon Way Bookstore and Restaurant in Newport, at three. Then I tore off to the Blueprint shop and begged those good folks to run off a hundred pictures of Lorna, like I had to have them yesterday! Back I raced to the wagon and tore off to Sean's house. I wrote a brief note, stuck it on the computer, and laid the computer on the covered porch *just in case of more rain*! Then I tried for a ticket on the way back to my apartment. I hastily packed a bag, toothbrushes for the three of us, food for M and M, and then I split to collect Sandy. Back I raced to the blueprint shop for the pictures, then over to the office to collect my crew, and off we headed for the beach.

Almost out of town, traveling west on 22, I gassed up at a Seventy-Six. Finally, my breathing having slowed, I filled the kids in on the possibility that Lorna might have been seen in Newport and where. The wagon is one of those old nine passenger jobs so everybody had a seat, if you count Mandy sitting on Ernesto's lap and Maggie perching on Biff's head. I told the kids to get some rest as we were going door to door on Newport's bay front until we turned something up. I purely hoped Frank Diddens had rounded up a whole bunch of his own troops. A quick glance won't show it, but there are a lot of homes strung out in the area back of the bay and I knew we'd be grasping at straws. Still, at long last, we might be finally getting our teeth into the hunt.

One of Mother Nature's gifts to man, on the way to the Coast, is Baskett Slough. It is a National Wildlife Refuge area. If you drive sensibly, or even take advantage of the turnoff to the observation center, you can spot oodles of your Canadian geese and Mallard ducks. Check out those White and Sandhill cranes. Look for Blue Heron. Count Fox and Coyote, stray dogs, feral cats, and beaucoup small birds. Best of all, nary a weekend gun happy bozo is allowed to shoot the little critters. During winter wet, large flocks vee holes in dark clouds and honk happy 'Howdies,' while flying gracefully over humans perched on land-locked feet. Having slowed, give a more careful look, might be your eyes will happy on to an occasional Swan. For all I know, considering the plethora of duckies wing-walking overhead, it could even be the ugly duckling that was! Fed guys have allotted citizens a restful spot to kick back and quietly enjoy wildlife. Stop a spell, you'll be back contending with exhaust stink and whizzing traffic soon enough.

When driving along in companionable silence, even though you should still pay strict attention to your driving, does your mind ever take little side trips? With important company seated by my side I can drive long distances and never utter a word, while my mind will be leap-frogging all over Cerebration Village.

When I was younger, on long journeys I used to ponder about girls. Naturally, that promptly led to erratic driving. Erratic driving though is risky on a two-lane highway so I don't do it anymore, at least not as often. Settled and sedate now I think of other things, like food.

Take today; I like to cook so I'm letting my mind plan a PDDB. What is a PDDB? Why, that my friend is a Perfect Danny Doyle Breakfast. Give a listen while I tantalize your taste buds. Besides, my offering will be three days of sunshine compared to a Bernie joke!

We shall begin with coffee, Mocha Java or Kona beans direct from the frig and freshly ground will do nicely, and while the aroma of perking coffee beckons I'll proceed with the rest. It is well known that the English constantly brag of their breakfasts. I am not into kippers, thank you, and blood sausage I suggest can take a hike! Nope, what you are going to get is my version of Canadian-American. How's the coffee?

I've checked the larder and, glory be, I have all the ingredients: one large beefsteak tomato, twelve button mushrooms, and four extra thick slices of bacon, two lamb kidneys, hash browns, two eggs, and two crumpets. First, I shall quickly blanch the tomato in boiling water and then dunk it in cold. I wish to remove the skin before I fry that lovely large beauty; bacon demands to be thoroughly cooked and left a shade north of crisp. Mushrooms, sautéed in the bacon fat; kidneys the same and left slightly pink in the middle; two eggs over easy, the yolks eager to run but with no gooey membrane chasing them; hash browns, deep and golden on the outside, still slightly moist inside. No skimpy slices of toast for me, I want crumpets: not those skinny little things obtainable in Portland, mine are Canadian: plate size, thick and hot right out of the toaster, browned like the potatoes, gleefully anticipating great gobs of butter which, while melting, shall be lovingly absorbed. Last but not least, thick slices of tomato fried until soft, but never mushy. I am most fond of scrambled eggs. The majority of eateries serve them overcooked and dry. That's why I fix mine over easy, then I proceed to cut them into tiny bites, whereupon the yolks immediately run and the final mixture is a delightful soft blend.

The feast, artistically planned to decorate a large warmed plate, shall appear as follows: mushrooms at seven o'clock, tomato slices at two; bacon shall stretch from three to five; kidneys five to six; hash browns seven to nine; eggs wend their way from nine to twelve and, precocious as always, flow willy-nilly toward the middle of the plate; crumpets, housed on a smaller plate alongside, take up position by the larger at nine o'clock; steaming coffee homesteads at three. I do believe breakfast is ready. Cholesterol? What, you wanna live forever? Pull up a chair!

Unfortunately, as musing is not like tasting, my taste buds remained unrequited as the miles slipped by. I did discover that a john break would be welcome though.

Watch for elk and deer in the Corridor. I once spotted a large herd of Roosevelt elk casually ambling along a forest road where she branched away from Highway 18, heading west. Lovely! When man is not allowed to invade and clutter up Ma Nature's domain, her home stays clean, pristine, and beautiful. She also does her own housekeeping. The Van Duzer Forest Corridor is one such place. I know I've already clued you in as to location but have I implanted a clear picture of it in your mind? Over the years and my many trips through the VDFC it has never changed. True, depending upon season, the Salmon River will either trickle by the highway or climb on up and give you a free car wash. Further back, a lot of the Coast Range has been logged out but not in the corridor. The four seasons are serious about visiting. I've seen snow three feet deep and also groped through ice fog, both while wishing I was to hell off the highway and safe at home. Sighted an abundance of fall leaves, enough to dazzle the eyes and force you to brag on them to those smog-covered city dwellers. Catch the spring budding— *including skunk cabbage*—flat out gladdening anybody pining for rebirth and the end of a wet winter. Instead, more heavy rain arrives, enough to float a flaming aircraft carrier, and then our blessed summer steps in bringing abundant sun along. The state is never loath to spend our money well, although not always wisely. When H.B.Van Duzer willed his property to the state they, in turn, installed Corridor Rest Areas; a wise move. All hail to the flaming bureaucrats!

Most, not all, of the peace and serenity you have been enjoying abruptly ends as you enter Lincoln City. Commercialism has taken over. The most important signs grab your eyes: directions to the casino; motel row; fast food locations; the factory outlet stores; all that, 'ya gotta know where they are' stuff. On the outskirts on the right resides a golf course. I call it Billy Goat Acres. No flat lies. You will get an over abundance of those downhill, side-

Bet You Don't Know Where Lorna Is!

hill, and uphill ones though! She comes complete with postage stamp greens. Do you ever watch the pros play on TV? From two hundred yards out they'll land balls on greens, each the size of Portland. They may have to putt for a mile or two but at least they are putting. On most public courses you can't even see the green from two hundred yards out. The weekend golfer complains, "By God, my game stinks!" Maybe not. After all, his club of choice needs to have built in radar to fly the ball to a green he can't see! You ever play the, 'I remember when' game? The first time I played on Billy Goat, she was only nine holes, same size greens, and three clams a round. A card was also issued; punched ten times entitled one to a free round. Now you got eighteen up and down holes, nothing is free, and you'll fork out twenty clams for the privilege of playing nine. You desire a cart? Pony up eighteen Washington's for each nine! Can I see the greens at my mature age? I have trouble just climbing up and down the bloody hills!

Most stores offering goods or souvenirs in Lincoln City would look better razed. If it weren't for the traffic I'd close my eyes as I pass. Thank God the inhabitants are nice folk! Architectural creations don't improve until one passes on by Taft and accelerates forward on the way to Depoe Bay.

I'm not sure what induces those eyesore creations. Back east, along their coastal shores, towns and villages at least follow a theme. Places are neat, clean and aesthetic. The west coast, if it follows anything like a theme, leans toward *anything goes*. If one finds an edifice in town with a little class, rest assured on either side of it will be derelicts washed up from the shore. Nor is anything sacred when it comes to slapping on paint. I suspect the artists (ha!) visit Goodwill and buy whatever is the day's surplus; have you by chance ever seen a whole building painted mauve or violet? Gaze but two or three stores away and somebody is sure to have made the raise on black, canary yellow, or purple.

Enough! Things improve upon entering Depoe Bay. True, the place is small re business establishments; however, on the east side newer buildings, a smidge aesthetic, give it a touch of class. Now if they would only lasso all those condos hogging the ocean view on the west side, and float them out to sea, the tiny town would look downright pretty. The bay is small, sheltered, and houses ocean-plying fishing boats along with Coast Guard cutters. Hey, my hat's always off to those intrepid people. I like Depoe Bay.

Newport, as she has plenty of room to expand north and south, is starting to bulge. The buildings are not as tacky as Lincoln City but here and there it isn't difficult to notice a disaster. Sixty percent of the United States economy comes from service establishments and Newport has her share: gas stations, restaurants, motels, tourist traps, the big guys markets—Freddie's, Safeway's, Rite Aid and Wal-Mart. They also have lumber yards, lighting, plumbing, and printing stores. One day I predict Costco will come to settle.

The Canyon Way Book Store rests east on Canyon Way which runs downhill toward the waterfront. I've browsed, bought books and eaten there many times. I have never been disappointed. Arriving there before three I took the troops inside for coffee and to explain strategy. We were going to cover as much of the waterfront area as possible before dark. During that time we'd hand out Lorna's poster and inquire for any sighting. Each of us taking a separate route seemed logical and safe in the daylight. I figured to take Maggie with me on the short drive over to the Marina. Mandy would stay to guard my lady. I also asked Sandy to wait for Diddens and crew, hand out posters, and inform him we would all meet back at the bookstore at nine. It would still be light then and we'd be able to share what info we'd gathered; I stressed *caution*! If anyone saw or thought he saw anything at all suspicious he was to get the hell out of there, scram to a public phone and call me on Sandy's cell which she had most sensibly brought along. Once I'd surveyed the marina and let Maggie sniff around I would hustle back to the waterfront and start canvassing stores. Everyone moaned that we were putting our hopes on a real long shot here.

"Think we got a long shot, huh? Try this one on for size," I said. "Remember in the movie, *Beau Geste*, where John and Digby and their two pals, situated high on a dune overlooking an Arab occupied oasis, are eyeing much needed water? Digby volunteers, 'I'll climb higher on this dune and blow *Charge* on my bugle. You guys fire your rifles at those Tauregs hogging the water down there and we'll run 'em all off.' At the sound of the bugle and the rifle fire, sure enough the Arabs jump on their horses and split. Now dig this: Galloping away one of them, bouncin' up and down in his saddle, like somebody's pokin' his arse with a cattle prod, looks back. Holding his horse's reins in one hand, he turns in his saddle. Raising a musket a half mile long with the other hand he aims it at Digby. All the time his horse is galloping over dune and down into wallow like it had a bee up its butt. KA-BOOM! The Bedouin, still bouncin' to and fro like a one-legged bull rider, fires once and some five hundred yards away Digby and his bugle bite the dust, literally, as he rolls all the way to the bottom of the dune stiffer than last week's doughnuts! Now that, my young friends, was a *long shot!* So let us make haste and away, might be our search will also turn out to be a flaming bulls eye." If I were you, I would be thinking:

"What the hell did all that have to do with finding Lorna?"

Absolutely nothing! On the other hand though, maybe a great deal. Here's my brain spin: Up to now we still do not know the whereabouts of Lorna. If she had been kidnapped and if she was the one the cop spotted, how come? The snatchers either had to be the world's dumbest or they were amateurs. If amateurs, who better than kids? Following that line of thinking should make it easy to find her. Only that I seriously doubted. Still, long shots do come in. 'Beat-the-Odds' Clyde will attest to that, albeit grudgingly. I wanted our crew to think and act positively. Lorna *had* been sighted right here in Newport and we were damn well *going* to find her. I merely tried to pump them up. Go get 'em gang! Improbable as it was, Friday turned up to help Robinson Crusoe, didn't he?

We were all frustrated. Sometimes a light mood, regardless of situation, awakens one, makes him more observant, more aware of his surroundings, especially if he is but hastening home for much needed shut-eye.

That's not one of mine; that touch of illumination, not the shut-eye, came from a cop writing me a ticket for running a stop sign at two a.m. on a dismal Sunday in May, 1978. The only flaming traffic was a stray dog, jaywalking on a cul-de-sac three blocks away; I pray for that cop's soul on a daily basis!

* * *

"What the hell happened? How did that sanctimonious bitch get loose? Taffy swore that everything would be kept under control until the proper time came to end it. Damn! Move it car. I've got to get there quickly and clean that mess up once and for all before the cops start nosing around."

* * *

11

Newport boasts of a fine marina, one that is truly worthy of brag. She will house your big and small boats, cruisers belonging to weekend sport fishermen, large fishing boats used by those who ply the ocean for a living, dinky ones with powerful engines strong enough to breast the surf and bob in the ocean, and some fifty and sixty footers who like to travel as far north as the San Juan's or south to San Francisco. Sailing sloops, some with motors, also sit cheek by jowl beside the large and small craft. I have a Coast Guard friend who often patrols the mouth of the jetty on busy weekends and holidays. He is always ready to haul to safety those whose engines quit or when ocean swells have been too much for the imprudent. His boat, small, possesses an engine powerful enough to tow a tug back to shore. Amazing how many landlubbers think they are sailors. Wallowing about the briny in an extremely quiet boat, because the un-tuned engine she's a no run, usually causes them to toss their cookies and gratefully grab at the rope my friend throws them. Their bods safely back on the secure dock they'll not return to tackle the ocean again for some time. Better believe monies allotted to our U. S. Coast Guard are always well spent!

June is usually light with Oregon vacationers most years and I didn't find too many folks aboard their vessels. None had seen Lorna. A crusty old broad, with a face like a beagle, informed she was one to mind her own business and encouraged others to do the same. She then invited Mag's and me to go partake of a refreshing swim in the bay! A big guy with a full head of caramel-colored hair stepped down to the dock off a rather large fishing boat. He had a face like a wet week. In addition, it displayed a furtive look. Still, trolling the sea for those dumb enough to swim with their mouths open is a tough way to make a living. The wary keep an eye peeled for the ones who come around checking licenses or for those looking to place liens on the boats of folks late with payments. Police, private or otherwise, are seldom welcomed by those intrepid people who brave the ocean for their daily grits. He was another of the totally noncommittal and likewise soon invited us to take a hike.

It is a large marina. There is more than one walkway to cover and they took a while to examine. One has to retrace steps to the entryway after each section has been inspected, walk over to the next down-ramp and repeat the process. One guy, his oilskins coated with fish scales, allowed as how he thought he'd seen Lorna up by the marina showers this morning, but his breath almost blew me off the dock. No question he'd been bending his elbow for hours. That lad was in no shape to even hit the deck with his hat, let alone recognize our missing lady! A notion tickled the back of my head on the last walkway but while I was trying to catch hold of it a seal surfaced smack in front of Maggie; she damn near jumped in the bay after it. I caught her when she was halfway off the dock. By the time I'd yanked the little mutt away from the seal—happily flippin' a flipper and blowing Bronx cheers at her—what was nagging my noggin continued elusive. I ended up with a throbbing headache instead. I had brought a scarf of Lorna's with me and Maggie had taken a good sniff. Her nose had turned up nothing when we'd been invited to board few of the boats; plus, the odor of bay brine blew

Bet You Don't Know Where Lorna Is!

strong. Beyond lengthy swearing at the seal, she'd barked but one other time and that had been at a saucy gull.

Regretfully, I turned my back on the marina and we headed for the wagon. Ah, hell, investigating is mainly the asking of questions and the receiving of shrugs—or other rude gestures—anyway.

I stopped at the Yaquina Bay Recreation Site, under the bridge, to allow Maggie an, 'I gotta go pee' break and a quick run. Next, I headed for the Coast Guard Headquarters just above the waterfront to drop off a poster and ask of any further Lorna sightings.

My Coast Guard pal displays a gray old buzzard, like me, and he no longer works full time, but I knew by using his name I'd get co-operation right away. The kid in charge, an Ensign, was full of P and V and eager to help. The Newport cops had been on the phone and advised them to check out harbor boats. Newport is not a big port but large ships do arrive from time to time. The *Yaquina*, Oregon State College's research vessel, berths there as do some of the bigger seiners. From time to time a vessel needing repairs will travel up the river to where she can be dry-docked. Ships with logs loaded in Coos Bay bound for the Far East will pass close to the Newport shore often and you'll remember that tanker ship the *New Carissa* carrying 400,000 gallons of oil that went aground off Coos Bay on February 4, 1999. By the time they finished with that mess she was in two pieces, 140,000 gallons of oil had spilled into the drink, her bow section had broken the tow, and she drifted in to Newport. Reattached and towed back out to sea, shelling and a torpedo from a submarine finally sank her. Half of her is now permanently parked two miles, straight down. The other half is aground off Coos Bay; seems like the *New Carissa* had aged pretty rapidly.

Have you ever read C. S. Forester's *The African Queen*? "Can you make a torpedo, Mr. Allnutt?" cries Rosie. And how about the movie, *Operation Petticoat*, starring Cary Grant, Tony Curtis and a bevy of Navy nurses? They add turmoil to routine and, when Cary Grant is about to sink a Jap ship, one of the nurses accidentally presses the firing button. The torpedo veers a touch off course, cruises up on the beach, and sinks a truck! Of course none of that is related to the *New Carissa*, except for the humor. It just tickles my funny bone that the Navy had to finally sink half of that ship with a torpedo. Ah, well, 'small things amuse small minds' as friend Bernie would say.

Newport's bay front is about what you'd expect. Depending on provender from the sea for half her economy, and tourism for the other half, she has your seafood markets, charters for deep sea fishing, restaurants featuring fresh seafood, ships' chandlers, art galleries, kite shops, and souvenir shops pushing trinkets relating to the sea: coral, seashells, glass floats, boat models, ships bells, lighthouses; it's all made in China and guaranteed to gather dust on your mantel. Really, she's a quaint place to visit and fun to listen to a bevy of barking seals begging for handouts from the tourists. It's not so joyful when looking for the missing. Maggie and I covered both sides of the street and about half the shops before sighting Sandy and Mandy. I bought my girl coffee at Mo's while we compared notes. She had nothing positive to report either. A couple of, "not sure's," and "maybes;" a few, "looks familiar," and that was all.

Sandy had already covered the other half of the business area so we decided to start working our way up Canyon Way toward Highway 101, inquiring at homes on the side streets as we strolled. Sandy and Mandy took

Bet You Don't Know Where Lorna Is!   127

one side, Miss Maggie and I the other. I think I'd rather suffer a snake bite than thump on doors! Some folks were willing to listen. Some just yelled "go away" from behind theirs. Some plain ignored my knocking. Some threatened to turn the dog loose! I was not going to let Maggie get into anything. She is a mutt who doesn't take crap from anybody; she also only weighs seventeen pounds. I noticed a few curtains move slightly and knew the folks were home even if they were not responding. A man's home is his castle, right? So what if the tax assessor doesn't think so! Regardless, this old boy was not about to venture where he hadn't been invited.

It was about to chime 8:45 P.M. as Sandy and I trudged wearily up to the bookstore. Diddens had brought six people including himself and reported failure as well. With the exception of Bill J., we were all there. Five minutes later the kid showed up. The restaurant was closing so I offered to buy dinner for the group at Mo's or at the still open Embarcadero. We opted for the larger restaurant as we could all huddle together and share notes and ideas. Unfortunately, not even a hot lead had been uncovered. None of the interviewed had been certain it had been Lorna who had entered or been pulled into the van at the Yaquina Recreation Site. Not one had admitted to seeing her on the bay front. Bill J. reported he'd seen a Porsche back out of a driveway on his street and drive away in the direction of 101. He thought there was something familiar about the driver but hadn't gotten a good enough look to determine whether they were young or old, male or female, or disguised, like in drag! Several of the disappointed mentioned it had been a *long shot* anyway!

We discussed strategy while eating. Despite our lack of success I was sure Lorna had been the one sighted. Short of obtaining search warrants for all houses in town, for which we did not have probable cause, we were stymied in Newport. I was also sure she had been kidnapped in Salem. It was there we would discover why. One of Frank's crew, Sam, was an ex-Green Beret with time on his hands. Close to tears of deep despair Diddens gave him money for food and a motel, told him to rent a car, and then discreetly stake out the house where Bill J. had seen the Porsche. Not to be outdone, and because I'm not completely stupid, I dug my camcorder out of Mandy's bed in the wagon and told him to film whatever moved in and around that house. If anything even slightly suspicious surfaced, he was to call me at any hour. My instincts were yelling we were far from through with that picturesque coastal town!

After dinner, for which the check meant I should now own a flaming piece of the Embarcadero, we boarded our cars and headed back for Salem. Notions, constantly driving down a one-way street, kept poking at me during the drive home, but nothing jelled. My gut response told me there was still something out there I was missing but, like the water which had imprisoned King Tantalus, it kept receding. I'm glad I'm not a swearing man; there are a few dandies I'd like to use along about now!

It was a quiet drive home and the silence was so profound in the wagon that everybody heard one of the passengers break wind. Immediately noses recoiled and window buttons were hastily operated. Whoa, did I ever state my little Maggie was without fault?

However, the silence gave me a chance to chase my thoughts. I'd talked to a few of the young at the marina, mostly college kids; receptive and eager to help they hadn't hesitated to gather round, pet Maggie, and study Lorna's picture. Other than the occasional whiff of marijuana, which had tickled my

Bet You Don't Know Where Lorna Is!

nose, and the sour tang of the beer they'd been quaffing, they were behaving themselves. Unfortunately, the viewing of Lorna's poster had not lit a fire, I still hadn't been able to get a handle on what was bugging me, and my dad-blamed headache kept jack-hammering the back of my eyes. You'd think with all the junk a woman carries in her purse she could at least have tossed in a couple of Excedrin! Thought chasing just kept circling so I flicked it in.

I tacked a mental note to my headache to check in with my hacker buddy, Sean, on the morrow re Lorna's computer files and decided for the rest of the trip to relax and enjoy the way Sandy had snuggled up to me. Subtly, I raised my foot off the accelerator a wee touch, too. One damn sure thing, as I'd sprung for dinner for half of Salem, friend Bernie was definitely going to get stiffed for the next go-round of bagels!

While I let Greg off at his house he handed me the list he'd made of Lorna's Junior and Senior classes, and said he wasn't sure I'd wanted the others to know about it so he'd held off till now. I'm going to make a detective out of that kid yet! Two names got my attention, one female the other male, I'll call them Jack and Jill. Nothing big time, in fact maybe nothing but a tempest in a teapot or a cruller in the stew. Jack was a junior at Sagen, not a math whiz, and had been known to crib on more than one occasion, but then he wasn't headed for MIT either. Jill, a senior, had ambition, she was opting for a Military career and some of her grades had been a whisker shaky. English had been receiving more attention lately and test results showed it, especially her final grade. She was no Valkyrie, standing five-four and weighing but 105 pounds in her skivvies. She rated higher in debate than in volleyball. Sandy pointed out she seemed likeable but didn't stand out in a crowd; some on the list had daringly jay-walked and sneaked a beer, even tried Mary Jane, and petted hot and heavy. Nothing that called for Alcatraz for any of them there. God damn it, why couldn't the guilty come forth, admit they had done the dastardly deed, turn Lorna loose and let me get rid of my rotten headache?

I finally got some Excedrin at Sandy's and maybe a little something else to boot. Whatever, my headache miraculously disappeared and I wasn't even mad at Maggie anymore. Mandy only raises my ire when, crowding the bed, she out snores one of those bay seals, the ones suffering from excessive post-nasal drip!

I have found in this business it is not wise to give in to anger but I was truly fighting mine. Lorna had been missing for way too long for this to be a kidnapping for money. Scum after ransom want it in a hurry, correctly assuming the longer they hold the victim the quicker the cops are going to get a line on them. In my mind these creeps weren't pros. If Lorna had gotten loose, and I felt in my bones she had, it had to be due to carelessness. Pros do not get careless, at least not to where the snatched manage to get away. Also, if the motive wasn't ransom what the hell was it? Why would amateurs grab someone who was prominent and not know their action was bound to raise a stink? What would have made them so desperate? And if they were not after money and not planning on killing Lorna, what were they going to do to her? If they still had her in Newport we had to have singed a few nervous butts today with our posters and canvassing. I was damn sure going to turn the burners up higher. A good friend in the Salem police had persuaded the Newport police chief to drive around the bay front bellowing on his bull horn, offering a reward for any information leading to Lorna's release; Sam had been clued to observe and film any activity in his area after the chief, repeating his message like a walrus with a cold, had passed on by.

On the morrow I'd head right back to Newport after I talked to O'Leary and stashed Maggie and Mandy with Sandy. I had a little breaking and entering in mind and those two would not be needed, I hoped! For those of you familiar with Lawrence Block's burglar, Bernie Rodenbarr, who gets his jollies heisting from the unsuspecting, I am not he! Breaking and Entering scares the living fazoot outa me. I know some of the tricks: Call from a phone booth and if nobody answers don't hang-up, let the receiver dangle on the end of its cord and walk away. Of course, you want to call from close by, a three mile hike and the resident could be home before you get there. If the phone is still ringing indoors when you arrive chances are he isn't home. Carry a dog whistle in case the owner's left Fido, usually a huge slobbering S.O.B. of a Rottweiler, on guard on the inside of the premises. Better yet, try to find out where the mark is at present and, most importantly, when he will be home. Best if you are seriously absent upon his opening his front door unexpectedly.

I caught up on paper work, checked my messages and crashed. First thing next morning I organized my notes. Then I called Sean to check on his hacking results. He, at an important finance meeting in flaming *Brookings*, couldn't be reached and would be gone for five days! I used some of those bad words that had been lying idle in my vocabulary for some time. I then ran over to the Salem City Library, latched onto a reverse phone directory, and what do you know, the phone number called in Newport by friend Bo belonged to a Chuck Drain. Where do you suppose friend Chuck lived? Right! The same address and driveway the Porsche had backed away from, the house Sam was quietly staking out.

For sure, when it was quiet, dark, *and nobody home,* I would be paying a visit to that house. Damn, I felt gay and alive for the first time in many days. Yeah, I caught your snort there, but do you remember the films: *Our Hearts Were Young and Gay, The Gay Caballeros and The Gay Divorcee?* They were all happy films. I agree with Orson Welles, it is a good word, it belongs in our vocabularies. Gay means to be happy, joyful, having fun. It should not be denigrated, nor should it be used to identify or label cupcakes! Flang it, you use the word your way and I'll use it mine.

I was not known to the Newport police. Most cops do not harbor warm spots in their inner beings for private eyes; can't imagine why?

Leaving the library, I drove over to the office and called my Salem Police buddy, Brozinski. After all they, too, had an interest in finding Lorna. He was in and from the sounds probably slurping coffee with his big feet up on the desk. I brought him up to speed re Lorna, our trip to Newport, and our poster handing-out session. Then I asked him to call his Newport colleagues and request them to run a check on a certain Chuck Drain. I said I'd wait in my office for his return call. Fifteen minutes later, my hollering phone woke me up. Oh, boy, good news! Chuck, while not as pure as filtered water, did not have a record. Other than a few bar fights there was no sheet on him. He'd never even had a traffic ticket. Double poop! A large chunk of my euphoria rose, hiked to an open window and, committing suicide, jumped out! I had bet me a ten-spot on Chuck being our boy and Lorna as good as sprung. Regardless of lack of Rap sheet, I'd still pay him an uninvited visit.

Paper work up to date, most bills paid, and my notes in order, I decided to take the dogs to Bush Park for a good run. As I was closing the office door, the phone squalled again. It was our man Sam, in Newport, checking in. He had nothing earth-shaking to report: Early this morning Chuck had exited his house and walked to the corner where a guy in a beat-up Honda Accord picked him up and away they went. Chuck was wearing his fishing togs complete with what the Limeys call 'Wellingtons.' Sam presumed they'd driven to the docks. I requested our watcher drive to the marina, quite casually sniff around, catch a few video shots if possible, and then hang loose. If nothing occurred in Salem I would meet him there at the stakeout around midnight. I also suggested he catch a few zees at his motel; he'd been on watch almost around the clock and had to be a tad bug-eyed by now.

I ran the dogs all over that flaming park until they finally flopped. Later we pigged out at MacDonald's. I'd overruled my decision re not taking my girls along, Maggie's priceless nose would be needed inside Chuck's digs.

Rhodenbarr may get a high from burglary but it flat out terrifies me. Hell, instead of a dog there could be a deaf mute, built like a gorilla, bunking in there; traction applied to healing any of my suddenly broken bones did not appeal. A tad after midnight I pulled in quietly behind a faithful Sam still on stakeout. He reported failure at the marina. Chuck had disappeared and he'd sighted no fishing boats heading out to sea. He'd given it two hours and then returned to his post. No one had entered or left the house while he'd been there. I thanked him and sent him off to his motel. What I was about to do was illegal, no need for him to become involved if my plan went awry. It was black and quiet as death when I stashed Mandy on a "stay" in the bushes in front of the house; she would not move now even for a tsunami. I planned on leaving the front door ajar and her loud growl would serve as ample warning to Maggie and me. I happened to have a set of lock picks in my pocket. Boy Scouts always prepare. Chuckie's garage had been attached to the house so that when it rained egress from garage to house would be a dry affair. Likewise, if one wished to bring something out (possibly a body!) from house to car, truck, or van, ain't nobody gonna see what you has done just brung out!

His house wasn't exactly surrounded by security devices. In fact, it took thirty seconds to pop the front door and twenty of those I spent pushing Maggie away, she loves to lick peoples' kissers, yuck! Quaking, I crept oh-so-quietly inside flipped on the pencil flash and then tried not to breathe. My God, it stunk in there. Friend Chuck was a pig: Dirty clothes, rotten socks, food curling on plates—unwashed since the last war—dirty bed linen, the strong stink of mildew, and a lingering whiff of marijuana.

Fortunately, as I was set and ready to dismember, nary gorilla one appeared. In fact, other than a fat rat or two, nobody was home. His was a two-bedroom joint, one of them, undoubtedly the guest room, reeked as bad as the likewise filthy master bedroom. Maggie and Mandy love to roll in sheep phewey-phewey. The stink of a long unmade bed posed her no problem. She hopped happily up and sniffed at length, but not excitedly. If Lorna had been held there, along about now her clothes would be in dire need of changing. No dirty feminine attire lay strewn about. Other than Filthy Chuck, no one else had been in that house for some time!

He did sport the latest in electronic goodies though: a 65 inch Mitsubishi TV in the living room plus a 48 inch one in the master bedroom. The high-fi, also a Mitsubishi, was the very latest; count two DVD's and a mess of CD films, many of them porno. The refrigerator, almost big enough to enter, was well-stocked including plenty of Henry Weinhard beer. Count a spanking new, glass-topped electric stove, the latest in coffee makers, and be

Bet You Don't Know Where Lorna Is! 135

my guest and admire all new maple furniture. Of course, it was all reposing in Pigsville! Go figure. Chuckie boy was doing right well in the fishing trade. Why was it that every time I took a step in this case it felt like I was slogging through fresh-poured concrete in bare feet?

Okay, you're hip and up to date on current forensic methods, so it will come as no surprise to learn that in addition to my garnering a certificate of merit from PI Breaking and Entering School, along with my lock picks I also carry a small magnifying glass, tweezers, and a load of plastic envelopes. Sherlock Holmes had his methods, I have mine. Besides, my eyes are in touch with cataracts today, I need a magnifier when searching for hair: head, body, or otherwise. I carefully examined dirty bed-clothing in the bedrooms and I also checked out the john and bathtub. The ring on that tub had appeared at the same time Mount St. Helens popped her top. It was now sprouting a lovely mess of fungi in an effort to commemorate that occasion.

I managed to scare up a few hairs. They, along with those from Lorna's hairbrush, would soon be DNA tested. Unfortunately, a complete test takes a lot of time, saliva or blood samples would be more accurate. Still, the needy accept what they can gather. Did I mention I also dusted for fingerprints? I am no expert but it couldn't hurt to grab a few here and there. Salem's finest would check them out muy pronto. I had hoped to find a check or deposit book but the rest of the house only yielded more dirt.

According to Bernie Rhodenbarr it purely does ease a burglar's mind if he *knows* when the person he is relieving of his worldly possessions is due to return to the safety of his hearth. Every second I'm illegally inside another's residence, even if he's celebrating at his own wake, only invites frequent trips to the bathroom! I collected Maggie, who was trying to force the filthy frig open with her nose in order to grab the large chunk of stale baloney she'd spotted when I first cracked the door, and we scrammed. I did take time to examine the garage. Inside, there was a new model blue van. It showed less than 3,000 miles on the speedometer. It wasn't locked and yielded neither bodies nor women's clothing. I did pick up some more hair off a foul smelling blanket that literally made my skin itch. Maggie wagged her tail, all over excited at that find.

Mandy was happy to see us. I was glad to see her. All I wanted at that moment was a long, cleansing, hot bath and then a half an inch of rum and coke in the bottom of that same bathtub! Mr. Rhodenbarr, take your chosen vocation and stuff it.

I phoned Sam at his motel and reported results; we decided to stake Dirty Chuck out for a few more days. Bushed, more stretched nerves than anything else, I purely wanted to get back to Salem. I drove to the rest area in the Corridor, let the dogs out for their needed break, took one myself and then stood for a few minutes by the river breathing deep, trying to rid my nostrils of the smell of Stinky Chuck. A question nagged, he didn't have a record so what was he into? Where the hell was the money coming from for all his goodies?

By the time the three of us crashed, and yes I damn sure took that bath and it was lengthy, it was almost time for the rooster to crow. The hell with him, I jammed the pillow over my head!

12

I'd taken the glimmer of an idea to bed with me and I awoke fresh and ready to examine it for action. In order to implement, I'd need to pay a visit to Bascomb's and collar Bernie. He was at his favorite table. You don't want to know what'd died on his bagel, especially if you've not had breakfast yet!

"Danny, me lad, I suspect by the long look on your kisser there is nothing good to report. You need cheering up. Have you heard the latest sage advice tendered to our esteemed oil moguls?"

As usual, without waiting for an answer, he proceeded to tell me anyway:

"Those darlin' lads, purely in the interests of progress and personal remuneration, continue to vie within their ranks to see who's ripping the most off the public, but you already know that. I've sent them the following."

"A motorist on a Sunday outing in Pennsylvania, undoubtedly one of his last considering the extortionate price of your gasoline, drove up behind a member of the Amish also trotting along the highway. Attached to the back of the fellow's buggy was a large sign which read: 'Kindly note! You are following an energy efficient vehicle. It runs on hay and grass. **CAUTION***: The observant should avoid stepping in the exhaust!' "*

* * *

Don't ask. I have no idea where he gets them.

"Put a sock in the jabber, Bern, and listen. I need a favor; didn't you blab to me at one time that you have a pilot's license? And don't you have a friend who owns a Cessna and is he not above loaning it to you?"

"That I do, me old son. I haven't been up recently, but it's like brushing your teeth, a good scrub once a week and you never forget how. How soon might you require the plane along with my services?"

"Like twenty minutes ago, pal. I'll pay for gas and all fees. Will you go and call your buddy? Forget about cutting your lousy grass today. If he says yes, call me at the office and I'll meet you at the airport in an hour. Also, I suggest you pack a toothbrush, we may be gone overnight and that bagel, curling on your plate, has been dead a long time!"

Thus the glimmer began to shine: I beat it to the apartment, packed quickly and called Sean, in Brookings. I got him out of a meeting by declaring dire doings and asked if he had his laptop with him? He had. If I brought Lorna's computer to him, could he not start hacking when his bloody meeting was over? Even bureaucrats run out of hot air, temporarily, and end incessant meetings when desiring food and fun! Sean agreed and told me he'd call and tell his wife to let me have Lorna's computer. He also advised I bring the floppy disk labeled Shazaam! It was the one sitting on his computer desk. I told him we'd meet him at Brookings State Airport, a mile out of town, in about three hours. To avoid having him sit around I promised to phone him from the plane twenty minutes before landing. Next I dropped the dogs off with Sandy. A dog having to make an urgent visit to the loo—at 3,000 feet up—is not a pretty sight!

* * *

The plane was a fairly recent version of the Cessna 150. A two-seater, she allowed for some gear behind the seats along with a separate compartment in the fuselage for extra. Wisdom comes with age, right along with skin that resembles parchment. I'd caught that bit from Bernie about not flying for a while, so I watched carefully as he pre-flighted. After all, his skin was definitely wrinkling and that could mean that pockets of dumb were happily nestling there among the folds! Bernie was thorough though and soon he was ready to crank her over. He opened his window, told me to fasten my seatbelt, and then said:

"Let me see now, how do you start one of these things? Relax, Danny, I'm just kidding. Why, before you know it I'll have you up there floating among the clouds."

At least he didn't say, 'Keeping company with the angels!' However, it soon became apparent that he knew his business. I was familiar with that flyers' phrase, 'There are old pilots and there are bold pilots, but there are no old, bold pilots.' Thankfully Bernie seemed of the former and once at altitude which he'd chosen to be 2,000 feet, and heading west, I began to relax. The blood even returned to my numb fingers before my pilot began to bend my ears per usual. A constant crusader in defense of teachers, nothing would do but I hear the latest in his ongoing quest for justice.

"Daniel, my boy, have you heard the latest squib that only a teacher could relate? I realize that laymen might not be fully in accord with it and if you have no desire to listen, you have my permission to get out and walk!"

With that, he launched into the following:

* * *

"A man in a hot air balloon realized he was lost. Spotting a woman below, he reduced altitude. Then descending a tad bit more he shouted, 'Excuse me, can you help me? I promised a friend I would meet him some time ago,

but I don't know where I am.' "

The woman below replied, "You're in a hot air balloon hovering approximately 30 feet above the ground. You're between 40 and 41 degrees north latitude and between 59 and 60 degrees west longitude."

"You must be a teacher," said the balloonist.

"I am," replied the woman, "how did you know?"

"Well," answered the balloonist, "I presume everything you told me is technically correct, but I've no idea what to make of your information, and the fact is, I'm still lost. Frankly, you've not been much help at all. If anything, you've delayed my trip."

The woman below responded, "You must be a school administrator."

"I am," replied the balloonist, "but how did you know?"

"Well," said the woman, "you don't know where you are or where you're going. You have risen to where you are due to a large quantity of hot air. You made a promise, which you've no idea how to keep, and you expect people beneath you to solve your problems. The fact is you are in exactly the same position you were in before we met, but now, it's my fault."

* * *

Bernie snickered for ten minutes over that one.

"I am heading west through the Gap, Danny, we'll come out over Lincoln City and then head south. Damn, it's good to be up in clear air not having to contend with stinking smoke from the field burning of a few years back. When I was a touch younger, and flying with a rescue squadron in Alaska, sometimes the smoke from forest fires got so bad we had to fly along the river to get back to base. I wasn't a pilot then but I got lots of air time parked in the right hand seat of Cessna's very similar to this one. My job as radio mechanic, after repairing one of the little beasts, was to test fly to see if it was again working properly. The pilot I often flew with was an avid fisherman. Once we'd checked out the radio, he'd spot a likely lake and, as we were equipped with pontoons for the summer, he'd land and we'd fish for awhile. Those were the days!"

"In fact that learning period stood me in good stead when, with a license of my own, I was asked by the folks at the Salem airport to fly down to Mahlon Sweet Field in Eugene with a bank jockey so I could help him repossess a Cessna 150 like this one. From aloft, we could see the whole damn valley was on fire from field burning and we had to weave our way among the plumes of smoke. Before landing he called a locksmith to meet us so as to unlock the plane. Once it was opened he, who had repossessed, prepared to take off again leaving me to fly the 150 back to Salem."

"I bellered, nay-nay, no-no, pal, not until I gas her up and preflight hell out of her. I started the plane, taxied cautiously over for gas, and checked her over. Everything seemed A-okay, but she'd been sitting for some time. I allowed for a long warm-up before I waved him away. Cleared for takeoff, I poured the coal to her and yanked our feet off the ground. Fifty feet up, *the bloody engine sputtered, coughed and gagged.* Jesus, I knew my time had come! Flying here today, nice and cozy, you know the engine caught again and she kept running. Smoke from the lousy fires was so thick it blanketed the whole valley; I could not see the ground. I don't have instrument rating, only VFR. I needed a reliable guide in a hurry. I hung a 90 degree turn to port, flew to the Coast Range, then hugged those lovely mountains all the way to the Gap, another 90 degree turn to starboard and I followed Highway 22 back to Salem. Besides a nervous tick I now exhibit during stress, and a tendency to black out when I fly, I recovered quite normally from that trip."

"Notice Baskett Slough below us? They even burned her one year. In a letter, I griped to the governor complaining of the loss of little critters which provide lunch for the plethora of birds housing in the area. Like all good politicians he shined me on and let an aide reply. His letter, full of BS, waxed endlessly about the need to incinerate fields in order to protect grass seed from disease; tough duff if wildlife starved to death in the process!"

"On August third 1988 a gigantic pile-up occurred on I-5 due to damn field burning. Over forty vehicles were involved and seven people were killed. Read William Wharton's book, *Ever After*. He lost his daughter, son-in-law, and two grandchildren in a mess that could have been avoided if the State Legislature had done their job. I only brought all that up Danny because today, as we enjoy flying, most but not all field burning in Oregon has been eliminated. So why the hell did it take a tragedy to end it?"

Bringing his sermon to an end Bernie then lowered the right wing thereby raising the left. He held us that way for about thirty seconds. Next, he repeated the maneuver in reverse, right wing up, left wing lowered.

"A wee touch rusty are we, Bern lad? Having trouble holding her straight and level, old sock?"

It should be considered criminal when old beaver teachers look down their snoots at their captives with such absolute disdain.

"Have you ever heard of the *Crowded Sky,* Mr. Doyle?" If you wish to continue living while flying use your eyes. Never stop looking for other aircraft. Small planes don't have much to fear from the jumbos, except around large airports, but at the altitudes we fly other small planes constantly flit and buzz about, especially in good weather, and like many motorists they

Bet You Don't Know Where Lorna Is! 143

don't concern themselves with the rules. Look up, down, and sideways. Be prepared to outthink the other guy and out-fly him, thus continue to live!"

"About twenty years ago the Oregon sky was less crowded. One Sunday, I took the wife up to examine and enjoy our sheep farm from the air. It was a clear, gorgeous day. The Salem tower was not manned on Sundays. Pilot etiquette dictated that, as one approached the field for landing, one should broadcast one's position over the radio. To wit: 'Any aircraft in the vicinity of Salem Airport, this is Cessna 19055. I am at 1,000 feet downwind on 16 approaching baseleg. I'll be landing to the north on 34 in five. Please be advised.' As one's landing progressed, one would continue to radio position and altitude. This I did. At approximately four hundred feet altitude, heading south and about to turn to port onto baseleg, an ignorant sumbitch, flying north, cut right in front of me on an angled approach for the field. No warning. No use of radio signaling his intention. No nuttin'! As I am now one of those *old* pilots I'd been scanning the sky for just such a jerk as him. I yanked us up and over to starboard, almost into a loop, like a flaming top gun! When my heart settled down to 200 beats a minute, I continued my approach, landed—not one of my best—and went in search of that guy. I found him in the restaurant."

"He'd decided, on a whim, to fly his granddaughter to the airport for their breakfast. Not bothering to turn his radio on he had heard none of my broadcast warnings. He had absolutely no idea I was also in the air over the field. I was so angry I was shaking and I came awfully close to decking him. I think if the little kid hadn't been there I would have. Just remember, me son, imbeciles also fly the *Crowded Sky*."

By this time we were through the Gap and almost over Lincoln City. Old

Bern took us out to sea a short way, advised me to eye-scan the waters for signs of whales, and he shut up for a change! The FAA allows a pilot an altitude of 500 feet over sparsely settled land, oceans, and lakes. 1,000 feet must be maintained over cities and towns. I must admit it was truly lovely soaring effortlessly over sand and water. Engine noise on a Cessna 150 is not very distracting. I did see a whale! Nobody was looking, so Bernic buzzed it. Lazing along, it did naught but spout off at us.

Once in awhile I do something right and in addition to bringing coffee, I'd also thought to bring along a pair of binoculars. Little did I know they were going to come in handy. I'd brought Bernie up to date re Lorna: the trip to Newport, my finding the door of Filthy Chuck's house *open*, the abundance of his material possessions, including the van, and what I had gathered for DNA testing. We both remained puzzled as to Chuck's source of monies. If the bum had a record I'd label him as being into nefarious doings. I wasn't buying he was too smart to get caught and I'd bet it wasn't an inheritance. I filed away another mental note to illegally check out his bank records, soon; then I settled back to enjoy the rest of Bernie's flying. Relaxed, eyes closed, window open, I set to pondering how constant wave motion and roar from yon restless inanimate liquid giant can so soothe the living. Prudently, I decided not to ask Bernie!

Shortly past Florence my esteemed pilot edged us slightly to port to the east in order to save time and gas. If I had figured correctly that would put North Bend-Coos Bay on our starboard side. We would be able to get a good look at ship activity in the bay. Don't ask! Call it a hunch, a nudge from above, maybe second sight. Actually, I have no idea why I wanted to give the area a careful scan; I just felt it would be wise to do so. The airport at North Bend does not possess a tower; however, they will answer on 122.8 and give current conditions along with wind direction. We already knew it was blowing from the north which meant, if we were to land, it would be a reverse approach on runway 34. The field is but a mile from the city. As our destination was still Brookings a landing wasn't planned. Not, that is, until I took a gander with the binoculars at a rust bucket in the bay just leaving the dock. I presumed she was now carrying a cargo of wood chips supplied by the mills at Coos Bay. We were too high for me to make out her name; regardless, my skin began to itch like that of the retarded town dog that had been foolishly playing hide-and-seek in a patch of poison ivy!

"Bernie, oh supreme among all pilots, what say you hook to starboard and take us out to sea a smidge, then call the folks down below and tell them you're going to shoot a 'touch and go' on 34. After baseleg you'll be bringing us back in over the bay. I can still look to starboard and get a lovely clear gander at that ship just before we land. Isn't that a terrific idea?"

I got a glare and a miffed sniff, but 'Ol Bern lifted the microphone and complied. They say the dangers in flying are but two, *the takeoff and the landing!* Intent upon the movement of the ship I paid absolutely no attention to the field as Bernie radioed position and altitude, then smoothly brought us in. With some forty feet of air left I caught the ship's name on her bow, YUKIKO MARU. She was an old rust bucket and would carry everything including wood chips, but not oil. Steam fully up, she was heading rapidly for breakwater. We touched down fifteen seconds later as smooth as patting baby's butt with talcum powder. Following the dictates of touch and go's, Bernie poured on the coal without leaving the runway. We immediately took to the air again, banked to port in a smooth 180, and continued to lazily fly south toward Brookings. The YUKIKO was also steaming south.

"So okay, Dan my man, what the hell is so important about that bloody old derelict down there?"

"You really have to be a detective to understand the mental nuances of the vocation my learned friend. Let me just say this about that, I haven't got the foggiest notion! My tiny inner voice just whispered to me to flaming well do it; as I usually find my hunches pay off, and having confidence in your flying abilities, we went ahead and dood it."

After leaving North Bend it was a straight run to Brookings so Bernie asked me if I would like to try my hand at the controls. He wanted to relax and think about what we knew, or thought we knew, about Lorna. Nothing ventured, as they say, and no money stashed in savings decided me. And with that I reached out and latched onto the controls.

"Jesus, Danny! Easy, easy; you're not steering a runaway truck down So Long Hill. Treat the flaming wheel gently, like you were bestowing a goodnight kiss on Sweet Sandy. We're not wrestling here. No sudden moves. No eager squeezing. Hold her straight and level with the fingertips. Save the bloody grabbing for after you're married. How the hell can I think with you rocking us up and down like a thundering big hippo rampaging his fat bod through a strawberry patch! Flit, like a butterfly, before we end up perched on top of a bleeding coast pine!"

I listened to his *calm* advice. Pretty soon, even if I brag, we were flitting softly through the sky so steadily and surely that he quit thinking and began to snore. That may be a small exaggeration but at least he stopped bitching!

Brookings' airport, while small, presented no problems and Bernie set us down carefully and easily. Sean was waiting. After I'd handed over Lorna's computer plus the floppy he had requested, and he'd promised to get cracking soonest on obtaining her password, we took off again for Salem. This time we headed directly inland and then followed I-5 north. I wanted to check some things in Salem and make some inquiries personally, and also by phone, before the end of the business day.

Bernie, once again, set us down ever so easy onto macadam and I hunted for a way to thank him.

"Bern, I owe you big. Tell you what, next time we meet at Barney's, you decorate a bagel with whatever disgusting mess you can think of and I'll buy. Hell, I'll even watch you eat it!"

"Why that's downright neighborly of you Daniel, and I accept. In the meantime, use care me old son. As Mister Sun said to the pumpkin, 'I seed you in the vegetable patch, you shorely gonna end up in a pie!' "

"Meaning what? Bernie."

"Meaning, without exercising caution, you keep poking your nose in where folks don't want to find it, they sure as hell gonna reach out and honk your horn. Remember: a grenade thrown into a kitchen in France would purely result in Linoleum Blownapart!"

No question, Bernie's been out in the sun without his hat again!

In the office, I called Diddens and regretfully informed him of the need for more money. A thought had been circling in my mind one I did not wish to contemplate but at this stage I'd consider anything which might help me locate Lorna so I asked him for her blood type. Type O+ is the most common in the United States. Type A+ is the most common in Asian countries such as China, Japan and India. Lorna was type A+. Then I called yon Oregon Science Center in Portland re progress on that DNA report I had requested; nothing definite yet on the DNA testing. Next I called a Norwegian friend of mine to ascertain if he was available for a little job I had in mind. This guy was a most interesting character: Six foot-four, two hundred and twenty pounds, he had a face, because of so many waterfront brawls, had decided to reform itself similar to the stern of a harbor tug. One eye, the result of a broken bottle, displayed a permanent quizzical look. His hands were large-knuckled, heavily scarred and strongly callused. Eric's head, if one were to ignore the knots and bumps, was large. Blue eyes pierced his universe along with anything or anybody standing in his way. Believe it or not, if you could keep him away from demon rum, he was a very gentle man. He had sailed the seas on whatever would float for over forty years before retiring. Social Security did not keep him comfortably at the Ritz, so he settled for digs at the Salem Blitz—as in blitzkrieg. Even the cockroaches there spoke in whispers in the halls for fear the walls would collapse. Still, Eric was a happy and contented man. He'd spin sea yarns by the hour and never repeat a one. I was very fond of him. Above all, he was trustworthy. I told him what I had in mind and he quickly volunteered. His fee, after he had accomplished the requested task, he quoted as being a bottle of good rum, plus expenses!

With Eric on his way, I called Sam in Newport for a report on scruffy Chuck's whereabouts. Sam reported our boy was at home, hopefully taking a bath, and he'd seen no one else going in or out. He had observed a large fishing boat gassing up at the Marina but had been too visible to venture close enough to get its name. He had drawn a rough sketch of it which might help though. I asked him to continue surveillance promising to cable him some loot. Then I called the Maritime Service in Portland and asked for all pertinent data on the YUKIKO MARU. As I'd thought, she was what the trade still called a tramp steamer. She plied between Hong Kong, the West Coast of the United States, and as far south as Guayaquil, Ecuador. Yukiko means, 'happy child' in Japanese. The only time that old relic would be happy again she'd be permanently attached to a dock! As I'd guessed, the old bucket would transport anything: hides, scrap metal, wood chips, bananas, tobacco leaves, you name it. The YUKIKO spent most of her time in out of the way seaports and was registered out of Hong Kong. Her captain was not known for humanitarian acts. He and the crew were mostly losers. The ship had just taken on a load of wood chips and set sail for South America. She would offload the chips at Buenaventura, Columbia. The YUKIKO'S next port of call would be Guayaquil where she'd take on a load of bananas. Then it was back to Costa Rica for coffee and on to Mexico for clothing and produce, all of it headed for San Francisco. Sans bananas, coffee, clothing and produce, she'd load electronic gear such as computers and software at Frisco and head back to Coos Bay for more chips intended for her home port. She would be off our coast again sometime around June 30th. Hugging the coast as far as Portland she will then turn toward the northwest; time at sea on the return voyage from Guayaquil, unknown; after Coos Bay, approximately ten days to Hong Kong. Time is never essential to those old tramps, breakdowns occurring regularly and nobody seems to give a rip.

So okay, a bit here, a bit there, nothing concrete. However, my instincts were telling me to keep digging. Lorna was a very attractive lady with a fine figure; however, she was also now past Jack Benny's age. My reasoning for her abduction canceled out the notion of an old letch with a yen for a taste of the young and delectable, but I sensed the answer was thumbing its nose at me from on top of the yardarm and couldn't care less that I always get seasick!

Mandy, Maggie, and Sandy were glad to see me so I ponied up for the grits: spare ribs at the Oyster Bar, then hot fudge sundaes for the humans.

I kept an ear tuned to the office phone. Irons in the fire, even though the speculating kind, were heating up and I eagerly awaited a report from friend Eric. I realize the hunch which had assailed me was so bizarre I have as yet avoided sharing it with you. Enough people already figure me for an idiot; I see no need to add to the list. However, Eric's report could do a lot to vindicate the reason my mind was slogging through dark alleys, those that reminded me of pits of despair, such as the ancient opium dens of San Francisco where shanghaiing was once rampant.

Meanwhile, I tended to the paperwork. Do you have any idea what the weight of junk mail amounts to on a yearly basis? We have to be crowding well over three hundred million plus folks populating the USA today. Exclude sixty million for kids and that leaves you two hundred and forty of the large. If each person receives twenty pounds of junk mail per year—has to be a low estimate—and you multiply that times two hundred and forty million of the overwhelmed ones, you come up with *four billion, four hundred million pounds* of ca-ca. No wonder planet earth is sinking!

Mail, bet your bippy most of which ended up in the circular file, urgently requested my services with another runaway, four skip chasers, and an alimony ducker; add a plea to locate a young lady who'd heisted the boyfriend's prize 56 Chevy convertible. Bring the car back, forget the broad! A pitiful cry to find a lost doggie. That one I'd heed, I am nuts about

Bet You Don't Know Where Lorna Is! 151

mutts! Finally, a wail to locate a fellow who constantly wrote checks on numerous accounts not belonging to him as they mostly belonged to little old widow ladies. I was truly looking forward to nailing that S.O.B.!

There had also been a phone message from Greg. His voice sounded funny so I decided to drive out and collect his message personally.

Greg was limping when I set eyes on him; he sported a split lip along with a shiner. Uh-huh, his girlfriend had said, "NO!" I'll bet. It wasn't that. Two pals, Bo and Bart had paid friend Greg a visit. They were not happy with the inquiries he'd been making. In their own inimitable democratic way, taking turns, they'd pounded on him as a way of reversing his direction, you might say. Now why should my junior detective's innocuous queries have upset those two stalwarts, especially as he had little of import to pass on to me? Rumor had it Bo would opt for a career in acting if not successful at entering West Point. Greg had not yet ascertained the name of Bo's amour but was sure it was not Sara P. I gave him a fin to buy a piece of round steak for his eye, told him to wear a football helmet whenever he ventured out among 'em, and further advised him to keep digging.

Frustration, once again, had me by the throat. I had a strong inclination to reach out and start swinging and to hell with anyone who got in my way.

Is it a sign of old age when a friend compliments you on your alligator shoes and you are barefoot at the time? If the reply is yes to the above, does a healthy rum and coke improve vision? If no, would three or four of those lovely libations help? Probably not, but by that time a pleasant mellowing undoubtedly takes over and at that point who gives a royal fadoot! I was in dire need of a healthy rum and coke! The flaming sun wasn't over the yardarm yet so I opted for a visit to Sandy and some female advice which, as all males will agree, is always going to be terribly sage, most valuable and definitely prolonged!

Sandy was receptive to my grumps, up to spiking my coffee, and more than ready to listen. Definitely my kind of lady!

Halfway into my third cup of coffee the phone rang. It was Diddens. He had just discovered a ransom note shoved under the rug on his front porch and, understandably, was all worked up.

"Don't handle that note with your fingers anymore than you already have," I yelled. "I'll be right over. We just might have a shot at them now."

Sandy and I made it to his front door in ten minutes flat. Frank, his face ashen, handed me the note. Correction, he placed it on the hall table and I picked it up with a pair of tweezers. It had been inserted in an unstamped envelope. After I read it I thanked the Almighty it had been delivered sealed because an idea had begun to beat against an eyeball. If the envelope's glue had been licked it would have retained the sealer's saliva. DNA could nail the puke if the envelope had captured a good sample of his luverly spit!

"The note wasn't there when I got home last night," said Frank. "I almost stepped on it on the way out to work this morning. Do you really think she has been a kidnap victim, all along? Do you think she is still alive?"

Unless I missed my guess the note had been computer typed, and this time they had tried to convince Diddens that they were foreigners with their ransom demand. And yes, I now definitely believed the lady was alive!

* * *

"To most esteemed husband of Mistress Diddens, be treating this with gravest of the attentions. We are having of her. She is most alive and in wellness. We are demanding of you three things only: (1) You must tell

fat old fuddy of detective to be butting out. He is poking his nose in where the mongoose will bite. Honorable sir, no other warnings shall be coming to him or you. (2) Do not show this note to FBI or bring of it to the attention of any other Police persons if you wish the lovely of the lady to stay in a state of wellness. (3) You are to be putting the sum of ten thousand of your American dollars in a large envelope and placing of that in one most big freezer bag. Do not trouble to be marking of those bills. We are not of the foolish and know how to check them for secret marks. Be placing of those monies under the third seat in the front row of the bleachers, which shall sit at the south end in the park of the Mr. Bush. Be doing this no sooner than Midnight of June twenty-first and no later than two-o'clock of the early morning of June twenty-second. Do not be failing to complete any of these very much important instructions. If all is done as we kindly order, Lorna Diddens, lovely lady, will be returned to her family still in a state of extreme wellness."

* * *

Gimme a break, that phony attempt at dialect wouldn't fool my Great Aunt Siphronie and she never made it outa the third grade. There was no signature. The paper, lacking an expert's perusal, seemed to me to be of the common variety and would be available in any Wal-Mart, Safeway, or Rite-Aid. I couldn't determine a watermark. I took the note and envelope from Diddens and told him to hang tight. We still had two days until the demanded delivery date and I wanted the FBI to examine note and envelope. If we had gotten lucky for a change, a DNA test would supply the blood type. Now to get some fresh blood samples and let the Feds do the rest.

On our way to taking Sandy home, I placed a call to Bill J. and outlined a devious plan floating around in my head as I owed Greg's attackers a small reward you might say. I also told him of my suspicions re his grade results. Next, I called Ernesto Escobar and told him to take an early lunch and meet me at Bill's. I told Bill to make a phone call first and if all was well not to call me back. I waved a hurried good-bye to a puzzled Sandy and, after a short stop at south Wal-Mart to make a purchase, I gambled on a ticket while beating it out to young Bill's. You're quite correct, that ransom note was begging to be analyzed. Don't worry, I wasn't about to overlook it, but first things first.

The two kids were waiting for me and for a change I figured things just might work out as I had planned. We all piled into the wagon and set sail for Sagen's outdoor basketball court. Presenting a pair of white cotton gloves each to Bill and Ernesto while driving with one eye on traffic, I filled in the details on my little scheme.

"When we get to Sagen's basketball court Bo and Bart, having been conned into a meet by Bill's phone call, should be waiting for you. Each of you choose one of them, inform the other of your choice, then think of a code: maybe bananas, bugs or peanuts. Hell, I don't know, pick one and decide who will use it. When you meet, don't let on you suspect them. Split the breeze with the two clods in a baloney conversation. Tell them anything, but pique their curiosity and lull them into relaxing with you. Be sure you are wearing those gloves. Having each chosen your victim, at the moment one of you spouts the code, and without any warning, generously belt them on their arrogant noses. Be sure they spill plenty of claret on your gloved fists even if you have to deck them more than once. Surfacing from behind the basketball court, fortuitously chancing upon the scene, I will protest such

Bet You Don't Know Where Lorna Is!

juvenile behavior, express alarm, threaten an arrest for unprovoked assault, and run you nasty fellas off. The dogs and I will then keep order. After I've expressed more shocked concern, offered commiseration, and tenderly kissed their owies, we will all meet back at the wagon. Be sure to identify your gloves with the name of each donor and put them in those two plastic bags I placed on the back deck of the wagon. Might also be a prudent idea if you both headed to the mountains for a couple of days. Trout are biting in Detroit Lake. Tell your boss you've come down with the three day plague Ernesto, or something equally convincing. I will pick up your camping fee and expenses as long as you two don't rent one of those rolling motels."

Don't you just love a good plan that works? Bo and Bart, completely surprised, bled copiously, swore loudly, and threatened death while I—purely tempted to use sandpaper—swabbed tenderly at the damage. I continued to cluck sadly and told the poor guys I'd definitely inform the miscreants' parents of their cavalier behavior. Hot damn, I felt good!

I dropped the assault team off at their homes and headed for the office, I wasn't going to delay getting the ransom note checked out any longer. No messages, so I called Sandy and asked if she was up to a trip to Portland and the FBI office. As enticement I promised a cheeseburger that would knock her socks off at a restaurant in Lloyd Center. I was going to beg, wheedle, plead, and get down on my knees if necessary, to get the Feds to run the ransom note through their lab as fast as possible. If the DNA on the envelope matched either Bo or Bart's blood samples, I had them!

The FBI office is in the Crown Plaza Building at 1500 Southwest First Avenue. The SAC was away chasing some bad guys but the ASAC, a pretty young lady, agreed to talk to Sandy and me; right off the bat, once I had told her about Lorna, she started to ream me out for not informing an agent earlier. I explained that up to that point it had only been a "Missing Person," and we'd been working with the local law. I further stated we'd just received the damned ransom note that morning and I'd brought it straight to her.

You aware a frog's eyes bulge so he can swivel them 360 degrees all at once? Prepared to jump an innocent bug, I figure for safety he can first check all directions to see if another predator, like a hungry fox, a feral cat, or the beloved tax collector, isn't preparing to pounce on him! The ASAC's eyes were also bulging, not because she was about to snag a fly though, I believe it might have been from the way she was examining the bags containing the gloves, the ones liberally laced with Bo and Bart's donations.

"Detective," she said, staring at me like I was *the* fly soon to become flattened on *her* desk blotter, "Just how did you happen to come by these samples? I certainly do hope they were not obtained illegally!"

Since when is it illegal to pop somebody on the snoot, unless it's your mother-in-law? I threw her my sincerest look and decided to reply honestly.

"Ma'am, do I look like one who would knowingly break the law? I'd not dare to even deposit spit on the sidewalk; however, I do believe it best you don't know how I got them. Trust me, those offerings came quite suddenly. Please to consider our beloved IRS, if I may. Having checked a happy taxpayer's returns and promptly demanding more blood, do they not always threaten severe penalty if it isn't forthcoming, tout de suite? Are not donors always eager to oblige?"

When I was a child, a neighbor lady once said I had the face of a priest. I laid my most innocent look upon the lady Feebie and waited for the storm clouds to pass.

13

After another of her bug-eyed looks had speared me, FBI Jane decided to let it go while we examined the ransom demand. She agreed the note was an amateurish attempt to disguise the kidnappers' identity and that it surely looked like it had been written on a computer. She liked the idea of testing the blood on the gloves for DNA. Right, the same thought that had puzzled me about the ransom demand elevated her antennae. If Lorna had truly been a kidnap victim why wait so long to inform the family and why demand such a paltry amount of bread? Ten thousand clams is chicken feed for a ransom. Also, why the unusual hours and date set as deadline for payment? You can play the guessing game forever. I'd started out feeling like I was groping through a maze. Now, I was bloody well hopelessly lost in it!

The young but tough lady agent promised to get cracking on analyzing the note and sending some of the envelope gum to the Oregon Science Center for DNA testing. She further promised to get the info to me soonest. The Bureau would also check the paper for identification dye, which could tell to whom it had been sold, maybe a chain or, hopefully, a small stationary shop, and in which city it was presently residing. I love forensics. When I was a kid, I'd always thought it was a fencing term. I was heavy into the Man in the Iron Mask and the Prisoner of Zenda in those days.

Sandy and I took leave of Edgarina Hoover and, crossing the Burnside Bridge, hung a left on Martin Luther King Boulevard heading for yon Lloyd

Center. There resides a restaurant just on the outside of that mall where I can order a half-pound burger cooked just the way I want it, nice and juicy. Since E. coli reared its ugly head at 'Jack in the Box,' fast food establishments, most burgers, slipped between two halves of a bun today, come thin as dollar pancakes and are about as tender as manhole covers. When I dine out, I'll either get one dripping down my chin or I'll cook the sucker at home and the hell with restaurants! While I thoroughly enjoyed my cheeseburger, and watched the juice from Sandy's drip off her chin, I also chewed on a vague thought about Lorna's case which had been nagging at me. Today was June 20th. Something about June that I'd shoved in my head's 'remember file' was not knowing where I'd put it. Fortunately, after our recent trip to the coast, Sandy had re-stocked her purse and it now included Excedrin. I always carry bottled water in the wagon in case an unexpected migraine came cruising through open windows to make my day. If perchance one arrived, it was a head-achy fifty-eight mile drive home!

Next day, too impatient to wait by the phone for Edgarina to call, I decided to check in with Bernie. I could hardly wait to view his next bagel creation! I checked my stamped and voice mail arrivals first and changed plans. An urgent message on the squawk box from Eric in Newport claimed priority. He was calling from the slammer and needed a troop with loot and impeccable character to come and bail him out! He was right on one out of his two choices. I hollered for my girls and headed the wagon for the coast.

Greeting Eric in the tank, I noticed he had a lovely shiner and skinned knuckles. I'll let him tell the story so you won't have to wade through any of my minor embellishments; well, maybe just a few:

"Danny, I bane do vot you say. I vos be in goot bar an' chust be drinkin' a brew or two, minding own biziness, yarnin' mit da fellers, ven dis pig pozo talk nod nice to me. He say all Norvegians vear panties und zing soprano. I say nod be true, only ugly fruidy cakes like him do dot. He say my mudder vas a jiraffe und I vas vun of her droppings ven I vas born. I yoost give him liddle push und he aggzidentally fall troo bar's vront vindow. He stops after his head go troo vindshield of dat Blazer parked der in front of goot bar. He don't giff me no more truble, but den bartender und tree udder fellers chump on me. Bartender going to be hokay ven dey takes dose pins oud uff his jaw. Vun of udder fellers maybe have vun leg broke. Da udder two chust resting in da hospital. I don't do nuzzing wrong bud dose police dey trowing me in dis cell anyvay. How zoon I bane be gedding oud of chail, Danny?"

* * *

Diddens was not going to be happy with Eric. Damages to the bar came to seven-hundred big ones. God knows about hospital costs? I purely hoped Eric's playmates had medical insurance! Might be there would also be other charges besides disturbing the peace. Though witnesses, one or two of them sober, said Eric had been provoked. I bailed him out and we got the hell out of the Newport City free motel.

I took him to Georgie's for breakfast. One of the newer secluded restaurants over on Elizabeth Street, it has a great view of the ocean and we could get a booth with a little privacy. I thought Eric might have worked up a small appetite after his little workout. No signs of hunger showed, once he'd polished off two three-egg omelet's, one with ham and cheese, one with sausage; add double side-orders of bacon, ham, sausage and hash browns; then lather maple syrup over two large stacks of flapjacks; Swig two glasses of orange juice, three of milk, and three mugs of black coffee! Around huge mouthfuls, he informed that "all vas nod lozt py golly." He'd found out quite a bit about Chuck. Seems more than one fisherman was curious about that boy's fishing habits. Many a night he'd been seen heading out to sea alone when bad weather threatened. The local fishermen knew that most fish, during storms, preferred the deep, and they shunned bait. Back in port he seldom unloaded a catch worthy of the risk. After those nightly sojourns he drove north the next day. Gossip held he went to Portland. He flashed money upon returning and inferred there was plenty more where that came from. I'd puzzled over his house filled with those expensive goodies myself. I'd also purely donate one of Maggie's ears to get a gander at his bank account. Unfortunately, without evidence pointing to complicity in a crime, neither the police nor yours truly could talk a judge into issuing a warrant to search his accounts. He does have a girl; she's reputed to be a dish and quite young but nobody knows her name or where she lives.

"If dat liddle missy effer shtays over vith Filthy Chuck den dey neffer have ozzer fellers or girls der at same time, py yimminy."

Lordy, I'd give a dozen of Bernie's rotten bagels to know what, figuratively speaking, floats Chuck's boat when it is dangerous for any fisherman to challenge mean-minded waves. The rewards had to be rich.

"Der is vun udder t'ing Danny, dose fellers calls him Daffy."

"Daffy?"

"Yah, py yimminy, chust like da candy vot vun chews."

"Candy you chew! Do you mean Taffy?"

"Yah, dat's vot dose bar fellers all calls him, Daffy."

Eric began to scan the posterior of our waitress, which more than amply filled her dress, with his good eye; no way was his look concerned with food anymore! Quickly, I dragged his beat-up frame out of there and I wore some tread off the tires heading back to Salem. At a state run booze dispensary I bought him a liter bottle of truly good rum, I believe the brand was Monarch, and then I dropped him off downtown at his digs. Neither of us mentioned his expenses!

* * *

It was high time to check in with Sean, but I wanted to listen to the message machine first in case Ms. Hoover had called. Both she and the Oregon Science Center had left messages. What I got was good and bad. According to results at the Science Center there was an eighty percent chance that Lorna had been in Chuck's house and that happily verified my gut instinct. I knew that pig was in this right up to his dirty drawers. Now, all I had to do was figure out a way to slip them into a Laundromat with him still in them!

Miss FBI related they'd been able to lift a really good DNA sample from the envelope. Unfortunately it wasn't one of the donors; neither Bo nor Bart had sealed that envelope. Bloody hell! They could still have written the damn ransom note though. Nothing else appeared to be significant about the envelope or paper, nor did they contain any fingerprints. Wal-Mart, Rite-Aid and Fred Myer all carried bulk piles of them. Odds were the letter had been typed on a computer. In fact, the dye indicated the paper probably came from Rite-Aid, possibly the one on South Commercial. Not much to go on but worth checking out; maybe they got careless with a credit card. I decided to go ask questions and show pictures after I checked in with Sean. How come they always showed Perry Mason having it so easy? Rin-tin-tin was even quicker at figuring out his canine cases.

Sean had some good news, I think! Soon as he picked up the phone he started to unload a mess of computer lingo on me and damned if he didn't try to do it all in one breath:

"Danny my son I've got it I thought I'd have to use a Bot at first but this guy is a Code cruncher not a Codeslinger he did crack Lorna's computer she doesn't have a firewall and he tried to Demon her but I checked and there was no bug in her Code . . . ."

"Uh, Sean . . . ."

"Well this guy is no Wizard and his hacking is mediocre he may be a MUDhead but he doesn't know Packet-sniffers or Phreaking . . . ."

"SEAN!"

"I'll bet he's mostly into Phishing the net but he damn sure is no Guru sure as hell he spends most of his time on the IRC he wouldn't know how to write Kludge even if he does know how to Root and I will bet he's into the Warez gambit for sure . . . ."

"SEAN, WILL YOU TURN OFF THE GIBBERISH AND JUST GIVE ME HIS BLOODY NAME! I have no idea what language you're using, or why you hate punctuation!"

"Jeez, Danny, you don't have to get snarly. Is it my fault you're too damn old and set in your ways to get into computers? You could learn a lot on the Internet. I could get you a good deal on a used Packard Bell!"

"SEAN!"

"Okay, already. Some people sure are a little shy on gratitude. Your boy is good old Bart. He and I suspect his pals did hack in and get Lorna's test grades. They changed five of them. Two guys, one named Ernesto and the other Bill J., actually got A's which were changed to F's. Barty boy changed grades from D's to A's for himself and a guy named Bo. He also changed an F to an A for someone named Jill. All the rest of the grades remain as Lorna had listed. I've made floppies for you. Little does that bum know I'm a Sysadmin. I connected with him on IRC and then slipped him an urgent ICQ. He bit and I got his E-mail address and name. You owe me bigtime Danny! I'll pick the place for the biggest, fattest, juiciest steak in town. A good wine will, of course, be included. And don't forget the cheesecake!"

"You got it, Pal. I'll even pay for the little woman if she tags along. You can leave the kids at home with Granmaw."

* * *

Finally a break and a big one at that, we now have motive and method. I also think I've figured out how they want it to end.

M and M were hogging the sofa, so with my feet on Sandy's lap over on the loveseat and a cold brew in my hand we planned strategy for tomorrow, the 21st, purportedly the day the ransom was to be paid. I'd already checked in with the Salem police who were going to have two cruisers staking out the vicinity. Bush Park has a plethora of rose gardens and trees among which a gang of kidnappers could easily hide. I had also checked in with the FBI. I did not want to take any chances on losing my license and, as kidnapping still remained a federal offense, figured I'd better clue in Ms. Hoover in case the Feebs wanted to be there. I am also a staunch believer in 'too many cooks . . .' and we could be tripping over one another and blundering around like a cattle stampede. I still thought the ransom note was a large crock. These were kids, damn it! Eighteen year olds. If they were smart enough to plan and then pull off a caper of this magnitude, which had all the believability of a skunk making love to a porcupine, I was much older than I thought. For sure, if by chance they were, we'd had nobody like that attending the schools I'd been thrown out of! Somebody in the educational field purely had to have been challenging their think boxes along the way. If I was right, the only adult in the group would be Chuck and I flat out couldn't see him being a member of the Menses! Besides, the ransom was still way too low for that much risk. Nonetheless, we had to check it out. Sandy wanted to be there, too. I said, "hell no." If they were dumb enough to try to collect, and got spooked, somebody could get hurt and it flat out wasn't going to be her. The cops weren't about to let Diddens come either for which I was grateful. If I were in his place and they dared to show up I'd be carrying a baseball bat, one I fully intended to use. Best if we kept things low key as possible. Besides, if we nabbed the little pukes they could always accidentally stumble into a police baton on the way to the pokey!

Ms. Hoover said she'd let the Salem cops handle it but God help them if they screwed up! I just love cooperation between law enforcement agencies, always reminds me of how much the Air Force loves the Army!

Participant adrenaline was pumping iron like the Furies when we all hove into view at the park at eleven p.m. on the 21st. We waited quietly. Sweaty palms nervously removed creases in slacks and uniforms. Believe it or not, nobody coughed, sneezed, or smoked for two and a half hours! Maggie and Mandy likewise didn't whine, growl or bark. Are they trained or what? Yeah, it was a total El Busto. Only a prowling tom, warily stalking the neighborhood, gave a yowl at the crescent moon. But one car drove into the parking lot and right on out. Turned out a priest on his way to administer last rites to a sinner had lost his way. I offered up a prayer for the sinner.

Some son-of-a-puke was making finger gestures at us, but why?

Bet You Don't Know Where Lorna Is! 165

Next morning, Bernie was at his favorite table filling his face and swilling coffee. I caught a quick glimpse of another mess lying dead on his plate, gagged, and quickly averted my eyes.

"My God, Bernie, what the hell have you desecrated that innocent bagel with this time?"

"Ah, Danny me lad, you are most fortunate to be gazin' at my latest creation. I guarantee it will catch on and sweep the country. Listen most carefully while I relate of the contents; I will also inform of a secret ingredient. You see before you a large raisin and rye layered with cream cheese, blueberry preserves and topped with some fresh raw oysters. Hidden between the layers of cheese and preserves I have placed a thin slice of jalapeno pepper to sort of keep the oysters company on the way down the old hatch. Now what do you think of that? Is it not a work of art? Wanna bite?"

"If you're the kind that can't go to bed without taking a long gander at a Jackson Pollock because you think it is art, be my guest. Most folks upon viewing a sight like that would just naturally throw-up!"

"Please, pal, cover it up with your newspaper, I have to talk to you and I can't while my eyes keep threatening to tell my stomach to toss."

Bernie is a good old stick and I began to fill him in on progress on the Diddens case while he kindly laid the latest page of good news from the third estate over his ungodly creation. I recited what I could remember of the ransom note and the meeting with Miss Feebee, and how she'd promised to cooperate with me and also the Salem police. I told him about the DNA results, the fact that the lab got a good example off the ransom envelope but that it wasn't that of either Bo or Bart. Bern was not surprised that the listed date for the payoff turned out to be a phony. I told him that Sean had nailed the hacker, who it was, and whose grades had been changed. We had pondered at length for the kidnap motive on our flight to Brookings and had pretty well agreed it must have something to do with grades if our culprits were the ones we suspected. The fact that we now knew grades had been switched made the motive definite and that kids had to be involved right up to their tushes. Unhappily, none of that brought us any closer to Lorna's whereabouts, the actual kidnappers, or explain the why or who of 'Taffy'?

When I related Eric's little brou-ha-ha and the number of citizens he'd sent to the hospital, plus the cost of damages, Bern laughed until his face turned red. Oh, yeah, I needed that. Constantly stuffing his face with bagels and only occasionally cutting his lousy lawn indicated a need for Bernie to exercise, even if it was only the movement of his belly, so I also told him how I'd collected blood samples from Bo and Bart. His jiggly parts immediately exercised for a further five minutes!

Bernie offered a theory that we weren't done with ransom threats or appointments just yet. We still could not quite pin that one down. Was it just a trial run, a bogus payoff to see if it would work? Maybe they were trying to figure out a better collection spot, and if they sent further notes would make it considerably more complicated while also demanding a much larger bundle of cash.

"Bernie, there is no denying you have strange tastes in food but I like the way you think. How would you like to come aboard as an advisor or consultant? The pay won't be much but you could be in on the finish. Mark my words: I am going to bring this case to a successful conclusion!"

"A consultant, do you say? Danny, me son, do you have the faintest clue

Bet You Don't Know Where Lorna Is!

as to what the rank and file in our esteemed educational system think of consultants? It shall be my pleasure to elucidate." And he was off again!

* * *

"A shepherd was herding his flock in a remote pasture when suddenly a brand-new BMW advanced out of a dust cloud towards him. The driver, a young man in a Brioni suit, Gucci shoes, Ray Ban sunglasses and YSL tie, leaned out the window and requested of the shepherd,"

"If I tell you exactly how many sheep you have in your flock, will you give me one?"

"The shepherd looked at the man, obviously a yuppie, then looked at his peacefully-grazing flock and calmly answered, 'Sure.' "

"The yuppie parked his car, whipped out his IBM ThinkPad and connected it to a cell phone, then he surfed to a NASA page on the Internet where he called up a GPS satellite navigation system, scanned the area, and then opened up a database and an Excel spreadsheet with complex formulas. He sent an e-mail on his Blackberry and, after a few minutes, received a response. Finally, he prints out a 130-page report on his miniaturized printer, turns to the shepherd and says,"

". . . You have exactly 1,586 sheep."

"That is correct; take one of the sheep," said the shepherd.

"He watches as the young fellow selects one of the animals and bundles it into his car."

Then the shepherd says, *"If I can tell you exactly what your business is will you give me back my animal?"*

"Okay, why not," answered the young man.

"Clearly, you are a consultant," said the shepherd."

"That's correct," says the yuppie, "but how did you guess that?"

"No guessing required," answers the shepherd. "You turned up here although nobody called you. You want to get paid for an answer I already knew, to a question I never asked, and you don't know diddly-squat about my business."

"Now give me back my dog!"

* * *

"Are you sure you want me as a consultant, Danny, lad? There won't be any danger of violence will there? I abhor the thought of somebody thumping upon bodies, especially my own!"

I hastened to calm his fears. "Naw, Bernie, I let Maggie and Mandy do all the necessary thumping. Oh, if I catch Taffy or the kids with Lorna I may not resist the desire and the opportunity to send a few heads into the outfield with a baseball bat, but nothing serious."

Bernie said to count him in and I told him to keep a phone handy, we might be called upon to make a quick trip quite soon. He was starting to raise the paper covering his plate about then, so I got the hell out of there.

Back in the office, messages checked and nothing new, I placed a few phone calls and then headed out south to check out paper dyes and their possible purchasers. I was also carrying copies of yearbook pictures from Lorna's senior class and a polaroid Sam had snapped of a possible 'Taffy.'

After I'd checked out Rite Aid, Wal-Mart, and Fred Myer, my feet hurt, my knees hurt, and my head was aching again. No one had recognized any one! Thoroughly pooped, and because Mandy and Maggie begged for a run, I took them down to Bush Park for some exercise. While there, we carefully explored likely-looking spots for yon ransom drop. Creeps who like writing ransom notes might tire of waltzing the local fuzz around the Mulberry bush and get serious. After all, what purpose is there in mailing a demand note if it isn't for personal gain?

In my business, I have learned to despise many types of criminals. The ones who kill perfect strangers for no other reason than that they are willing to take a life for pay. The ones who, under the guise of phony patriotism or because they are gullible enough to believe the puke who, while carefully keeping himself out of harm's way, exhorts them to go and commit terrorist acts of barbarism. The CEO who thinks it is clever, not criminal, to rob the working man of his life's savings including anything he might have had if he'd been allowed to retire after a lifetime of devotion to the company. The rotten S.O.B. , an already rich horse owner, who will kill his animals for the insurance. Claiming accidental death, he kills the animal by shoving a bare wire up the horse's rectum, fastens another one to the victim's nose and then plugs the cord into a wall outlet where, as the poor creature is electrocuted, its agony is unspeakable. The cowardly bastard who uses bombs to kill innocent women and children in crowded market places, churches and theaters. Serial killers like Bundy who, we are told, deserve pity because they are sick. The miserable little creep who takes guns to school and mows down teachers and classmates over some imagined slight. The pervert who captures, tortures and kills again and again. Why? 'The devil made me do it!' But the one I truly hate the most is the despicable kidnapper. His victims are so often the young and the innocent.

Horrific mental anguish suffered by victims can be insurmountable; scarring is for life. Pain experienced by those families, helplessly waiting, praying for a safe return of their loved one, often to no avail, is unspeakably and horribly cruel.

"Do away with capitol punishment," cry the ones not suffering, "it won't return the dead to life." Of course, the bewailers are absolutely correct; the dead will not return. However, sending their killers to hell assures *them* of their own lengthy conversations with the Devil. Ever know of anyone who swapped lies with the Devil and won? If I have anything to say about it, capitol punishment stays!

Hey, all you hand wringers out there, what about Lorna? You gonna spend equal time sobbing for justice for her?

My thoughts had been dwelling more and more on that missing lady. Today calendars as the fifteenth day she's been gone. Imagine being held for fifteen days in the hands of scum. What must be going through her mind? How is she coping with her fear? How long will a reasonably healthy person be able to hold up under terror? And, the worst question of all, do I really think she is still alive? Or is it just that I want her to be?

14

Who is Lorna? What was she like as a little girl? Did she play house with her dolls? Did she have a favorite? What about pets? All kids want pets. Was she wanted and loved as a child? How about neighborhood kids, did they get along? Who was the boss? Was she the teacher even then when they played 'school'? How does a young girl handle fear? Was she good at her studies or just average? If average, did she have to work longer and harder than the other kids to keep up? Did she ever worry herself sick over grades? Did she ever fail a test? Did she often cry herself to sleep over little things—to adults—awfully serious to children? When she went away to college, did she become homesick? How many times did she want to throw in the towel and run home to the warm, loving arms of Mom or Pop? How did she overcome her childhood and adolescent fears? How the hell do any of us manage to finally lay them to rest?

Was she scared the first time she had to give a speech? When she spoke to her audience was she afraid her knees could be heard knocking way off in the back of the auditorium? Was she popular with peers? Did her first boyfriend ever break her heart? When and where was her first time for a kiss? Did she think she'd immediately become pregnant? Later, all grown up, what did she fear then? What, what, what?

Is there such a thing as mental telepathy? Does she know somebody is looking for her? Oh, God, I do hope so. Don't you dare give up hope Lady

Lorna! If what I like to pass off as a brain is functioning, and my inner voice is right, you won't be away from home much longer.

*   *   *

Early next morning, I was parked in my office hoping the phone would ring. Sam, or somebody, would then inform of a break in the case. To while away the time I was studying my bible to see if anything worthwhile was running at Santa Anita. Mandy was snoring on her pillow under the desk. Once in awhile she'd sigh and smack her lips. No doubt she was dreaming of my luscious lamb stew. Maggie was on the phone. I don't mean she was talking on the damn thing, she was sanitizing a dab of peanut butter off the receiver. Breakfast had been interrupted by a call from a jerk wanting to erase flying rock damage off the wagon's windshield. When I slammed the phone down a glop of jelly departed the sandwich and landed on Maggie's nose, the peanut butter took up residence on the receiver. What, you never have a PB&J sandwich for breakfast? Do not knock it if you haven't tried it. At least I hadn't lathered sardines all over it!

It was kind of quiet and peaceful. I hadn't even noticed roar and stink of city buses passing under my window, nor heard the squeal of my office door until a gravelly voice resonating from the doorway interrupted my reverie.

"Are you thuh detective what is fer hire?" inquired a voice, reminiscent of Marjorie Main's.

"Depends," sez I, right back. "What needs doin'?"

She was wearing a yellow and orange polka-dot blouse followed by blue jeans of the almighty large size. Sandals the size of wagon wheels imprisoned bright red socks which, in turn, covered her feet. Completing that ensemble, an old straw bonnet with dangling tassels perched impudently on top of a mess of gray curls. She reached behind her and hauled forth what I was sure would be Pa Kettle. Instead, a female version of what old coots like me call 'the younger set' appeared, dressed like a Goodwill reject. The kid's short skirt started about three inches below her bellybutton and ended some four inches shy of her tush; a torn tee-shirt began covering four inches above that. Her green hair looked like she'd latched onto the bare wires of an unforgiving wall outlet. Naturally, she sported rings through her nose, upper lip, and bellybutton; a tattoo of a chartreuse butterfly landing on a sunflower prettied up the left side of her face. Purple lipstick completed her decor. She presented charming. Barely preventing a quick shudder I immediately recalled one of Bernie's many lengthy sermons.

"You don't have to tell me I'm rapidly approaching late middle age, but Jesus, what the hell has gotten into these kids? The wife says they are just going through a phase and will grow out of it. How do you grow out of tattoo's and rings through lips and noses? I know you won't believe me, but I've even seen open mouths expose diamond (probably glass) doodads on tongues that have been drilled; those pointed jewelry things have then been shoved through the holes and fastened on the other side! Must be a real challenge when they feel inclined to tackle a cob of corn!"

"Don't forget the boys. They, too, are so into this modern nothing style they're also piercing ears, eyelids, lips, noses and tongues. Almost any body place will do to hang gee-gaws on.   The kids wheedle Mom and Pop into ponying up a hundred clams for a pair of Levi's. Then they cut holes in the knees, fray the bottoms, bleach hell out of the remainder, and trot off to school wearing the latest fashion, including a green or orange Mohawk haircut. In my day 'Our Gang' kids wore hand-me-downs like that out of ye olde necessity, certainly not from choice. What ever happened to pride in and of appearance? Daniel, before you wind up and throw the cat at me, I have not uttered a contradiction. I did say many kids are getting better looking all the time. I also said that they were the ones who took pride in themselves and were truly interested in learning rather than wasting valuable awake time on silliness. Idiotic behavior from the losers drives me up the wall. Flang it, I'm gonna go out in my garden and assassinate some bugs!"

* * *

Gotcha, Bern, let's get back to Marjorie.

"My daughter here's got a twin sister that ain't been home fer a week. Think yuh kin find her? We ain't got much money, but I seen you were studyin' a racetrack sheet when I come in; if ya take us on and find my other little girl, I'll give yuh a winnin' tip on a horse is runnin' today in the Queen's Plate Trophy at Woodbine, in Toronto, Canada. Thet horse flat out ain't goin' tuh lose an' the odds are gonna be 82-1. Thet's high enough up there tuh tickle thuh tops of his pointy ears! If yuh laid a twenty on his nose, even in Canadian dough thet will add up tuh a right nice piece a change!"

I had enough on my plate hunting for Lorna without taking on any more side trips, but I like to eat and bills have to be paid; besides, I kinda liked this old broad.

"Why don't you and your lovely daughter make yourselves comfortable in those chairs in front of the desk dear lady, you have my full attention."

Fortunately I didn't have to warn either of them about the danger of leaning too far back, as both ladies sat primly. Mother because it was in her nature; daughter because, in that skirt, she could definitely be arrested for causing population eye strain, if she didn't.

Bet You Don't Know Where Lorna Is!

"My name is Jessamine Tooley an' I'm married to Jacob 'Make a Bet' Tooley, mebbe you've heard a him. I an' he met at Saratoga in New York. I've liked tuh be 'round horses since I wuz weaned. When I wuz young I could generally be found workin' in thuh stalls; muckin' out an' feedin' an' curryin' when I wasn't out exercisin' them broomtails. While runnin' the track one day on a fractious colt, he thrun me an' I landed smack dab on top a Jacob. He was a-timin' the colt fer speed an' we right off become attached, so tuh speak. My Jacob is famous around all thuh tracks cuz his percentage of winners ain't never been matched by anyone who follers thuh sport a horse racing. Yuh can take thuh tip I'll give yuh to the bank, mister. When 'Make a Bet' says it's a sure thing, best to go an' put yer money down!"

"This here's JoBeth, her sister's called JoLene. JoLene kinda likes tuh run around a mite. School comes easy tuh both my girls. In fact, JoLene is on thuh honor roll an' can purt-well have her pick uh colleges. She ain't intuh rings in her nose, dyed hair an' short-shorts like her sister. She wears jeans an' sweat shirts an' likes tuh hang out around horses on weekends jest like I did. Some of her friends ain't of much account though, an' now that school's out I'm feared she's gone an' stepped in a peck uh trouble."

"In case thuh long shot don't come in, which ain't gonna be the case, I kin pay yuh twenty-five dollars now an' mebbe three more a week until we pays yore 'hole bill. Will yuh find my little girl fer us, mister detective?"

"My dear lady, I will be happy to take the case provided you understand I am heavily involved in a crime of kidnapping at this time and I will have to, temporarily, put your needs on the back burner if anything breaks on that one. What did you say the name of the long shot was?"

"I ain't said it yit, but his name is T J's Lucky Moon, an' if yer wise you'll bet thuh farm on him. Kin you start lookin' fer JoLene right quick?"

"Indeed I shall, dear lady. Now, how about some particulars? Do you perchance have a picture of JoLene? Does she go by any nicknames? How about racetracks, which ones would she be inclined to frequent? Is she into hanging out at county or state fairs where livestock is shown and where a few even schedule horse races? Can you put a name to some of her friends, boyfriends in particular? Do you by chance have a picture or two of the swains? Could any one of the lads have a record, or done time? Is little JoBeth here acquainted with one or two? Could the twins have attended school with any of them? Might JoLene be attracted to one because of his fondness for horses? Does your missing one have any allergies which require prescription drugs? Has your daughter ever been in trouble with the law? Some police protectors look askance at pierced portions of anatomy today and are not at all loath to spend time rousting those who have them."

I was running out of breath from querying, so I shut up and looked expectantly over at Mom Jessamine. Of course, right along with the questions I had already asked was one bouncing about in my noggin that I hadn't. Like, if old 'Make a Bet' was such an expert at picking those winning ponies as Jessamine had said, how come they were hurting for money? Could it be he was rolling around in horse puckey rather than in clam dip? And if he truly was loaded would not his spouse also be able to porpoise through those fat bowls of clam dip? So why slip me but twenty-five fish down plus but three more a week? As stated, I liked this old broad. I wish I knew what the hell was making me so damn suspicious!

Mom did have a picture of JoLene and said it was a good likeness. Joly was her nickname. Jessamine didn't know of any racetracks her Joly liked to frequent, but the kid had always been one to attend state fairs and, most days, could be found hanging out in the livestock barns. Ma and Pa had done their best, including a few whuppin's, to discourage JoLene from doting on horses 'cuz they figured there was no future for a girl in hanging out with our equine friends, short of becoming a jockey where she was sure to break her neck! I refrained from mentioning training, showing, veterinary careers, or horse breeding. Last time I looked some women were doing quite well in all those fields, not to mention equestrian trials.

Her best friend was a girl named Bootsy who spent her summers on her grandparents' farm out in Aumsville. Bootsy was into horses in a big way, including gymkhanas. Grandma and Gramps raised horses so JoLene often went out there to ride. Jessamine had already checked with Bootsy who hadn't seen Joly for two weeks. Joly had been slinging hash after school for the last two years at the Red Lobster on Lancaster. Mom had no idea what the kid did with her wages and tips but she never seemed to spend any, and JoBeth had as much chance of borrowing a few shekels from her as the Oakland Raiders have of ever fielding a decent football team again!

The only boy who pined after her sister that JoBeth could name was a fella name of Jerry. He, too, was fond of horses; in fact, he had a face looked a lot like one. He also carried a full load of acne which immediately brought good old Bart to mind. Naw, there surely couldn't be any connection there. No way could coincidence wrap itself slantwise like that!

JoLene had no allergies, bathed in no makeup except soap and water, and couldn't even stand flu shots let alone have her body parts pierced.

"Okay, Mrs. Tooley, I'll look into your daughter's disappearance for you right away. Do you have a phone and address where you can be reached? I try to keep clients apprised of progress quite often so don't be surprised if I call at any time of the day or night."

She slipped me the twenty-five fish, took her receipt, latched onto JoBeth and on the way out the door reminded me that T J's Lucky Moon was racing today at 5 p.m. Eastern time. As they rose, JoBeth spied one of the picture posters of Lorna lying on my desk.

"Me and JoLene seen that lady not long ago," she said.

I bolted up in my chair. "You have! And where might that have been?"

"It was after classes the Thursday before the last week of school. JoLene and me were waitin' outside Sagen for her boyfriend to show up. He goes to Sagen too only he ain't smart enough to be in an advanced English class. Me an' JoLene is, only we ain't in Miz Diddens class neither. The teacher was talkin' to two boys standin' beside a Toyota Camry on the school parkin' lot. The boys was acting pretty excited an' kept pointing down the street."

I yanked the Sagen yearbook off my desk, turned to pictures of Bo and Bart and asked if those were the two?

"We didn't get to see their faces as they was turned away from us. We could see the teacher's face real clear though an' she looked kinda surprised. We never did get a good look at the guys except we seen they was urgin' her to get in the car. After some more of their hand wavin', she got in the front seat an' they drove off away from us down the road towards town. She didn't look scared or nothin', just worried like maybe somebody was hurt or somethin'. I didn't think nothin' more about it until JoLene told me later she'd read in the paper that the lady was missin'. I hope you find her mister, JoLene's boyfriend says he's heard she's real nice."

* * *

Bet You Don't Know Where Lorna Is! 179

It was only ten a.m. Pacific time after they left so I had plenty of time to call 'Beat the Odds' Clyde if I desired to drop a twenty on the longshot. I also decided to enlist Clyde's help. He knew most of the bookies at all the West Coast tracks. For a mere pittance, like another mortgage, he would fax JoLene's picture north and south in hopes one of his cronies would spot her. Meanwhile, I hotfooted it over to Sandy for a cup of coffee and to ask her to check out addresses of all the likely local tracks including the Multnomah Greyhound Park. Ya never know. If Joly couldn't find work with horses— dogs are nice. There's not a whole lot of difference between mucking out a dog pen and a horse stall either, if you're wearing waterproof boots!

Do you have any idea how many racetracks there are in the northwest, and we aren't talking yet of the ones where quarter horses run? How about state and county fairs, horse shows, equestrian meets, and dressage events in the months of June and July alone?

I left Sandy punching a keyboard and took me off to make a few phone calls; still nothing from Sam in Newport. No sign of Dirty Chuck; nada with any of the police departments. No more ransom notes for Frank. Greg hadn't seen hide nor hair of Bo or Bart. Ernesto and Bill J. called to thank me for straightening out their test results. Sagen had reported they were looking into all the grades plus illegal computer habits of a certain acne-faced kid. All kids had been advised of their corrected grade. If Lorna were alive, and being held against her will by those clods, what could possibly be gained now? Kidnapping, besides being a no-brainer, carries a stiff rap; were they crazy enough to add bodily harm to the charges? In a way I hoped the scuzz we wanted were professionals and not kids, at least those creeps know when to cut their losses. Regrettably, that mostly turns out to be to the victim's detriment. Jesus, I hope Sandy still has some aspirin when I return!

* * *

We'd heard from Fairplex Park, Pomona, CA; Hastings Park Racecourse in Vancouver BC; Los Alamitos Race Course, Orange County, Ca; Southern Oregon Horse Racing Association, Grants Pass, OR.; the Josephine County Fair Race Meet, Grants Pass, OR.; plus Emerald Downs in Auburn, WA. Seattle is called the Emerald City so I guess it's no surprise they chose to name their track after one. No info on JoLene from any of them. The only thing of note is a tad bit of trivia about Emerald Downs. The track is now owned by the Muckleshoot Indian tribe which also owns the largest casino in Washington. There now, and wasn't that interesting?

Portland Meadows e-mailed a possible sighting some three days ago. The track's had a fairly bad year, attendance and wagering both off. I found that hard to believe. True, Oregon at 8.5% unemployment is supposed to be coping with the highest in the nation, but latch onto the following:

This information is off the internet and supplied by the Washington Thoroughbred Industry: In the United States in 2001, $14,550,000,000 was wagered on Thoroughbred races. Over $467,400,000 lovely clams in revenue was returned to states just from Thoroughbred racing (does not take into account the Standard bred Quarter Horse or any other breed's racing statistics). $1,067,490,193 was distributed in purse money. Count some seven thousand, three hundred and forty-three racing days (that's gotta be adding up racing at all tracks, because I learned how many days to a year in school!) during which 55,127 races were run. Add that all up and we ain't just talkin' a load of hay here!

I can go on but who wants to wade through a mess of stats? Simply said,

Bet You Don't Know Where Lorna Is!

folks flat like to gamble and that in turn makes for variety in jobs. It figured a youngster named Jolene would be found among 'em, especially as a little more digging turned up the fact that most high schools in Salem had approved and supported equestrian teams. Not too far down the educational line, the Oregon High School Equestrian Teams program will seek official sanctioning by the OSAA. The state of Washington has formed THRUST—Thoroughbred Horse Racing's United Scholarship Trust—it was awarded to college freshmen and above for the fall of 2003. Top award equals $10,000 over a four year period. Students may attend any college or university but, and here's the catch as far as Joly is concerned, they must be residents of the State of Washington at time of application. Applications had had to be postmarked by February 1, 2003. I would think it has been in effect long enough now for them to have worked any bugs out.

Now, it seemed to me that while giving out with background material, Jessamine had informed of a sister, name of Jennamine, who resided in Spokane. She and JoLene had always hit it off. If the kid was bunking up there she would have plenty of time to establish the required residence in order to comply with the rules, and apply for the scholarship. According to mom her grade point average was equal to the task. There would be a personal interview and a written, video, audio tape, or film response to a question: The query for 2003 was: How has the expansion of gaming in Washington state (tribal casinos, mini-casinos, MegaMillions, etc.) affected the Thoroughbred industry? Piece of cake, I could have written a book on that one myself! I have no idea what this year's question is; probably, "Do you think horse racing should be reinstated in Iraq on weekends?"

Anyway, if JoLene is now residing in Spokane, Jessamine will be in luck.

Happens I have a friend lives in Spokane. She has her own detective agency, loves mysteries, and is a little bloodhound when it comes to hunting for answers. I asked Sandy to send her a photo fax of JoLene along with the particulars. If anything was stirring at Playfair Race Course in Spokane Mary E. would find it!

* * *

No messages re Lorna so I hied me over to Bad Bascomb's. Sandy was too busy to play hooky. I figured to talk Bernie into taking a run up to Portland Meadows with me. If any time permitted we'd also scoot over to Multnomah Greyhound Park and check out the dogs. He was at his usual table, a cup of Java to the side. I risked a quick look at what he was eating. Lo and behold, his bagel was unadorned except for a small dab of butter.

"What gives, Teach? Your plate usually looks like something just died on it, why a plain bagel today?"

"No real reason, Dan my man, the old stomach has been off a bit lately; no doubt a touch of the summer dismals. I'm just taking it a little easy for a while. As a kid I always used to get sick for a brief spell during these warm, lazy days. Probably the horrible thought that school would soon be starting again triggered them."

Right! I didn't need to be a croaker to know exactly what triggered those dismals he was suffering through; however, I am a gentleman. Though I truly had to fight myself, I refrained from outlining them.

I gassed up the wagon and we headed north. While Mandy drooled in Bernie's ear as we cruised up the freeway, I filled him in on my latest case including the tip on T J's Lucky Moon. The race was long over by now, there being a three hour time difference between Oregon and Toronto.

Bet You Don't Know Where Lorna Is!

Yeah, he was ticked I hadn't let him in on it and wanted to know how much I'd put down. I explained that I was a tad doubtful of the info as Jessamine's source, her old man, reputed to be the world's winningest horse bettor could only afford twenty-five clams down and three more a week for my fee. I did promise to call 'Beat the Odds' for the name of the winner upon returning to the office. For another ten minutes Bernie kept licking a pencil stub as he tried to figure out, on a notice to pay electric bill, how much bread he could have won if he'd put a Lincoln and a Hamilton on the nag's nose. Finally finished adding, he sighed deeply and told me the latest horse racing joke making the rounds on the internet:

* * *

"Seems like a Preacher wanted to raise money for his church; upon being told there were fortunes to be made in race horses he decided to use a touch of the congregation's money, pony up for one, and enter it in races. However, at the local auction he soon found out the going price for broomtails was steep, so he ended up buying a donkey instead. He figured that since he now possessed the animal, and feed and housing cost dough, he might as well go ahead and enter it in a race."

"The next day the racing sheets carried a headline, 'Preacher's Ass Shows.' The Preacher was so pleased with his donkey that he entered it again and this time he won! The paper's caption read, 'Preacher's Ass out in Front.' The Bishop found that kind of publicity unsettling so he ordered the Preacher not to enter the donkey in another race; another headline graced the front page, 'Bishop Scratches Preacher's Ass.'"

"That was just too much for the Bishop and he ordered the Preacher to get rid of his animal. The preacher decided to give it to a Nun residing in a

nearby convent. Another headline the next day stated, 'Nun has the Best Ass in Town.' The Bishop fainted. He informed the Nun that she would have to dispose of the donkey immediately. She found a farmer who was willing to buy it for $10.00. On the morrow, the paper bannered, 'Nun Peddles Ass for Ten Bucks.' They buried the Bishop the next day!"

* * *

I chuckled all the way to the turnoff to Portland Meadows over that one. The track can be reached off Schmeer road west of 99E and east off I-5. As tracks go, Belmont she isn't, not too bad she is; only being a touch rundown in places and flat out reeking from too many untended stalls. Recollect the oldie? 'She was only the coachman's daughter, but all the horse manure!'

The last time I'd placed a bet had been back in November of 2001. We Can Move—out of Drag Butt and Evicted—was a sure thing. I put a clean Hamilton on his nose. He blazed in eighth out of a field of seven if you catch my drift! Portland Meadows was dry at this time of year and while they were boarding a few runners there was no racing. We checked with most of the barn clan. A few thought they had seen JoLene mucking out stalls a week or two ago but none of them would swear to it. One toothless, bearded, skinny old swamp rat, related she'd headed off to California to bunk with her aunt JocyLynn. Mother Jessamine had mentioned no aunt named JocyLynn. I figured this old beaver had been imbibing a touch too much mescal and his hindsight was mixed up with his foresight resulting in gear shifting sans clutch. No transmission would put up with that!

Bernie and I thanked one and all. I then pitched a carrot at We Can Move who, I'd been informed, had been retired. Inhabiting a stall with a view he was not going anywhere which came as no surprise! Bern and I trundled off to check out the greyhounds. No one at Multnomah Park had sighted JoLene and the only thing I noticed at the track was that the rabbit scooted around like a coyote who'd accidentally set his tush down on the business end of a cactus. No living dog was going to catch that sucker! After sniffing Joly's scarf, obtained from Mom, neither of my dogs had been able to smell her out. Mandy had spied a pile of horse manure that looked appetizing and Maggie, unloading her imperious bark on me, yearned to take on the rabbit; nothing productive there, so we flicked it in and headed out to the parking lot. I let the wagon follow her own course to the freeway, put her on cruise, and we headed for Salem.

I realize one can never fully relax while motoring any highway, but at one time I-5 was a dandy freeway all the way from Ashland to Portland. One could truly savor Oregon's beautiful scenery then and still drive safely. Not anymore. I-5, due to excessive traffic, is definitely showing her age. Keep both eyes on her lest an errant chuckhole toss you on your head into a trash loaded ditch.

Enjoying one another's company, Bernie and I rode in companionable silence. Letting my mind drift, as one is wont to do from time to time while still staying alert to the traffic, I wondered, not for the first time, why I had become a detective. I remember as a kid I was pretty good at figuring out whodunits on the weekly Perry Mason series, and by an astute following of clues, along with tracking the travels of our cross-eyed Siamese cat, I'd found my Ma's ruby ring where not a single other soul would ever have thought to look. It was under her bed!

I really think I took up the career of sleuthing because I like to be my own boss. I'd tried my hand at selling gas, greasing cars, flogging groceries, peddling auto parts, concrete construction work, carpentry, the military, and picking, eating and selling strawberries. In every case, someone else was always dying to tell me what to do and where to go. The where to go part got picturesque at times! I tend to be curious and I also get mad when innocent people get hurt, so I guess I just naturally gravitated into trying to right a few wrongs.

If that explanation doesn't cut it, my almost all time favorite film is a tossup between *The Adventures of Robin Hood,* starring Errol Flynn; *Four Feathers,* the early 1939 version with C. Aubrey Smith; and of course I refer once again to *Beau Geste,* with Gary Cooper, Brian Donlevy, Ray Milland, and Robert Preston. Who can ever forget the hyena-like cackling of J. Carroll Naish up in Fort Zinderneuf's tower? Right, you didn't ask. I'll tell you my favorite anyway: *Singin' in the Rain;* Gene Kelly, Donald O'Connor, and a very young Debbie Reynolds. Who will not forever relish Jean Hagen's superb performance as Lila Lamont? She should have received the Oscar! Even though that offers no explanation as to why I chose to fight crime as a profession, I make no excuses for doting on that dandy old movie. Isn't everyone entitled to dwell in a touch of fantasy?

After awhile, bored with my own thinking, I asked Bernie what he had been doing lately that had been exciting?

"Well, the wife and I just spent three days signing our books at the Salem Art Fair. In fact, of the five top sellers, we came in fourth with *Mojac's Megan.* We both renewed acquaintances with former students, friends, and parents of former students. That was really nice. I've told you before, Danny, teachers don't rake in the dough but when a student you had in class some thirty years ago steps up and not only remembers, he or she greets one fondly and with warmth, then that, my son, is money in the bank! By the way, old lad, you are not the only one with a fondness for a flic. One of my all time favorite movies is *Goodbye Mr. Chips* starring Robert Donat and Greer Garson"

"I have also been trying my hand at more writing. Titled *Crosetti's Curse*, it will be a murder mystery; so far it has been hard to get down on paper. I write true stories about what I know. Other than the occasional yen to off a politician, what do I know of murder? Most of the novels on stands today show authors hunted for artistic ideas in sewers. Try the following."

* * *

"It is dark on a rain swept street. Suddenly a shot rings out followed by a cry of agony. A body staggers, stumbles and falls into a gutter. A young good-looking lad is sauntering south on that same street. Notice a lovely young lass strolling north. They meet by the body. 'Shocking,' she cries. 'Bummer,' he answers. She bats her eyes demurely in his direction and quips, 'Race you to the sack!' They exit off stage and for the next two chapters, while the stiff in the gutter grows cold, they play hopscotch under the covers. The author relates that those two pursue every acrobatic contortion known to man, some even experimental. He describes it all in exquisite detail. Some of the mentioned twists and turns a flaming octopus wouldn't even be fool enough to try!"

"Chapter three begins with the investigating detective and his female partner standing over the corpse. He proceeds to spew forth every dirty word ever penned, even to the extent of creating a few new ones. His partner, rather than washing his mouth out with soap, contributes some epithets of her own. Got to be one of the 'guys,' right? Another two lengthy chapter's sewer on by. They do nothing but stink up the pages"

"Chapter five begins: Those two sex explorers, considerably bleary-eyed, stagger out onto the sidewalk. The stiff is gone, but out of the corner of Romeo's eye he spies the killer driving away in a souped-up Hummer. Betcha the fiend doesn't know that the kid has his own gas hog hot-rod. Whenever he changes gears, his car is able to leap tall buildings in a single bound. The two sack wrestlers limp into Big Lover's car and the chase is on! During three lovely chapters: two busses collide head on; another jumps a bridge; sixteen taxicabs find themselves headed for a wrecking yard; the subway train jumps the tracks; two Caddies, two Navigators and a Mercedes intertwine forever, and two cats, three little old ladies and a mangy dog learn to fly in one easy lesson. As excitement progresses, the author manages to elicit sixteen gallons of blood from both good and bad guys which, of course, is allowed to flow with abandon. Finally the culprit, trapped, races down an alley and flies off a dock into the Hudson, or whatever river is handy to the locale; naturally this does him in."

'I guess that taught him a valuable lesson,' trills Juliet. 'Right on,' baritones Romeo. 'Race you to the s . . . !' Fadeout."

* * *

"While channel surfing on TV the other night, I tuned into a movie featuring two prominent actors, I'm talking Oscar and Emmy winners here. During the five minutes I watched, both of them tried to outdo each other in the use of filthy language. Presumably, that's telling it like it is. I don't doubt we all tread in the muddy field of cussing from time to time, especially when under tension, but certainly not in front of twenty to thirty million people! How sad those two care so little for their profession they willingly wallow in filth.

Bet You Don't Know Where Lorna Is!

There is neither rhyme nor reason for that, especially as it's just filler for lack of a plot. What kind of example are they setting for young hero worshipers? They should be thoroughly ashamed of themselves."

"I'm not into that kind of trash, Danny, and I sincerely hope the majority of the people who read aren't either. I want to try to make my stories interesting, believable, enjoyable, and humorous to read. That's what I have been attempting to do lately and I haven't even been able to come up with a good plot yet! And while I'm on the subject of that which remains unanswered, are you going to tell me if you bet on that damn horse or not?"

"What horse was that Bernie, me old squash?"

Muttering something that sounded suspiciously like, ". . . concrete-headed detectives . . .!" the old geezer slid down in the seat and pretended to catch some zees. Except for his snorting and wheezing, I was alone once more with troubling thoughts. What the hell were the kidnappers up to?

I called Sandy from the mobile phone, heard nothing encouraging re Lorna so I offered to feed Bernie at Chili's in Wilsonville. At least it wouldn't be a God-awful concoction desecrating an innocent bagel! Bernie ordered chili and beans with sausage bits, cheddar cheese, doubles on the minced onions, sour cream, and three Jalapeno peppers. He washed it down with one mas grande root beer float made with spumoni ice cream; so much for those summer dismals! I settled for a grilled cheese and coffee. Afraid Bernie was going to lick the dregs of his spumoni ice cream from the dish; knowing (figuratively) humans are tasked to watch out for one another, and because I also genuinely like ol' Bern, I offered him, purely in the spirit of gratis from the brotherhood, advice on his health:

"Bernie, old sock, are you into homilies?"

"Not particularly, especially when they come in the form of lengthy and boring lectures, such as yours!"

"Good, I am glad you asked me to relate this one. Did you not inform me that, as a long time graduate gourmet, your constant fantasy is to attend The Cordon Bleu School in Paris, France? What I shall clearly recite now was written for those with a passion for fatty foods, definitely you! Ah, you accuse me of dithering. Okay, already, listen while I declaim."

"*Lord, grant me the strength that I may not fall into the clutches of cholesterol. The road to hell is paved with butter. Cake is cursed, cream is awful, and Satan is hiding in every waffle. Beelzebub is a chocolate drop and Lucifer is a lollipop. Teach me not the evils of Hollandaise, of pasta and gobs of mayonnaise. And crisp fried chicken from the South? If you love me Lord, shut my mouth!" (Reverend Tom Walsh)*

The above received a glare and silence from my chubby companion!

* * *

Back in Salem I dropped Bernie off in plenty of time for him to cut his lousy grass and headed back to the office to check on messages. I wanted to call Mary Elizabeth, my little bloodhound of the north, she had never let me down yet and my poking-into instincts were hollering that Miss JoLene would be found shoveling out stalls in the Spokane neighborhood.

You've heard the bit about dynamite coming in small packages, right? That describes Mary E. to a T. She probably doesn't weigh an ounce more than ninety-two pounds in her skivvies, but she wouldn't be afraid to take on The Bears ex-tackle, 'Refrigerator' Perry. A safe bet is she'd dump him on his can, too. I once saw her grab a full grown, snarling Doberman by its ears and toss it clean over a six-foot chain link fence!

15

Mary E. isn't too much in accord with telephones; thus, one can expect the unexpected upon calling: I dialed her number and after three rings:

"Drogan, Drunken and Draggin' Detective Agency; tell your troubles to Mother; you got thirty seconds!"

"My, my, even for an old bag we are just a touch frivolous on the phone today, are we not? Ah, I get it; you've got Caller ID, right?"

"All modern and successful detective agencies have it, my good man, and watch that bit about 'old'!"

"I don't have it."

"I rest my case!"

"Mary E. leave us dispense with the pleasantries and get down to business, I am in need of your inexpensive services!"

After another few jabs, she decided to listen and I quickly filled her in on the Tooley problem. She knows Spokane like the runs in her socks and promised, once we'd eliminated the word inexpensive, to check out the race track and surrounding areas for me.

Playfair Race Course is over on N. Altamont and E. Main Streets in Spokane. Racing doesn't begin until September 26 and it runs through December 21. The nags will run Friday, Saturday and Sunday. At this time they were conducting workouts there; JoLene may well have signed on in order to get some pin money while, and if, she is establishing her residency.

I also needed to consider this kid has committed no dastardly deeds. In fact I kind of admire her. I believe she is following her dream. Not afraid to work she is also doing it with pluck. Wouldn't Mom and Pop be surprised, and yeah I think proud, if she gets a scholarship through THRUSH?

Even though I'd felt I should tell Mary E. to walk softly with the kid, I trusted the old broad's judgment. She can be as soft as butter when she isn't confronting a sleaze. No news is no news but I decided to leave her to it. When she was ready I'd get a collect call. In the meantime I truly wanted to turn my attention back to Lorna. That's where the real fire smoked.

* * *

I had just started to go through Lorna's file one more time when the phone rang. I was ordered to meet the three o'clock afternoon Greyhound coming in from California. My San Diego buddy had collared the runaway and was personally escorting her home. When they disembarked, other than having previously examined a photograph, I got my first good look at Carly Draper. She couldn't have been more than thirteen and, other than looking a tad skungy, she just looked scared.

"So, how come you brought the kid back yourself, Marine?" I asked.

"I am overdue to visit my sister in Lincoln City," he said. "And besides, this is a good kid; I wanted to make sure nothing bad happened to her on her way home. She's all yours Danny. My bus is loading for the Coast and I'm already tired of looking at you, sayonara."

He's a great kidder, I think! The kid had made no move to scram so I took her gently by the arm and headed us for a bench inside the depot.

"Let's have a little chat before I take you home, Carly. I want you to know I am on your side but I do need a little information. Was anything bad

Bet You Don't Know Where Lorna Is! 193

happening to you at home with your folks, like beatings, abuse, or even nastier stuff? Tell me about it. If it proves out I will see that you find a better place to live. I gotta tell you, when I talked to your parents I got a strong feeling they love you very much. I know they are worried sick over you, so what's your side of the story?"

"Dad was mean to me. He wouldn't let me go out with my boyfriend any more. He said I was too young for serious dating and Freddy, that's my boyfriend, is too old for me. Mom sided with him and they threatened to ground me if I disobeyed. I just couldn't bear it, I love Freddy so."

"So no one was thumping on you or anything like that?"

"No, my parents have never hit me or been mean before."

Sure didn't seem like a major problem here. Could be her folks had a good reason to shunt her away from the boyfriend. In my book thirteen is still awfully young for serious stuff.

"Your boyfriend got a last name?"

"Oh yes, it's Randall, Freddy Randall. He is so dreamy!"

Puppy love! How many memories does that bring back? Most of them bad. I decided to check one more thing before I took her home. I needed a belt. She was too young. So I put her in the wagon with my girls and headed for a Baskin-Robbins over on Market. She could have a soda and I'd forego my belt while I made a phone call. The Drapers were home.

"Mr. Draper, Danny Doyle here. I'm still investigating your daughter's running away. Tell me, does Carly have a boyfriend or somebody close she might have elected to go stay with?"

"That's what most of the fuss was about Mr. Doyle, Carly was going with a much older boy and it worried me. I checked him out; he is a bum and has been arrested three times; once for possession of cocaine; twice for suspected rape. He has been in trouble with the law since the age of twelve. Now twenty or older, he is surely headed for jail and will take Carly down with him. I tried to tell her but she wouldn't listen. Have you discovered anything yet? I'm afraid her disappearance is going to put her mother in the hospital. Her heart is not strong, you know."

"I'm pretty sure I am making progress Mr. Draper, I'll get back to you as soon as I can pin her down. I promise it won't be much longer."

I gave Carly a chocolate soda when I returned to the wagon. She soon had foam all over her mush and had drained her soda dry by the time the mutts woke up too late for dibs. I decided to play it straight with her and hope this kid was just young and innocent, not dumb and pig-headed.

"Carly, I have friends in the Salem Police. Your Freddy has a record and he is not what you think. He's a loser. Sooner or later he will end up in jail. Your parents were quite right to worry about your relationship with him."

I filled her in on the details of why Freddy was headed for the slammer. I also told her I understood how she felt. We all go through the same stages. Most of the young, hopefully including her, by using common sense will survive those adolescent pitfalls and enjoy productive lives as adults.

"Carly, you are only thirteen. That's awfully young to be making major decisions, especially the ones that could most likely affect the rest of your life, probably not for the good. I know you think adults are pretty stupid; I did too when I was your age. Not much later I learned better. Your parents will welcome you home today, not with yelling and threats but with hugs and kisses. I am going to leave it up to you: go hug mom and dad or, if you prefer, I'll find another home for you, one provided by the state. Nothing to get nervous about, like a reform school. It will be a good home with foster parents that I will approve of, or they won't get you. Either way, I cannot allow you to roam the streets on your own you are too nice a girl for that. Your parents are lucky to have you and I honestly believe in their own way they are trying very hard to show you their love. I would like to take you home Carly, what do you say?"

Her empty soda glass flooded with her tears and after awhile I took her home. Occasionally, the fox loses and the rabbit returns safe to the burrow!

You saw for yourself how far overboard my gyrene pal had gone in returning the runaway back safely to me. My blasted conscience began to pummel me, as always happens when friends perform good deeds for me, and I knew the stipend I had previously decided to pay him would have to be increased considerably. I wrote a mental note to kick it up to 45 clams.

* * *

I checked calendar and clock in the office. Both read late on June 23rd. There were no messages from cops, Diddens, Sam, or the tooth fairy. I know what you're thinking: After all the time Lorna has been missing, how come the great detective with years of experience hasn't come up with a flaming solution? You suppose I haven't already berated myself over the same damn question? What could I do that I already hadn't? I am not one of those Travis McGee kinds of fellas who off the bad guys just for the exercise. I totally despise violence. Dripping blood makes me nauseous, especially when it turns out to be mine! Don't misunderstand, if I'm facing a perpetrator whom I know without a shadow of a doubt is guilty, and the guy is giving me trouble, I won't hesitate to deck him. I will also take great satisfaction in doing so. But, lest we forget, a private-eye had better operate within the law or it will be so-long license. I had my suspicions, sure, but proof was another matter. If I was right, there would be another ransom note and it would give me a few more days to find and free Lorna.

At the Coast, faithful Sam was still keeping a close eye on Dirty Chuck and I checked in with him twice a day. In the meantime, as I've already said, a guy has to eat, though it wouldn't be gourmet on a few bucks a week! I would continue hunting for JoLene for awhile longer while always ready for a call from Sam; when he hollered, I'd be over there listening to and enjoying a sounding ocean again before he could hang up the phone.

As a matter of fact, and thanks for reminding me, though I hadn't solution one yet there was still something else I hadn't checked. So, next morning I decided to investigate Miss Jill. Sandy was up to her tush in JoLene sightings. You have any idea how many bookies 'Beat the Odds' happens to be acquainted with, and how many of them are near-sighted? JoLene had been spotted at Saratoga, Belmont, Hialeah, Woodbine, Santa Anita, Del Mar, Hollywood Park, Churchill Downs, Arlington and even Caliente—all on the same day! What, the kid has her own jet?

I collared Bernie before he got seated at Bad Bascomb's and promised breakfast if he'd go with me, the only stipulation would be, no loaded bagels. He agreed, provided he could pick the restaurant. I figured he'd opt for the Original Pancake House on south Commercial. For my money, they put out the best omelette in Oregon. Of course they don't give them away. I have a hunch breakfast there will set you back more than anywhere else in town; however, the place is immaculate, the omelettes are huge, the stainless steel tools used to fork the grits into one's mouth are sterilized in a container resembling a rock tumbler, and the coffee is Boyds; all in all, she is a far cry

Bet You Don't Know Where Lorna Is! 197

from Denny's. Surprisingly, Bernie chose Shari's on the corner of south Commercial and Kuebler Blvd. When I asked the reason, Bern fooled me.

"The Original Pancake House is great, but they give you too much. I've asked for a senior menu but they don't have one. I can fall face down in their ham and cheese omelette, only if I do I'm never able to come back up! Shari's has a senior menu, it is non-smoking, and the hash browns come the way I like 'em. A hundred years ago in the Air Force in Alaska, we had a guy from New York in our outfit. Name of Skadora, promptly dubbed 'Skidrow', he used to say: 'Da only way ta eat ya hash browns is merst'; for those of us who speak English, try reading that 'moist.' 'Da outside hasta be crispy and da inside hasta be merst.' I like mine crispy and merst also. The coffee is good here, my omelette is not too big, and I can also get my toast cremated! When the check comes—to YOU—you won't need to take out a loan either. Any more questions or comments?"

"Just one request, Bern, please don't ask them to insert raw oysters into your omelette!"

Breakfast was enjoyable, the day was gorgeous, and we were ready to go brace Miss Jill. According to the address from school records, she lived out by the Creekside Golf Course in another one of those poshy places. Head west on Kuebler Blvd. to Lone Oak Rd. Hang a left then hang another left onto Mildred Lane. Wander awhile and eventually you'll come to it. Check out a curving driveway going on forever; manicured lawns; these only covered an acre or two and gave Bernie the 'green eye.' The front of the house covered three city blocks. It was a three story with brick and granite façade; small, maybe only twenty rooms. A humongous entryway comprised of two huge oak doors was inscribed with family crest.

"Sheez," burbled Bernie, "take a gander at that, those front doors are hanger size and wide enough to permit egress for the Spruce Goose!"

You got your three car garage, apartment above. A Caddy parked within, a Rolls Royce out. The chauffeur was shampooing the Lord's Rolls. I'd learned Miss Jill's father happened to be a surgeon and much in demand. I believe the doc's specialty was overhauls: like heart, lung, and kidney replacements all at a modest thirty-five gees a pop. Busy, busy, busy, he would be seldom seen by his loving family.

Leaning on the front door bell did not make it go ping-pip-pong. Instead, visitors became tuned into London's Big Ben laboring under a bad case of adenoids, BO-N-N-G, BO-N-N-G, and B-O-N-N-N-G. I was tempted to ask the butler if Parliament was in session.

The woman who opened the door, butler's day off, displayed what is often termed a severe figure, six o'clock straight up and down. Her mouth was wide and tight. Picture an old-time front-door mail slot and you've got it. Her voice, when she graciously deigned to notice us, had welcomed many a martini over the years and planned on greeting a whole lot more.

"What, may I inquire, is the nature of your visit? If you are salesmen your entrance is around back, be sure to wipe your shoes."

Mom was a precious jewel. If she tried to look down her nose any farther her neck would snap. She was already wearing enough jewelry around her throat to put a bow in the neck of a giraffe!

I hastened to elucidate. "We are neither of us salesmen, Madam. I am a private detective and would simply like to speak to your daughter, if I may, in regard to a most urgent matter. Might she be at home?"

"My daughter isn't home this week and most assuredly she wouldn't wish to be acquainted or have business with either one of you!"

"Please do not misunderstand, Madam, Miss Jill knows neither this esteemed gentleman nor my humble self. My name is Danny Doyle. Mrs. Lorna Diddens, a teacher from the high school, is missing. Your daughter was a student in one of her English classes this year; we are simply here to inquire if your daughter has any information which might be of help to us in locating the teacher. Mrs. Diddens has now been missing since late afternoon of June seventh. Understandably, her family is quite worried as are we. The students usually participate in a little celebration with staff after the final exam for the year. Possibly Mrs. Diddens might have mentioned some of her plans for the summer at that time. I understand Miss Jill acquitted herself quite well on the finals' test. Mrs. Diddens would have been pleased and would have undoubtedly extended her congratulations except that she went missing before issuing her final grades. May I inquire where your daughter is and when you might expect her home?"

"Good heavens, surely you don't think we socialize with teachers!"

I coughed warningly to Bernie and fought with, "Perish the thought you snooty old hag, Bernie and I would sooner party with a skunk inflicted with a bad case of herpes!" I settled for one of what Sandy calls my furious non-committal stares and then, in my very best teeth-clenching-so-tight-my-caps-are-going-to-shatter calm voice, I said: "Madam, I realize my friend and I are taking up your valuable time but if you could just share your dear daughter's whereabouts with us, we will trouble you no further."

"Wait here," decreed her highness, and she closed the door in our faces.

"Why thank you very much for your gracious invitation dear lady, we shall be most pleased to enter such a delightful abode and escape the heat of a warm day," I snarled, as the solid oak doors slammed shut.

Five minutes later one of the doors abruptly opened. Mrs. Sweetness had returned with another imperious order:

"Follow the walkway over there on the left to the back of the house. My husband is relaxing by the swimming pool. He is an important man and needs his rest; however, he will allow three minutes for your questions. Make them short." The door thudded closed one more time.

"So much for 'Goodbye and have a nice day,' eh Bern; got your hiking shoes on?"

"Forgot to bring 'em, me old son. You toddle off. I believe I will just stay here and police the driveway for herself. Later, perhaps she'll offer a glass of cold milk for one of the overheated laboring class."

The swimming pool was big enough to have daunted Johnny Weismuller; besides a bathhouse it also presented two diving boards, a flagstone surround, wrought-iron outdoor tables; chairs and chaises; umbrellas positioned in regal splendor over the tables, all refusing passage to the sun. Doctor Dad, outfitted in expensive sport clothes, was reclining on a thickly padded chaise reading a book; probably one relating *How to Replace Human Organs for Fun and Profit.* He was sipping a tall drink.

Remember how regal Walter Pidgeon could look, especially in the movie, *Mrs. Miniver*? And how his voice would roll sonorously and masterfully; sounded so good you almost wanted to make a sandwich of it. If that guy informed the multitudes that the earth was flat, who was gonna doubt him? Well, by grab, good old handsome Walt looked up and actually spoke to me:

"Now then sir, just what are you accusing my daughter of doing? She is destined for great things; I have no desire to hear of the mundane or sordid."

Bet You Don't Know Where Lorna Is!

He didn't invite me to sit or offer me a libation, even if it was only ice tea. Along with that came disappointment numero uno: The timbre of his voice resonated like Walter Pigeon's only if Walt used to bray like a donkey! Tree-top high, old dad's screeched like a rusty gate. Ever suffer through chalk scratching on a blackboard? Numero dos, dad's breath was strong enough to make a skunk cringe and he had the bedside manner of a pissed off hippo! The crusher! A luxuriantly thick silvery rug of natural hair decorated the top of his dome. My head, now showing roughage from yearage, had long ago pushed past most of my curly locks. Would you say I am one of those whom others can irk easily? You can't be serious! Regardless, tired of standing awaiting another chewing-out by the principal, I sat down without an invitation and the hell with him.

"Your wife has it dead wrong, sir. I do not bring tidings of sordidness. I also accuse your daughter of nothing. One of her teachers at Sagen is missing. I am but pursuing any leads available in an attempt to locate her. I simply desire to converse with Miss Jill in the hope that she might possibly be able to shed a little light on Mrs. Diddens disappearance. I understand from your wife that the young lady is not here today; perhaps you might inform me of her whereabouts. I won't take up much of her time. I believe she and the teacher had a good rapport. I'd like to think your daughter would be willing to help if she could."

Once again the gate screeched, urging me to go hunt up the WD-40.

"I strongly doubt that Jill can be of any help to you at this time. She won't be home for the next two weeks. She and some of her school chums are staying over at our beach house in Florence for the next few days. From there they plan on visiting the Wildlife Safari at Winston. Some shopping in

Medford is planned after that and possibly a further jaunt on down to San Francisco. Mother and I expect her back around the tenth of July. You might try calling her at 541-988-3039. The housekeeper will know where she will most likely be. And now, sir, I bid you good-day."

Promising myself not to stomp on his rose bushes on the way out, I said:

"I thank you for your courtesy, Doctor. Would it be possible to acquire the address in Florence in case we do not make contact via the phone? I have to trek over to Newport anyway and the little extra distance would not be out of my way." Jesus, once again my ears cringed, if I only had a handy can of 3-in-One, I'd pour some in his lousy iced tea!

"Very well, our cottage is in a gated community called Splendor by the Sea. Turn right at the first stoplight and at a four-way stop, turn right again. Turn left on Salmon Drive. Follow it until you see a gate. Our place is number 102233 on Rolling Dunes Road. It faces the ocean. Make your visit brief!" He waved his drink like a wand and stuck his head back in his book.

When the day comes that I sprout a wart on my nose he won't be the bloody doctor I call to remove it!

I had the satisfaction of neglecting to offer a farewell and took myself off to round up Bernie. He was sitting in the shade of an Umbrella tree and, like most old geezers who have recently dined well, was nodding off. I filled him in on Pater and asked if he'd earned himself a glass of milk.

"Nay, me old son, I had no intention of cleaning up after these arrogant sods. However, one can oft gather bits of this and bits of that from the hired help. Yon chauffeur is a veritable chatterbox and Miss Jill is not one of his favorite people. It would seem she, bound on becoming the first female four-star general in the Air Force, is a trifle steel-minded; she commands the peasantry to jump about, willy-nilly, and is not above lying to Mater or Pater if her orders are not promptly obeyed. Father presented her with a lovely Porsche for her last birthday. Mom is often away poshing about with country club cronies and their doings. Dad is swapping somebody's organs every other day and is seldom home. Neither parent pays much attention to Miss Jill; the little darling pretty well does what she wants and goes where she wants. Seems to me a certain horse-playing, chunking-up, mediocre detective would benefit from a touch closer look at that youngster."

And I hadn't said one word all day about his disgusting bagel-eating habits. Mediocre! Now that was a low blow.

* * *

Bernie had to go to a teacher's retirement do of some kind and couldn't make the trip to Florence with me. Sandy, Mandy, and Maggie jumped at the chance. On the drive over to the coast Sandy kept reciting the names of the racetracks she'd heard from because every time she got to Hialeah Maggie barked. How the hell do I know why!

I'd absolutely no intention of trying to touch base with Miss Jill via the telephone, when we engaged in a chat it was going to be eyeball to eyeball. I definitely wanted to personally gauge her reaction to my questions.

If you promise not to breathe a word of the following to tourists, and be cautious about even confiding to little Fido or Pussums, I'll let you in on a little secret. The Oregon coastline is outrageously gorgeous, especially from Lincoln City and thence heading south. Florence perches approximately seventy-five coastal miles further on from Abe's namesake. Sadly, like all the other quaint beauty spots along our state coast, she is growing and rapidly becoming crowded; true, north of Lincoln City is pretty much inland until you reach Garibaldi, Manzanita and Cannon Beach. But south, you got breathtaking vistas almost all the way to Brookings. Little towns: Yachats, Reedsport, Port Orford, Bandon, still bid the visitor, pining for an ocean view, a cheery welcome. And all along the way the ocean knocks itself out waving at you. Paradise? Oh, yeah. But I have to be straight with you. It *rains* during what is laughingly dubbed the wet season. Last year she started in late November and bucketed for fifty-six days straight. I mean RAIN, not snort, sneeze, or drizzle. If you decide to pay a visit, buy a drip shedder. Not one of those Chinese umbrellas which turn inside out in a slight breeze. Pony up for a Limey bumpershoot. Those jobbies will not only turn the bucketies aside, they'll threaten them. Dig deep for pond waders, an extra large hanky, windshield wipers for your eye-glasses, a wee flask of brandy, and you'll turn into a flaming duck like the rest of us.

After some turny-twisty on 101, we rolled into Florence. As directed, we turned right at the first light, drove about a mile, hung another right, then a left on Fishy Drive up to a big gate. You got a card with the correct code, use it and enter. No card? Park and flaming well walk; it's only a mile or two. No big hill for a stepper!

16

Some years back we had a governor name of Tom McCall. Tom believed the public had rights. Using political clout and cajoling the legislature he got a bill passed. *The public shall not be denied access to the beaches anywhere in Oregon!* Bless you Father Tom. Since that time nobody, and I mean nobody, has been able to lock off the beach to the peasants. She ain't like some California folks, where the rich run fences down to the waterline then turn and give the public the well known finger gesture. No sirree babe. Here in Oregon you want to walk on the beach, go walk on the beach. If desired, and Ma Nature provides no obstacles, grab hold of shank's mare and trek all the way from the California border to the Washington border.

Also, some years back a group of Las Vegas heavies built a resort called Salishan. Below the Siletz River, it lies south between Lincoln City and Gleneden. Those bozos erected gates on the west side of the highway blocking public access to sand and surf. Loaded honchos immediately flocked to the ocean side and built posh abodes out on the Spit. Tch, tch you lowly citizens, if you have no card or written permission from the owners, access is denied to our Spit and our beach! Along comes a winter storm. Abodes are highly disturbed by big waves; some even practice floating!

"Help us," moan the owners to the state, "Yon ocean is waving us away!"

"Get stuffed," hollers the state right back. "You had no business building out there in the first place!"

I often find myself praying for the repose of the soul of Tom McCall.

Faced with a locked gate, I parked the wagon and Sandy, Mandy, Maggie, and I forged west toward sand and sea, hung a right and proceeded to walk, beachside, into Splendor by the Sea. From time to time I headed inland intent on checking addresses. After a short half-mile we came to what Doctor Dad had called their cottage. She was just a modest two-story, right on the ocean front; large, big-beamed rooms. The cook needed roller skates to bring hot food from the kitchen to the dining room. Put a figure on her? Try a million plus at today's economy prices! Two-car garage; too-big, too-posh; too much for we lowly proletariats.

"Miss Jill is not at home," belled the housekeeper. "She and her friends decided to visit Winston today. I do not know when she shall return. Perhaps you would like to leave a message. Her calendar is quite full; possibly a few minutes later in the week could be arranged. Leave your card." This she handled as though it was emitting a slight touch of leprosy.

I'd had sense enough to bring Lorna's scarf. Maggie and Mandy gave out with loud sniffs of back, front and garage doors; nothing. Not that I really expected Lorna to come to the door. Doctor Dad was not averse to spoiling his daughter, but I believe he'd take a decidedly dim view if his little love had decided to develop and flaunt her kidnapping skills.

Damn and God damn! How I wished I could belt somebody. I could not remember a case which had frustrated me more. If it weren't that I was truly concerned about Lorna I'd have said, "To hell with it," then taken a hike over to the Sandpines Golf Resort and attempted to put a dent in my new driver. Instead, I put a lock on my tongue and took my three girls to Lovejoys Restaurant and English Pub, for yo High Tea; two of the dear girls

Bet You Don't Know Where Lorna Is! 207

remained outside, wagon-slammered, albeit with future promises of mouth-watering delectables. I had heard Lovejoys was a dandy joint to sip the English brew (unfortunately we ain't talkin' beer here) and munch on cute little finger sandwiches. I know what you think, but ladies are into that sort of thing. Why anyone would order those fingerling bites where the crusts have been cut off and itsy-bitsy ingredients featuring watercress, smoked salmon, or cucumber, is beyond me. Who can ever figure out broads?

Later, Mandy spit her cucumber sandwich in my lap. Miss Maggie scoffed her salmon and watercress and looked around for more. I swear that dog will eat anything not nailed down and come back for seconds!

I rang the bell at 102233 Rolling Dunes Road one more time at eight p.m. that same evening.

"Miss Jill has not returned nor called, try the latter part of the week."

Might it be polite for one of us to retort, "Thanks ever so, and may an asp build its nest in your nose!" Yep! I cranked up the wagon and headed for Newport and a quick report from Sam. He, too, must have gone off as he wasn't at the motel and also didn't answer his phone.

I'd given some thought to trying to run Jill to earth at the Wildlife Safari in Winston. Unfortunately, like all good, well prepared, detectives, I'd forgotten and left her class picture in the office. I hadn't spent much time studying it as yet and wasn't sure I'd recognize her. I could pay the entrance tab though and just drive up and down dusty wildlife lanes crying:

"Yoo-hoo, Miss Jill, are you out there playing Hide-n-Seek with the BIG kitty-cats?" And if I were to then shout "Ali ali oxenfree," would she, knowing that that phrase tells all hiders the game is over because one of the players has been caught, kindly step forth giving out with a lovely smile and a, "Golly, gee-whiz-darn, you son-of-a-gun I guess you've found me."

With my luck a bloody great rhino would come charging out of the brush and play his favorite game of Pitch-n-Toss, with *me*! Besides, the bloody preserve would be closed for the day long before we got there.

"Sandy, I'm going to flick this business in. It's not like the old days when it was easy to nail the perps; when the truly tough, those offered up by Dashiell Hammett and Raymond Chandler, nailed rotten scumbags fast and flaming well permanently."

"What do you mean, easy?" replies my love, "I thought detective work was always difficult and very frustrating?"

"I never said that. Give a listen to one of my famous, easy cases: Five friends, named A, B, C, D, and E had been buddies for years. One day A and B got into a fearful row. Insults were hurled that could never be retracted. Late that night, a furious B went over to A's house and offed him. He then planted clues that would implicate C, D, and E but not point at him. The cops interrogated the three but couldn't pin the killer down. I was hired by the father of one of them and, though I spent twenty hours a day on the case, I couldn't nail the guilty one either. Some time later C, who was no dummy, figured it out. He confronted our killer with definite proof and naturally B offed him as well, planting more clues to implicate D and E in the process. I upped my hours to twenty-two and still failed to nab the sucker. D, a summa cum laude in pocket billiards, also came up with the answer. Right, B offed him, too. With but two left E, knowing he was completely innocent, hastened to B's determined on answers. Didn't happen, B, expecting the visit, was out front hiding in the bushes. By that time lights and bells had gone off in this old boy's noggin. B naturally must be the killer. "Why," you say? Because flaming B always comes before E!

Unfortunately, during interrogation B was shot while trying to escape. Case closed. See what I'm saying here, crime was easier to solve in the good old days."

Now what's with Sandy air-mailing me perplexed looks?

All the way back up 101 I pondered on how I'd present an acceptable work resume to Salem's Sanitary Service, and to hell with detective work!

After I got stuck for dinner at the Oyster Bar, at least it wasn't cheese paste and grass cuttings, I dropped Sandy off, headed home and crashed.

Early on the 25th, I headed to the office to check on the latest race track sighting of young Joly and, of course, yesterday's joyful messages.

"I am here, where the hell are you?" squalled the message from Mary E. "I found your girl and you, you dimwit, aren't there to hear about it. Ring me!" My ear cringed as the phone bounced resoundingly on its cradle.

Gentle rings, four or five, a click and, "Yeah, who cares what you're sellin' today or any day? I have an appointment with the Rajah of Rottenpore in ten minutes, he is nuts about my curry so you got thirty seconds to grovel before I hang up!"

"Is that any way to speak to your employer, Miss Mary? Against my better nature I go to the trouble of hiring you in order to keep you off the dole and what do I get for my generosity? Nothing but insults. You wound me deeply. Further, your bonus is now definitely in jeopardy. Do you flaming well have any good news for me or not?"

"Touchy aren't we? Are we in need of a little Ipecac or are you just snarly when the moon is full? Yes, I have found the little doll right where you figured, mucking out stalls at the racetrack; man, horsy odors emanating from some of those cubicles would bring tears to the eyes of a dead jackal!"

"The kid is doing her damndest to qualify for the Thrush scholarship and I think she might have a chance. I will put her on a bus if you insist but for what it's worth I think Mom and Pop need to butt out and let the kid have her head. She's not in any trouble. I took her over to bathe, bunk and get fed at the aunt's. Why not prod Mom or Dad to give the sister a call? If Auntie says, 'Green light, go,' maybe they'll leave the little squash alone. Go talk to them Shamus, I'll pay my phone bill and you can call me back sometime. Meantime, I'll still keep an eye on lil' JoLene. I like her and, naturally, I will also continue to charge for my time."

"Has the gumshoe industry's bright horse player had any luck lately wagering on the broomtails? I nailed my bookie for six Lincoln's the other day on a nag called Step-n-Fetch-It in the sixth at Santa Anita, and no, I won't count that as part of my fee! Later."

Have I not said that little feist is a winner? Her advice was sound and, hallelujah, the case hadn't been complicated. I started to pick up the phone to call Jessamine with the good news when it rang. It was Frank Diddens and he'd received another ransom note. I called Sandy and asked her to buzz the Tooley's, tender Mary E's suggestion for the kid, and tell them I'd touch base with them a little later. On the way out to the wagon I also wrote a mental note to check with 'Beat the Odds' re the results of the Woodbine race; I'd forgotten to do it when Bern and I returned from the Rose City.

Diddens was beginning to show the strains of kin trying to contend with the kidnapping of a loved one. Haven't I said I hate kidnappers above all criminals? I wouldn't hesitate to tar and feather the whole rotten bunch and that includes the scuzz I was figuring were the ones who'd grabbed Lorna! I swung by Bad Bascomb's to collar Bernie. After all, he had accepted the position of consultant he might as well be useful. I never even glanced at the latest bagel desecration I knew he'd be stuffing into his stomach!

Diddens didn't speak, he simply handed me an envelope. Same system as before, it had been placed un-mailed against the front door. I handled it very gingerly though I was sure there'd be no fingerprints. This note was brief:

* * *

"Tell fat detective to hurry to Hazel Green School mailbox. He is to be following instructions he shall there be of the finding."

* * *

Bernie, Mandy, Maggie and I piled into the wagon and set sail for Hazel Green. I headed northeast on Portland Road and hung a right on Hazel Green Rd. Not much more than a mile further on, we came to Hazel Green School. It's not green or hazel. A small rural job, it is named after a former, well-liked principal. Bernie rode herd on fourth and fifth graders for over ten years out there. I asked him how come they hadn't named one after him.

"Probably be a school of correction if they ever did," he said.

The mailbox sits back just off the road and would be easy to pilfer if the school ever got any mail worth heisting. Bernie said all they usually got were cartons of reports of administrative meetings, about as useful as rubber boots on a duck. Waiting inside the box was another envelope addressed to **"The Fat Man."**

Once again I fished it out carefully, gingerly popped the seal, and read:

* * *

"You will now be, oh so safely, driving to that City of the Mount of the

Angel. Proceeding to the cathedral called Saint of the Mary's, go inside. Be of the walking to the first confessional on the left. Enter and look under the kneeler. Be then following of the instructions you will be finding. Hasten!"

*   *   *

I gunned the wagon east on Hazel Green Road which Bern said would lead me to Silverton the back way and, by cutting off to the left before hitting town, we could head directly over to Mount Angel.

"How come the kidnappers chose to leave a note in that school mailbox Bernie? You suppose they attended Hazel Green and are known to you?"

"Not likely, Danny, I've been retired for sixteen years. Even if they were fourth graders then they would now be age twenty-six to twenty-seven, too old for me to have taught our suspects. There may be relatives living in this area though. The school is buttoned up for the summer but you could call Sandy and ask her to inquire of the administration downtown for names of students in attendance during the last eight to ten years. The school district must be aware of Lorna's disappearance by now; you've bloody well spent plenty of time out at Sagen asking questions about her!"

Ho-ho, maybe the old boy will earn that one bagel, which is all I'm gonna pony up, for his consultant fee! I hauled out the cell phone and gave my love a yodel. I also asked her to call 'Beat-the-Odds' and check on the broomtail's run in Toronto. Bernie wouldn't stop bugging me for the results. I haven't the foggiest notion why, as he hadn't been alerted in time to lay farthing one on the nag.

Close to Silverton the dogs noses began to quest and mine began to cringe. We were approaching a dairy and the odor, floating wild and free off a loaded slurry pond, would gag a cage full of baboons. Mandy and Maggie couldn't get enough of it. I closed and locked all the windows. As we passed I could see a whole bunch of what looked like large doghouses. Contributing further to my education, Bernie told me they housed the newborn calves. Naturally they were taken away from their mothers right away, no bonding would be allowed. Most of Mom's milk was to go into bottles, not the mouths of their calves. Ain't progress wonderful?

Two hundred yards on, when we could all breathe again, the old geezer sat up and pointed to a road heading to the right:

"Follow that for a mile or so and you'll run into Silverton Rd. Take a left and after a half-mile you will pass by the small farm of a guy I used to teach with at Hazel Green. Most all teachers, taking home but a pittance while laboring in the professional field, need to moonlight in order to continue to support just the military defense bill! My pal farms about five acres. He and his wife grow tomatoes and straw flowers. The wife and I went with them to Sisters for a couple of years because those mountain folks put on a fall festival every year for arts, crafts, flowers, quilts, jams, and veggies. My pal used to sell out their straw bouquets in double quick time. Mollie-O took some of her watercolors along as well. She didn't sell many but we had a good time chatting to the folks who came to browse and perhaps buy. Dan, do you suppose everybody in the world loves to shop, like Americans?"

"We played golf one time at Billygoat Acres. He used a Big Bertha on the eighteenth tee and wailed hell out of the ball. I watched it land smack on the green, the ninth green that is! He was already beating my butt royally so I hastened to point out his error. After I showed him the flag he should have been aiming for, he cranked out another one. That one flew over the correct green and halfway up the hill. My drive ended up thirty yards short; no doubt you've probably noticed he's maybe a page or two shy of a ream but we always have a good time together. No charge for that trivia, Daniel!"

* * *

Like everywhere else in Oregon, Bernie could also conduct tours of Mount Angel. The Catholic cathedral there is quite old. Their cornerstone was laid in 1910 and the edifice was completed in 1912, to the tune of $85,000. She exhibits a two hundred foot bell tower visible from almost anywhere in the valley. In March 1993, along comes an earthquake, magnitude 5.7. Surprisingly, none of the windows imploded nor did the bell tower fall on its face in the street; however, damage to the church was severe. Repairs were accomplished in 1995; those are reputed to have cost the insurance company *one million smackers!* You suppose John Hancock jumped at the chance to renew their policy?

It is a truly lovely church, somber and quiet inside. The twenty-six stained glass windows are absolutely beautiful. Only goes to prove that talent turns up in the most unexpected of places. The church architects, members of the parish, were two brothers: Engelbert and Emil Gier who originally hailed from Texas.

German Catholic settlers greatly influenced the growth of Mount Angel because the founder, Mathias Butsch, advertised in German newspapers for kith and kin to hie themselves out to the hidden "Paradise of the West." Und py golly, dem relatives dey upped und packed und den dey comed!

I entered the designated confessional, fished out another envelope and rejoined Bernie and the dogs, happier now to have had him take them for one of their short necessary breaks. Again, the envelope read '**Fat Man.**'

When I catch up to them, I'm going to take that sobriquet they are so fond of using, enclose it within my fist, and fatten a few lips with it! The note inside this one stated:

* * *

"Fat Man, you perhaps could be of use as a postal of the employee. You will now drive to the Silver Creek Falls State Park. Be going to the South Falls Day-Use Area. Pay of the three dollar entrance fee, then proceedings to the South Falls Lodge. Be inquiring of the person at the desk for an envelope which shall be addressing to 'Mr. Stout.' Follow, oh so very carefully, all the most kindly of instructions to be finding inside. We are growing most tired of the Mrs. Diddens and are wanting to be rid of her! Remember: be following of all which has been stated here quickly if you are wishing to see her of the alive again!"

* * *

Has the thought of becoming a detective ever crossed your mind? You think it is exciting. One performs lots of derring-do, rousts bad guys, solves crime, and head homes at night highly content with one's self, right? Wrong! Detective work, in the main, consists of chasing after false trails, standing out in the rain on surveillance picking your nose, listening to a ton of lies, reading gibberish by the box full—mostly like the above—accumulating bunions from the walking and piles from the sitting. Investigation work is enervating, frustrating, disappointing, and tedious. Bright and early the next day, a case successfully concluded, a visit to your bank is in order. Guess what? The check bounces!

Thirsting for the glamorous life are you? You would be far better served by becoming a sword swallower, an acrobat, or a lion-tamer in the circus!

Friend reader, I beg you, pick a vocation other than that of detective.

* * *

Leaving the cathedral, we headed for Route 214, a stout two blocks away. There, we hung a left and headed for Silverton. I like that little town: one motel, two elementary schools; nice folks, Homer Davenport Days, and she is now the home of the Oregon Garden. Bernie knows where all the damn libraries are and he pointed it out as we were now driving out of town on the Cascade Highway, which is still 214, and beginning to climb up toward the park. High in the hills, Bernie identified the local Grange Hall where the community puts out extra large portions of strawberry shortcake during the summer for people who flat out hanker for a calorie loaded dessert; so much so, they'll drive out from the big town, Portland, to pig out. Visitors come all the way up from Eugene. Many cruise over from the Coast. Chartered bus loads often travel over one hundred miles to make it their destination.

The big luscious berries are donated by nearby growers. They couldn't be fresher unless they picked themselves. It is a big event during early summer and most of the proceeds go to benefit Silver Crest School. I truly do admire folks who go and do it for themselves without relying on the dole. Bernie said he and the wife worked there during the summer. She had one of her drawings in the cookbook which featured lots of mouth-watering hill-folk recipes. He usually got stuck to wash the berries or go out on the truck to help bring 'em in! I told him it was nice he finally had to do some sweat work. I'm not gonna tell you what he told me to go and do!

17

Bernie perked up at Drakes Crossing and told me to slow down so he could point out his old farm:

"Good, the pond is still full and I see the tree my ram used to butt, looking a smidge concave now, is still standing. Damn, the new owners left the sheep squeezer out in the rain!"

"Bernie, quit waltzing us down Memory Lane. If folks want to know why your dumb ram kept thumping his head on a tree they can read all about it in *Mojac's Megan*. I need some skinny on what to expect at the park."

"Go ahead and stomp on my nostalgia, Dan my man, but lest we forget, that used to be a sweet little farm and sheepishly claimed ten and one-half years of my swiftly passing life! As you insist though, I shall inform of one of the loveliest state parks you'll ever have the good fortune to visit. You might wish to visit the falls while here and take eleven, free, chilly outdoor showers. Silver Creek Falls State Park lies about twelve miles southeast of Silverton; she sites right about 1800 feet above sea level. When valley folk tire of baking summer heat they drive up and grab a dab of cool. She is the largest state park in Oregon, encompassing close to 9,000 acres. You got your hiking, biking, and horse riding trails; count the eleven falls, many of which dwindle to trickles when summers are dry. But remember, we had fifty-six straight days of sobbing clouds last winter and many of those falls will still be flowing today. She boasts campgrounds and RV parks; add your youth camps such as the Ranch and the YMCA, where for many a year I brought two hundred wriggling fifth and sixth graders for a three day outdoor education experience. I still shudder when I dream about it."

"The South Falls Day-Use Area supports a restaurant and conference center in the lodge; add a swimming pool, play area and picnic tables. The South Falls, biggest in flow at a height of 177 feet, purely is one mighty appealing sight. Folks argue that Double Falls at 178 feet is just that, two falls and they won't be bullied into counting it number one. Who cares? They are all lovely and the park is a place that flat out cannot be beaten. The Chamber of Commerce invites, 'Why don't all you perspiring citizens, assuming you would prefer not to wilt, drive on up here and listen to your skin dry! Bring your pets, there are but a few areas forbidden to them and those are remote.' "

I forked over three clams and we entered the park. I would have really liked to take time to enjoy some of its wonders, but I wasn't on vacation. I scribbled another mental note to bring Sandy up here after Lorna had been returned safely to her family and we hastened over to the lodge. A pert young thing, hell they're all pert at my age, smiled and inquired of my wants.

"Oh, yes, sir, I believe it was delivered not long ago. A nice young boy brought it in. Here you are."

She handed me a grimy envelope. Yep, it was addressed to "Mr. Stout." In vain hope I asked if the delivery kid was still around or was known to her? Did I get lucky? Do Eskimos suffer from heat prostration in the merry month of December?

Kidnap note number two read as follows:

* * *

"To the unluckiest of persons married to mistress teacher, Lorna Diddens. We are of the last time writing most nicely to you. She has grown to be of the big pain in the butt! She is also in most need of changing of the clothes. Because you did not follow our last friendly instructions, the monies owed us will now be of the $50, 000 dollars. You are to be placing of them in a large shopping bag. Put changing of the lady's clothes: shirt, slacks, socks, under of the wear, in bag also."

"Not to be using of dyes or radio buggings in bag, monies, clothings. We will scan and if hearing any chirpings or seeing funny coloring of monies, good-bye to Mrs. Lorna."

"Fat detective is to be delivering of the monies. NO DOGS! He is to be taking it to the Riverfront Park in Salem. Knowing you of the carousel there? Exactly at midnight of the June 30th, the fat man is to be opening the fronting door of the carousel, not to be worrying it will be left unlocked, he is to enter and be placing of bag under seat of ride called Chuck of the Wagon."

"NO POLICE ARE TO BE THERE! Fat man is to leave same way he comes in and must walk away. We will be watching him most vigilantingly and silently. If all is done properly this time, Mrs. Lorna will be soon sending to her home, safely and unharmed. Be failing to follow our most polite requests and the poor lady will never be seen again. We are of the promising of this! Also, fat man detective is to be carrying a flashlight. No lighting will be permitted on in the carousel! If all is not done on time, the bad results will be on your heads! We will keep our promise. Vishnu reigns forever!"

* * *

No signature again. I'd handled the scungy envelope gingerly but I knew, other than the desk girl's and the kid's fingerprints, there would be no others. I handed the note over to Bernie without comment. After reading it he said:

"Devious, nasty, sods aren't they? Sheez, as teenagers the only time we ever dug heavy into the sneaky was during Halloween and only to bug the neighborhood grouch. You know the one: he is forever shouting at kids to keep off his lawn, keep the damn dog out of his bushes, and stay the hell off his property. Retired, he devotes all his time carping at the legislature to pass a law demanding quadruple trimester abortions!"

"Halloween Eve, the entire neighborhoods' dogs always want out early to take care of pressing needs. They have not enjoyed enduring prolonged past pain induced from loud thumping of drums and pans, along with the loud cries of costumed kids hollering 'Trick or Treat' at doors where the porch light had been left on. The mutts will sleep under the bed tonight, thank you very much!"

"In preparation, the studious among us would then gather up shovels and go out on poop patrol. Once we had filled a large paper bag with offerings from 'Man's best friend' we would sneak quietly up onto the grump's porch, lay the bag against his front door, set fire to it, ring the doorbell, then run like hell and hide nearby; close enough to clearly see him stomp on the burning bag and enjoy his hollering as the old goat blistered the air with words we sometimes didn't even know! Our machinations wouldn't rate up there with Einstein, but we now could tolerate the grouch for another year."

"Will you quit with the ancient homilies, Bern. What's all this jazz about the Carousel? Why would they pick it for the drop? Is there anyway we can smuggle somebody in to a closet or john, beforehand, then grab those creeps going out with the loot?"

"I seriously question that, Daniel. The building is surrounded by nothing but open, which is why I suspect they chose it. It will be easy for them to keep entrance and egress under observation either from buildings across Front Street or along the riverbank above the Willamette. There is a gift shop adjacent to the merry-go-round, but I doubt if they'd forget to cover it. Outside you have wide areas of open grass almost encircling the carousel building. Add to that the large parking lot. Plenty of places for them to hide and observe, especially as it would be late and little activity would be taking place at that time. I do not know if the services of a night watchman are required. I should not be surprised though, the hand-carved and hand-painted horses, all work done by volunteers, must be quite valuable. That carousel is an attraction Salem should be and is proud of. I hate to think that our culprits would do it harm."

"There is the possibility that members of the law, attired in camouflage clothing, might secrete themselves under tarps out on the grassy area close to the rear doors but, as we follow daylight saving in Oregon, it remains light until at least nine-thirty. Dark doesn't really settle in until sometime after ten. I suspect our kidnappers will have the place staked out long before full dark. Possibly the police or FBI have a way of installing an undetectable signaling device, perhaps in the waistband of Lorna's clean slacks, the collar of the shirt or inside the wire of her bra? How about placing one in a false bottom in the bag?"

"Recently, the wife and I enjoyed a ride on that carousel. Why the guffawing? You're never too old to listen to hurdy-gurdy music in comfort, while an inanimate horse painlessly elevates and lowers your butt! I happen to flaming well like carousels. Besides, that's not my point. The Salem merry-go-round is located so as to be quite exposed. The only nearby buildings are the johns and a kids play area to the south. And don't forget, I already told you to west, north, and south open grassy areas almost surround the joint. Southeast is the parking lot. The whole shebang sits about forty feet in from Front Street which, running north and south, parallels Riverfront Park. I don't envy any minion of the law who, charged with orders to remain incognito, will attempt to pussyfoot in unseen. It's too much for my hibernating brain, Danny. I recommend a Clint Eastwood solution. Make the day of the Salem Police and throw in the FBI for good measure!"

Entering Salem, I cut off Lancaster onto State and we cruised down to the park for a quick look-see. It was just as Bernie had described. Only two of the detectives had a wonderful time and they turned out to be Mandy and Maggie as they enjoyed enough grassy area on display for them to play on and run for damn near a mile!

I dropped Bern off at his home. For a news flash, he wanted to water his lousy lawn. I headed on over to the Police Department. They would have to be filled in, and after tonight we had but four days left to prepare. I know the note said, "No cops!" Tough duff! They had to be involved whether the kidnappers liked it or not. Ditto that for the FBI. I've stated it before, but it bears repeating, a PI's license can be revoked toot of the sweet and often for very little reason. Bet you've never noticed most cops have no sense of humor! Besides, I had a few plans of my own I needed to flesh out.

After talking to the police and planning temporary strategy, it was late. I ran the jalopy out to the Diddens home, showed him the current note and filled him in on what was being planned; I also told him I truthfully believed

Bet You Don't Know Where Lorna Is!

we were on the down hill pull and his Lorna would soon be home safe and sound. He brightened, wiped a tear from his eye, and promised to gather up a change of clothing for her. He would then package and deliver everything to my office.

It had been a long day and I was tired. The dogs needed to be fed and then taken for a run. I needed to be fed and then allowed a snooze. Before all that important stuff though I had to check messages at the office, call Ms. Edgarina of the Feebs, call Sam in Newport, call Biff and Burt to set up a little job I had in mind, call my pal Bill for another little job I had in mind, call Mary Elizabeth to thank her for all her good work and maybe mention there would be a very little something coming in the mail. And finally, call Sandy for another job I definitely had in mind. First though, I had to call the Tooley's and elaborate on what Sandy had informed them about JoLene.

Jessamine answered and as I was sure she would the old girl agreed to let the kid follow her dream. She had already talked to her sister in Spokane; between them they had arranged for JoLene to call her Mom on the morrow. Mom said she and Pop were going to take a little jaunt up that way anyway as there were some pretty good broomtails, now in residence at Playfair, that they both wanted to look over before racing season started. It wouldn't surprise me a bit if the kid couldn't point out a few good runners herself that might add a tad to the old exchequer if, come opening day, old Make-a-Bet laid the family's wagers correctly.

All in all, there was one case that turned out just fine. And I hadn't even laid eye one on the subject. Mom felt so good, she said she was going to send me a check for four clams rather than three for my first week's work.

"Yeah verily, thee truly righteous shall surely prevail," sayeth I. So what if my expenses had amounted to two, well-worn Franklin's. It's the good feelings one experiences for a job well done that counts! Besides, as we all know, it's the bill collectors who are always stomping around after money, the rest of us have learned to get along just fine without it.

Beg pardon, I thought I just heard you voice a question? Ah-ha, you've been listening to Bernie's crabbing and you, too, wish to know if Jessamine's tip worked out. Did T J's Lucky Moon cross the finish line first and had I laid a clam or two on his nose? Shoot, in all the fuss over the ransom note I plumb forgot to tell you. Sandy had indeed called me back with the results right after Bernie and I had entered Silver Creek Falls State Park. That four-footed speedster had indeed breezed home in front and at eighty-two to one. In Canadian dough that amounted to $166.00 for a two clam bet. I haven't told Bernie yet. As to whether I had put a little something on his nose, you'll have to ask 'Beat the Odds' Clyde for the answer. Come up on his blind side when you pose your query though, he's been awful grumpy lately!

* * *

Ms. FBI insisted on looking Riverfront Park over for herself. I mentioned the risk. The perps, knowing I'd already picked up the ransom note, might now have the place staked out.

"Not to worry, detective," she trilled. Then, figuring we'd find the park busy and full of tourists at that hour, she arranged to meet me in the Oyster Bar parking lot at twelve noon.

"I will be prepared and I don't believe those rotten bastards will peg me," she added. Such language, and from such a dainty wee thing, too!

I got there early; they put out a decent cup of coffee at the Bar and after the prior long day my eyes were in need of propping open.

When she showed up my eyes awoke in one hell of a hurry! I had to definitely concur, the perps would never place her. She was adorned in so much make-up it tilted her head forty degrees forward. Her pants were so tight I despaired of her bending over and knew if she ever did modesty would have to cover its eyes. If she was wearing underwear, it had to have been almost nonexistent. Her blouse rode a full five inches above her navel and her pants reposed another eight below. On her belly—clearly displayed for all to view—there appeared the damnedest tattoo I've ever seen. Outlined in glorious Technicolor was a big sassy robin. Tugging mightily with its beak, it was hauling on a worm protruding from her navel! No question, that tattoo was an eye grabber and conversation stopper, totally!

"Is this kid a tree hugger?" I wondered. "If so, I wish I were the tree she was currently enjoying hugging!"

Why did I think she was an environmentalist? That flaming fat robin was yanking on an *earthworm*. She was also sporting a pony tail which I thought had gone out of style back in '63. Most passersby would rate her a cute little airhead and go on about their business. Hopefully, the clods we were after, after prolonged gaping, would also ignore her.

"Stay here and have another cup of coffee, Dad," she ordered. "I'll check things out and get back to you." At least she didn't call me Fatso.

It was a three-block walk west to reach the park. Four fender benders occurred in the first block as gawkers, their awestruck eyes glued to her derriere, forgot to watch for oncoming traffic. Female young, green-eyed her in envy. Stoplights went unnoticed by walking males and more than a few flirted with a trip to the hospital. Sandy, love, I also have to confess that as I watched her sashay down the street in that outfit, lecherous thoughts of a desert isle for two stampeded through my aging noggin. Not to worry, after twenty minutes those runaways settled down for their mid-morning nap!

I'd warned Jane, yeah that was her name, to be most careful and casually pointed out we had but three and a half days left according to the kidnappers schedule. It now read June 26th on my calendar.

I downed three more cups of coffee and paid two visits to the loo before she returned; seemed like PI and FBI were of like mind. It would be extremely difficult to stake-out the carousel. Coupling her views with mine we proceeded to think out and lay tentative plans: The use of a camera mounting a five hundred millimeter telephoto lens coupled with extremely fast film, the photographer stashed in a window of a building directly across Front Street, was chosen as one idea. Two Feds keeping company with horribly lethal rifles—faces painted and bodies attired in the current camouflage—would crawl ever so stealthily up from the riverbank and thence over grass toward the mechanical, musical, horsy contraption upon the arrival of full dark. Remember, in Oregon in June, this does not occur until well after ten. Jane would also take time to liaise with the Salem police as to our plans. It would never do if the Feds ended up shooting the cops, or vice versa!

I wondered aloud, "Possibly the city fathers might be able to convince a traveling carnival show to quickly take up residence on the Park's grassy acreage? Carneys usually go full blast up until eleven and don't turn lights off until close to midnight."

"Everybody and their Aunt Saphronie would probably come. Workers are constantly on the move during a carnival. I bet a gaggle of roustabouts, unobserved, could sneak a coiled cobra into the carousel building during all the noise and activity!"

Jane gave me what I suspect in Feebie looks was a, "Jesus, why me? There are no reprimands in my file and I haven't asked for a transfer or a promotion in almost a month. How come I got loaded down with this schmuck?"

"To continue, Miss Jane, you got your Ferris wheel and bumper cars. We wouldn't need another carousel. You got hotdogs, hamburgers, popcorn, peanuts, candy floss, pizza slices, and soda pop stands. You got games: Ring Toss, Knock the Bottles on Their Arse, Shoot a Hole in a Duck, Pitch a Penny in a Dish, Cover the Circle with the Cards, Dart Yo Defenseless Balloon, Ring a Goldfish Bowl, and Drop the Clown in the Water Tank."

"In those midway tents you got your bearded lady, your half-man-half-alligator, your stunted dwarfs dolled out as Leprechauns and Jo-Jo, the Dogface Boy. You got Bong the Bell with a Hammer, Guess Your Weight within 3, and Snap your Picture with a Pal. Don't forget all those cutesy ladies in Arabian underwear doing the Hootchy-Cootchy. Small Carney's don't furnish mangy lions, but they'll sometimes use a chimpanzee to collect tickets for the Ferris wheel. Dear lady, you could hide a lot of Feebees in among all those folks."

Her coffee cup stopped halfway to her mouth and I got another of her looks. This one I figured she read promising:

"Well peel me a grape, now there's almost a good idea. This old beaver may not be in his dotage after all."

Possible I lost a little in the interpretation there as I was busy enjoying the movement of her adorable mouth. Swaying palms from that far distant South Seas isle beckoned me again. Might have even missed a word or two.

"Won't work," she said, "although, on the surface, it has merit. I flat can't see us rounding up a carnival in time, and the City Fathers would have to schedule committee meetings up the dump stump just to consider it. They'd also have a hissy fit over the damage that would be done to the grass. Still, I will present it to them, they've had far too peaceful a summer up to now, and to hell with their lousy lawn when a human life is at stake!"

We parted, she eager to tackle the tiger, me eager to stroke the pussycat. Ah, if I were but twenty-five—make that thirty—years younger!

Feeling guilty for enjoying my bad thoughts, I walked over to See's on Liberty Street and bought Sandy a two-pound box of soft centers. Next I headed for the police station. For what I had in mind a substitute, a fella built like me, so round, so firm, so fully packed, would soon have to be garnered from their ranks. He wouldn't have to be as good looking though.

I called Bernie; oh, yeah, he was cutting his bloody lawn, and told him to hang loose for the next three days. I had a hunch I would soon be in need of his services. Next, I went shopping. There were one or two items I'd need and only the big city could provide them. Don't laugh, the first time I laid eyes on Salem she counted a population right around sixty-three thousand. We're talking State Capitol here. Trot out your Texas toting-up tool and make it read, as of the year 2,000, one hundred and thirty-six thousand, nine hundred and twenty-four. No wonder I can never find a parking space!

My mind, fearing a coming hurricane, floated apprehensively like a chained dory bobbing up and down at the dock. I was pretty sure what I'd figured out would turn out to be right, but there's still a big difference between absolutely sure and pretty sure. What to do next? I definitely wasn't going to go watch Bernie insult his stomach, stuffing another of those bound to be condemned bagel concoctions in it, at Bad Bascomb's; which is where he said he'd be after manicuring his effing lawn!

Sandy was now using my name in vain and working out on her exercise bicycle. How did I know she'd scoff half the flaming See's box at one sitting? She could have told me to take the candy back and bring her a carton of skim milk instead. Women!

When pondering weighty matters, along with fighting nerves, I like to eat. I decided double Mac's and fries for the three of us wouldn't hurt. Mandy scoffed hers, tried to shove her nose into mine, and drooled. Maggie cleaned up the crumbs and also ate the paper on hers. It dawned on me my two pals hadn't broken their fast since breakfast yesterday. Big Guy in the sky thanks ever so for dogs. Always loyal and uncomplaining they truly put their masters to shame. To atone for their unintentional fast, I sprang for once more around plus extra thick strawberry shakes for my girls. Naturally they smeared the froth all over the upholstery, side windows, and the windshield.

While eating I compared the kidnappers' ransom demands with my own plans and, on the whole, decided to go ahead with mine. After which I immediately came down with a case of but what if I've guessed wrong? Is it possible I'd be putting Lorna in even greater peril? So okay, let's cover the bases one more time: Bill had been alerted and would be ready; Sam would be doing his part; Biff and Burt were awaiting my call; Greg, before he'd gone out to check the neighborhood, had passed me a smidgin of news. He had finally pinned a name to Bo's steady, she went by name of Gina Pallino. She was a junior at Sagen and hadn't been a student in any of Lorna's classes. I figured her to be a completely innocent miss and could now cross her off my list. Good for my reformed booster. Junior grade detective Greg was showing definite promise. Who says Mandy and Maggie aren't a good influence on the young!

Furthering preparations, Sandy would make sure all phone batteries were fully charged and with spares ready at hand. She would also keep in up to the minute contact with the Salem police and the FBI. Bernie was raring to go and had conned the wife into cutting his ever growing, over-fertilized lawn. There was a miracle indeed, enough to raise Rootitout, the patron saint of perfect lawns, from the dead!

I had already collected all the tools I'd need, including a pinch bar. Mandy and Maggie, as always, were raring to go. So okay, everything ready all guns loaded, and decks cleared for action, kindly explain to me why, still fighting the wobblies in my stomach, I seriously contemplated an immediate flight to Bali?

18

Late that evening, my cell phone rang. Jane reported the city fathers had turned my carnival suggestion down. They had discerned an obvious flaw: While a plethora of law enforcers could hide in the crowd, nothing would prevent the perps from also hiding among those warm bodies and, if flushed, to hold a few of the innocent as hostage while affecting an escape. No, they preferred, if you'll excuse her atrocious pun, to leave things in the dark. She and the Salem police had scheduled a meeting for the morrow to finalize preparations and my presence would also be required. In the meantime, as her tight pants were killing her, she was heading home to shuck herself out of them. I allowed five seconds to pleasantly visualize that scene and was tempted to ask if the robin had finally nailed the worm. In an attempt to duck out of going to confession though, I blinked rapidly and took the dogs and myself for a long run over the pristine grass of Riverfront Park.

Fortunately for my state of mind the next three days hastened by. Starting off, the meeting with Jane and the Salem police went well. Hoping we'd covered all bases, I next checked the office for messages. Three had been logged by that clever machine. A Reginald Plumbfer desired an immediate conference. Seth Lowell allowed as he'd like to visit fer a talk, and Mrs. Barney Piccolo wished to talk to me soonest about a most private matter. Before the sun dropped into the sea that day, I had signed on three new clients:

Seth, of the second message, opened my office door just as I ended listing phone numbers for all callers. Seth was in a misting sweat for detective Doyle to find his prize ram. Seemed like he had been on the way to the Border collie trials in Scio. On the way he'd stopped off in Turner where an enterprising breeder of sheep had advertised a top of the line purebred Suffolk ram for sale. Ol' Seth had bought the handsome fellow. Happily, he had then piloted his old cargo-racked Dodge pickup, carrying the newly purchased and incarcerated subject, to Burt's Diner in the thriving metropolis of Scio. There, he planned to partake of a small breakfast prior to viewing the sheep trials.

"Border collie trials are educational," he'd informed me, "and a must for a breeder of sheep as the damn things are always getting lost (the sheep that is, not the breeder or the dog), a well-trained findin' dog along with a ewe-inclined ram is essential to survival."

You are aware we are speaking here of the farmer's longevity, are you not? Anyhoo, while he'd been pigging out on ham and eggs some sleaze had purloined his new prize ram right off the back of his flaming truck. Seth had just laid out five Franklin's for the future papa of his flock; he damn sure wanted him back! I know what you're thinking and you are wrong. All sheep do not look alike! Bernie has often discussed his sheep raising days with me. He swears that whenever he entered the large pasture on Mojac Farm, where viewing of the flock would be of quite some distance, right away he could pick out Buttercup, Molly, Old Blue and Gutface. He could also distinguish Beau from E. Flynn, a mile away. The missing ram I'd be chasing would also be easy to spot; he had a gray streak on his left ear and of course, if I got close enough to read it, the inside of that ear had been tattooed. Doubtless, my reward for this one would be a lovely lamb stew for

Mandy! I had a hunch the perpetrator of this kidnapping would probably turn out to be a disgruntled neighbor. You purely have no idea how jealous some livestock growers are of their colleagues, especially when a competitor's stock entry looks to be a sure winner over theirs at the Oregon State Fair.

I accepted a fifty dollar retainer from him and, as I'd time to spare, I decided to start ram hunting right away. I planned on checking out Seth's bailiwick first. If I spotted a likely prospect grazing in a nearby field, Mandy would round the sucker up and bring him in close enough to where I could check for tattooed numbers in his ear. Maggie would stay confined in the wagon. I didn't need a yapping mutt biting on that ear as she eagerly chased an innocent farmer's ram into the next county! The blasted phone rang as I started to pop the latch closed on the office door.

Reginald Plumbfer, client number one, lists in my book of strange cases as one irate, transplanted Limey. A rotten thief and killer had stolen his birdseed; in the process the killer had knocked off his beloved King Charles spaniel. Said killer shall be caught, then drawn and quartered. Money would be no object! I copied directions to his digs and, preparing to put Seth's ram on temporary hold, reached out for the door handle again. The damn phone shrilled for attention again.

Client number three, by name of Hortense, wife of Barney Piccolo, was in the most urgent need of an astute and clever detective, namely me, to immediately locate her missing diamond brooch. Not just any brooch mind you; this, a fancy one happened to be one of her husband's most cherished family heirlooms, if she failed to recover it hubby dearest was just naturally going to break her jaw!

"How might such a troubled damsel have lost said trinket?" inquired the detective.

"I felt lonely and so I went to a party last night." Barnums (her choice, not mine) hadn't attended. Occupying himself with the loan sharking business, the compassionate fellow had been in Las Vegas checking on lapsed loans.

Doubtless friend Barnums, engaged in pursuits monetary, was busy hammering the knees of welshers into shapes concave! A gentle reminder to those of us who, frequently in need of loans but always lacking necessary collateral, are escorted quickly to the outdoors by unsympathetic bankers. Thus there becomes a need for Mr. Piccolo's ready services. Later, not only must the vig be paid, one definitely should desire to pony up the total tab to good old Barney on time because he and sympathy for the unfortunate had never become acquainted! I began to work up some empathy for this lady.

"Might Ms. Hortense have tippled a tad at the party?"

"Uh-huh."

"Might Ms. Hortense have gotten a tad smashed?"

"Uh-huh."

"Might Ms. Hortense have played Post Office with a few male guests?"

"Uh-huh."

"Might Ms. Hortense, housed in a strange bed, have also awakened to the sound of chirping birds outside the window of an unknown bedroom? If so, had her slumbers taken place in the same abode where had occurred the lovely party?"

"Uh-huh."

"Might Ms. Hortense recollect whether her pin had gone missing before or— ah—after she retired?"

"Thank you for putting that so delicately Mr. Doyle, but the answer is, I haven't the foggiest idea."

"Might Ms. Hortense be able to list the names of the male players and tender them to the nice detective?"

"Damn straight!"

"Might Ms. Hortense be up to forking over a few clams to the nice detective to aid him in recovery activities?"

"Uh-huh. Mr. Doyle, when you come to collect your retainer you'll find the front door open. Please enter quietly and *don't slam the door*, I have a rather beastly headache. Do you suppose you could also fetch me a bottle of aspirin?"

Acquiescing, and with directions, names, party place location, I then hied out the office door. On the way to the wagon, in my mind, I listed clients in order of need and preference: Reginald first, Hortense second, Seth last.

I'm not going to bore you with the nitty-gritty of how I solved all three cases before the cock crowed on the 30th. Suffice to say, I nailed Reginald's dog killer exactly half an hour after crunching across his drive.

His house was a pseudo Tudor. Oregon really isn't heavy into Limey architecture, although both areas suffer the damp. It had a lovely den, walnut paneling on the walls, massive oak coffee table, gun cabinet; a large black walnut bar along with high-backed stools. Bottled booze was plentiful; I counted twelve bottles including Glenlivet scotch and Bombay gin. Reginald looked like he sounded: Standing ramrod straight, thin, he presented a ruddy complexion; add a prominent beak, thick eyebrows, mustache, white shirt, checkered vest, plaid trousers, regimental tie and polished oxfords. He definitely had a mad on over the loss of his mutt; close to where his impeccable English suffered, he'd almost drifted into stuttering. He pointed out where the crime had occurred and also indicated where Chesley was now buried. There were tears in his eyes as he talked of him and I knew just how he felt, I've also lost my share of special pets.

Actually, Mandy spotted the killer right away. He had been pilfering the seed and peanuts Reginald had put out for all our bloody welfare birds. Ensconced high above in a massive fir tree, he now snoozed replete. Masked robbers, the suckers are tough fighters as many a dog has found out to their sorrow. Mandy could have taken him but I didn't want her scarred up in the process. I simply called the Fish and Wildlife service and gave directions and location of the thieving raccoon. In the den, I collected fifty clams and thanks from Reginald, then headed for the wagon and the site of Mrs. Piccolo's downfall. Reginald was heading for his gun cabinet when I left. A lovely Purdey over and under resided therein and I had a hunch, if those Wildlife folks didn't hurry, Master Ricky Raccoon wasn't gonna be in healthy enough shape to surrender to them when they arrived.

* * *

The lady Hortense lived in a better than average neighborhood in South Salem, not far from Myer's school. As informed, the front door was unlocked. I made sure not to slam it upon entering. From what I could see Hortense was a bottle blonde in the neighborhood of thirty-five. I couldn't tell much about her figure; she was tightly swathed in a bulky chenille robe and was stretched out on a huge sofa,—resembling one of the dead—an ice bag decorating her noggin. I handed her two aspirin and poured a generous slug of gin from a decanter on yo glass coffee table to help chase them down into her queasy stomach; must have been a lollapalooza of a party. Wheezing painfully, she thanked me for coming, extended a clutched fist containing a curled list of the male party goers, asked me to kindly close the blinds and, although I'd introduced myself in a whisper, to please not shout. Scanning the list I recognized no names, so I tore a page off her notepad, wrote that I'd get on her case right away, picked up the hundred clam retainer lying on the table, and gently closed the door on my way out. Her list contained five names. Four were married. Why the hell weren't the spouses at the party? Three of the listed lived within five blocks of her. Upon answering my knocking, the first two revealed over-the-hill paunchy Joe's crowding their doorways. Answers to questions I asked convinced me they were not involved. How did I know? After awhile in this business you just know. Number three was pumping iron at the local gym. Not guilty. The last two rented condos on Kuebler Road, west of Commercial St.

I nailed number four, the bachelor, for the thievery. Upon entering his abode my skin began to itch. Nothing jumped out, it was just a feeling. His place, while nicely furnished and definitely not threadbare, conveyed the sense of a troop living close to the edge. Credit cards probably maxed out, paycheck to paycheck survival; a guy fighting to keep up with the 'in' crowd and fading fast. His digs also displayed massive furniture, including a stout rolltop desk in the den. While conversing, we stood over by that desk. A hinged box, like a recipe holder, claimed space up front on the far left. For no real reason I placed my right hand on the desk close to the box. Pleasingly plump people do those things, has to do with the need for support for fallen arches I've been told. I'm going to tell you how I nailed him but I know damn well you won't believe me. Just recently I had enjoyed watching one of my favorite movies for the umpteenth time! Do you remember the classic film, *The Adventures of Robin Hood*, starring Errol Flynn? (Hollywood has made many different versions since then, but his is still the best!) Close to the climax, there was a scene where Sir Guy of Gisbourne (Basil Rathbone) barges into Maid Marion's boudoir because the Sheriff of Nottingham, Prince John, and he suspect she had overheard them plotting to kill King Richard. That she had. She'd also just finished penning a note to Robin Hood to warn him of the plot. Her lady in waiting was going to scoot out of the castle the back way and deliver it.

Gisbourne thumps on her door before flinging it open, which just gives her time to hide the note in a box on her table. Nasty Basil questions her with his hand resting on the box. She denies all but grows nervous and keeps looking at the box upon which Gizzy had placed his hand.

"Ah-ha, you lie, Madam!" he bellows. And with that, he pops open the box to find her note.

Hey, you don't need to hear me relate the whole movie. Just know suspect number four grew more nervous by the minute the longer we talked. He also kept glancing down at the box.

"Ah-ha" I cried, and then reached out and flipped his recipe box open. There lay the darlin' brooch twinkling in the light almost like it was smiling gratefully up at me. I didn't even break the bum's arm, just his nose.

Damn, that Basil Rathbone was a hell of a fine actor. With his deep voice, like Lee Marvin's, and a schnoz a block long, he still got the job done.

Upon the safe return of her brooch, Hortense-in-the-Dark thanked me profusely but painfully, threw her gin decanter at me, and told me *not to slam the damn door* on the way out!

Bet You Don't Know Where Lorna Is! 239

* * *

Recovering Seth's ram took a little longer and resulted in a few bruises accruing to my aging frame. I blame Mandy!

After leaving Hortense, I stopped at Sandy's and took her to lunch. I filled her in on the results of both cases while disposing of a Clubhouse at the Oyster Bar; I've already bragged there's none better in the whole state!

"I am happy you solved both puzzling crimes," said my significant other, "but why in the world did Hortense throw her gin bottle at you?"

"Well, I knew she was happy to get her pin back, but I could see she was still suffering and that the ice had all melted in her ice bag, so I told her a story to help cheer her up."

"Why did telling her a story make her mad?"

"Beats the royal fadoot outa me, maybe it was because she laughed while her head was still aching,"

"Uh-huh, so tell me the story and let's see if it makes me laugh or brings on a headache."

"Okay, but you have to pay close attention and not interrupt:"

* * *

"There once was a thrifty tradesman, a painter by name of Jock. Now that lad, a Scot, was interested in making a penny wherever he could. Quite often the canny fellow would thin his paint to make it go a wee bit farther. Happened he got away with this for some time. One day the Baptist Church decided a big restoration painting job was overdue on one of their biggest churches. Jock put in a bid. His price was so low he got the job."

"He erected all his trestles, set up planks, bought the paint, and yes, I am

sorry to say, he'd thinned it considerably more with turpentine. Then, standing on his scaffolding Jock painted contentedly away. The job was almost completed when suddenly there came a flash of lightning and a horrendous clap of thunder. The flash knocked Jock clean off the scaffolding. He landed in the church remembrance lot smack dab amongst the gravestones. The Sky opened and rain poured, it washed all the thinned paint off the whole church. Looking dazedly around, Jock saw he was surrounded by telltale puddles of the thinned and now totally useless paint."

"Jock was no fool. He knew this was a judgment from the Almighty. Forcing himself up on his knees he cried, 'Oh, God! Forgive me! I have offended thee. What do you require me to do as penance?' Forth from more tumultuous crashing thunder roared a mighty voice . . . ."

"Repaint! Repaint! And thin no more!"

* * *

Midway through a large bite of her sandwich Sandy choked and coughed. Half strangling, she fought for air. Her body shook dislodging a slice of tomato from her BLT which, unfortunately, fell into her coffee. I live right, there wasn't anything handy on the table for her to throw at me that wouldn't have killed me! But I beat a hasty retreat to the men's room just to be on the safe side.

19

I came away bruised from case number three because I got careless. After two days of driving around fruitlessly in the vicinity of Aumsville, Stayton, Scio and Sublimity, listening for the baaing of a lonesome ram, I wised up and started inquiring for current sheep farmer chatter at local food markets and gas stations. It wasn't until I had further worked my way through Jefferson, Brownsville and Lebanon that I got lucky. My feet were sore, my butt was sore, and my voice was sore. Two precious days had flown the flit by the time a grocery clerk in Lebanon, a 4-H'er raising his own ewe to enter in the State Fair, told me to check out a farmer in Turner, name of Stanley Scroggs. He didn't think Stanley had snatched the ram but that old geezer knew everything and everybody having to do with pedigree sheep, and he knew them up and down the whole Willamette Valley. If anyone knew the skinny on Seth's ram it would be Stanley.

Scroggs checked out a scrawny old boy with a prominent Adam's apple that slid up and down his throat like a yo-yo; wire whiskers decorated a sunburned face. If the little woman happened to plant a smooch on his kisser, the dear old lady would end up badly lacerated. He wore clean, but many times patched, baggy overalls circa 1860. They were fighting proudly, but desperately, to hold him together. The weather was late June warm and he still wore an old flannel shirt over long johns. In spite of the heavy duds he wouldn't dent a weighing machine past 122. I'd bet his false teeth were bought, fitted, inserted and had not been removed since the Civil War!

Stanley rolled his own 'makin's'. If his yellowed fingers were any indication he smoked a bundle of them. His voice gurgled like a flushing toilet. After spending the time I do turning over rocks, his honest look, coupled with kind blue eyes aimed my way, not only made my day but they flat made my month! I liked him on the spot.

His acreage ran to about a hundred of the gently rolling kind. It was fenced and cross-fenced and I guessed housed around a hundred Suffolk ewes. His was a century farm which came as no surprise; I pegged the old boy at right around three digits himself. He told me he'd won so many ribbons competing at fairs he raised his sheep now purely because he loved them. Bernie, too, is another guy who's told me he has a crush on woolies.

Stanley couldn't swear to it but, seemed like chatting with local gossipers opined that a couple of fellers over toward Sweet Home had come into a right purty pedigree ram jest t'other week. If story were true, t'was a big Suffolk. Couldn't say iffen it had a streak uh gray on its left ear, or even iffen t'were tattooed. Stanley still punched holes in his stock's ears, didn't shed no blood though; it were all in the knowin' how an' where to punch. Hadn't been no rams bought at the Turner or Scio sheep trials an' the State Fair weren't a-gonna be hummin' till late August. Them two fellers was not extra special stock themselves iffen I caught his drift, best to come up on 'em quiet like. Them two had about eight acres t'other side uh Sweet Home. Name on the mailbox would read, Purdy. I thanked him and headed for the wagon, prepared to move out. Friend Scroggs musta been watchin' a Clint Eastwood film last night. Thuh one called, *Maggers Force*, or somepin like thet. Iffen I felt the need fer backup, give uh yell an' he'd be plumb proud tuh provide her.

Bet You Don't Know Where Lorna Is!

I do believe that old boy would be more than the Purdy's could handle, but the elderly are also subject to sudden heart attacks, so I pointed out my two deputies in the wagon, thanked him again and, pulling a John Wayne, I saddled up and headed out.

Sweet Home lies southeast from Turner and about halfway 'twixt Eugene an' Salem. I drove south on I-5, then hung a left onto 20, the Santiam Highway. Reposing in the foothills of the Cascade Mountain Range, Sweet Home is a picturesque little town. Seed from grass would be the principal industry. From the center of town a major leaguer could throw a rock into Lake Foster, maybe even the larger of the two, Green Peter. It lists plenty of recreation, wildlife, waterfalls and the Santiam River. Bernie says they have some really nice campsites on the lakes. He used to go boating and fishing there until one year the smoke from field burning got so bad it completely blocked out the sun.

"After a long winter of clouds, rain, and no sun, anyone who blocks out Oregon's summer smile can go to hell," he hollered. So he cranked up the car, took the pass through the Cascades until he located the Deschutes River. Over there, he had a lovely time in the sunshine!"

Lately, you'll remember, growers have cut way back on field burning. Oregon provides two-thirds of the world's grass seed and Linn County contributes almost half. Okay, already, I agree this isn't a lesson in civics.

Some twelve miles east of the town, I turned south off Highway 20 onto Dead Burro Road. At milepost 5, I headed east on Dumb Ass Lane until I ran into a dead-end at Kicking Mule Hill. The Purdy farm sited in a pretty spot at the base of that hill. Their farm, however, was anything but pretty! The owners were pigs! Trash: A year's garbage, tin cans, broken equipment, falling down fences, a house that would have been condemned during the Mexican War, and an equally dismal barn in the rear littered the landscape.

I wouldn't have been surprised to see Bathless Groggins sacking out in an ancient rocking chair on what passed for the front porch, but the only howdy I got was a swishing tail attached to a one-eyed Calico cat, and a half-hearted growl from an emaciated coon hound. I wasn't sure how I wanted to play it so I left Mandy and Maggie on stays in the wagon and 'hallooed' my way around the dump. As I approached the barn, a gate swung open and the Purdy brothers, Will and Phil, stepped out to confront me.

"You lookin' fer somethin' mister?" asked the one who looked like Ernest Borgnine in *The Wild Bunch*. The other guy, a dead ringer for Hannibal the Cannibal, just stared and picked his nose.

"Good afternoon, young gentlemen," enthused the detective. "I represent the Parker Packing Company, purveyors of quality ham, bacon and lamb. A young man at the feed store in town opined that The Purdy Farm raised fine hogs and sheep and the owners were quite often of a mind to sell a few head. Dare I presume I have the pleasure of talking to the Purdy brothers? My company pays top dollar for good quality livestock."

"Huh?" elucidated the talker, who turned out to be Phil.

"Whut?" added Will.

"I am on a buying venture today, young sirs, and especially interested in purchasing young rams and ewes. Perchance I've come at the right time and you have a good ram for sale? I have my eye on a lusty boy back in Lebanon but was led to believe your stock rates higher, being of the pedigree variety. I was further given to understand you knowledgeable young gentlemen are raising the Suffolk breed. I'm also aware that Suffolk's, upon their demise, weigh out in prime meat. May I have the pleasure of viewing the excellence of your flock?"

The only flock I'd seen so far had been a scrawny rooster and two old hens, all more than ready for the stew pot. Not to fret though, while I'd been prattling away, my ears had tuned into a 'baa' emanating from the barn. I stepped forward preparing to enter Dogpatch, but Will forced himself to refrain from picking his nose long enough to stay me.

"We ain't got no rams or no ewes fer sale, mister. I 'spect you better ease on down the road right smart. Our dog don't take kindly tuh strangers."

"Most disappointing, young sirs, my company has been paying up to five hundred dollars for prime rams this summer. Regretfully, I won't be back this way during the next six months and but two rams and two more ewes would fill our quota. You are sure you've nothing for sale at this time?"

The two exchanged questioning looks, but then Phil hunched his shoulders, showed a lovely yellow growth of fungus on his teeth, and said:

"We done tole' yuh mister, we ain't got nuthin' fer sale. Best yuh git tuh headin' on outa here."

With nothing for it, I headed back to the wagon, cranked up and dusted on out of there. Damn, had I overplayed it? I'd bet a purty those two weasels had Seth's ram stashed in the barn and that meant the girls and I would have to go back and pay a nocturnal visit. I hate that! On those occasions, almost always a guard dog eagerly desiring to chew on various parts of my body shows up! I hid the wagon out of sight half a mile away, took the dogs for a required break, and then curled up on the front seat to await the dark. Of course I zonked! Acting is hard work. So is thinking!

My dashboard clock read ninish of the evening when I awoke. I'd roused because Maggie, perched on my stomach, was licking my face. I hate a lickin' dog! But she was right, it was time for action. I hauled out the flashlight, including extra batteries. I had been down that lonely road before when the bulb yellowed and then died at the worst of times.

Allowing for another potty break for all, we were then away. I had scouted the area enough to figure out where to reach the farm from the back. Yon moon was full which, as I gave thanks, allowed me to watch where I placed my big feet while pacing through the pasture. It is truly amazing how growing grass happily thrives in a pasture due to the contributions of but a single cow! Fortunately, every time M and M stopped to sniff mounds, this old boy knew enough to go around them. After a considerable walk, along with snagging my jacket on a few barb wire fences, we came up to the backside of the Purdy barn. Its falling down status helped as I stepped easily inside through a large hole. I put Maggie on a 'stay, don't bark' by that hole. Using the flashlight sparingly Mandy and I inspected the barn. More sheep than I had estimated were in there. No doubt the bigger ones were rams. I counted five of them. Quietly and skillfully Mandy ordered each one to the rear of their pens and then held them there while I inspected. Number four rolled up a lovely seven! I spotted a gray streak on the outside of its left ear and my numbers matched those of the tattoo appearing on the inside.

Planning on then leaving I started to turn, when suddenly the lights went out, those I use for inner vision that is, and I dimly heard a voice exclaim:

"I done tole yuh thet stranger were up to no good, Phil. Hev yuh kilt him dead? Oh, dad blame it. **OUCH!** Git this varmint offa me!"

Naturally, I'd had to fall face down into a pile of cherry pits (Bernie says that's what he and his farmer cronies call sheep droppings). At close range, I failed to see the resemblance; immaterial of course because I'd also dropped the flashlight and at that moment I couldn't see anything too clearly. Damned if I hadn't been cold-cocked upside the head, all because I'd put my sweet, gentle girls on 'stays.' My ears had no difficulty discerning the hullabaloo though. Groggily I propped myself up, groped for my saving light, retrieved it and shone the bright beam around the joint. Off in a corner, Will was screaming while desperately trying to remove a snarling Maggie who had latched onto a most important item in his pants front, one he could ill afford to lose! There shouldn't be much risk of infection though. As you know from the time of her puppy hood Miss Maggie's teeth have been brushed every day. Mandy wasn't fooling around like her sister; she had already removed a chunk of Phil's left leg and was worrying hell out of his right shoulder. When I could use my voice again, I called both dogs off. The Purdy boys almost tore the barn door off its flaming hinges in their haste to put distance between themselves and my peace-loving pals.

"Best to skedaddle fellas," I shouted after them, "the sheriff is on his way and you've got some explaining to do. My twelve gauge here, loaded with slugs, is also purely itching to part some hair. The dogs will know if you come back. By the way, the rams in here all got loose and took a fast hike out the back door. Ya' all have a nice evening now."

Once I truly had called the sheriff on my trusty cell phone, I placed another one to a waiting and hopeful Seth.

"Seth, my man, this is the detective you were wise to trust. Grab a harness, collect a couple of stalwart chums, hop in your pickup and come collect your handsome, healthy ram."

I gave Lowell directions to the Purdy dump, advised him to keep his eyes peeled for the turnoff and, in the meantime, I prayed those two louts wouldn't set fire to the barn. With my two chums reposing vigilantly on either side of me, and enjoying a mental picture of the Purdy boys collecting barn door splinters off various parts of their bods, I settled down to wait.

When the Linn County sheriff arrived two hours later, he photographed the rest of the loose Purdy stock rambling around in the pasture, took a lengthy statement from me, patted both dogs, and laughed a lot. Then friend Seth and his crew showed-up. Profuse in praise of the brilliant detective he was deeply grateful. His only regret, he hadn't been there to see my two girls in action. Like I've often said, "who needs a gun when apprehending sleazebags?"

Seth delivered two lovely legs of lamb to me the evening of the 29th. I informed him Phil and Will had been arrested at the Sweet Home hospital by the sheriff. The doctors there were still shaking their heads over the most unusual location of Will Purdy's wound. Upon arrival, Will had related how he hed plumb falled offen a hay wagon an' landed on a roll uh barbed wire which his dumb brother hed left layin' in thuh field. Sound like a plausible story to you? That time bro Phil was picking his nose.

I fixed the dogs' one of my humongous, gourmet lamb stews. I'd also made sure there remained plenty for Sandy and yours truly. I even shook the moths out of the wallet for two bottles of the 2001 Laetitia Estate Pinot Noir. That dandy little winery is located in Arroyo Grande in California. A touch of trivia: Laetitia, in latin, is an expression of joy and happiness. The only thing that could bring me greater happiness after solving three not terribly complicated crimes, besides marrying Sandy, would be the arrival of the day when I escorted Lorna safely up the steps into her home once again.

20

There would be a waning full moon the evening of the 30th. Couple that with no rain and please, no fog! I'd checked and double checked plans. Still, I was nervous as a jumping frog having to explain to a herd of cattle how come I'd landed in their watering trough! I had called Jane and the police chief to inform of where I would be during their stakeout. For their part of the operation the substitute *me* was ready. The ransom, half of which had been contributed by Diddens' boss, was packed and ready. Ms. FBI Jane was more than ready. I was tempted once again to ask if the robin had been successful in its daunting, prodigious task, but I refrained. Slight as she is, I do believe that little lady could bench press me without breaking into a sweat. The Feebs with rifles were ready. Were the lousy kidnappers ready?

The sun would set about nine-thirty, full dark would creep in at ten-twenty-two. I had told Bernie I would pick him up at his house. My eyes, in definite sympathy with my stomach, were definitely not about to watch him threaten his stomach with capital punishment at Bad Bascomb's.

 Sandy had begged to go. I'd said 'no' for the same reason as before, she could be exposed to real danger; besides, I needed her at the police action where she could keep me instantly informed if I'd guessed wrong.

Sam was on duty at the coast, watching. Bill was standing by. Greg was staking out the suspect's house. Biff and Burt were on their way to the Baskett Slough National Wildlife Sanctuary on Highway 22. They would be able to park unobserved up on the hill and still have an excellent field of view during daylight. I'd also loaned them a pair of binoculars. Until dark, they were to keep watch for just two particular automobiles.

The girls and I had taken care of grits and ablutions earlier and by eight I pulled up before Bernie's digs. It was still light enough that I noticed his lawn needed cutting! I had allowed plenty of time for a good reason. Offing a deer in the Van Duzer Corridor could blow the whole operation; therefore, I planned on the wagon moving at a sedate fifty per. I was going to enjoy the scenery, maybe spot an elk, or a bear, and to hell with any impatient drivers crowding me from behind.

I wasn't up to much chatter, nor was Bernie. Too much was riding on my theory and I kept running it through my head along with what Bern had informed me about kids. She boiled down to this: If the kidnappers were the ones I figured them to be they could not afford to let Lorna go. First thing she would do is blow the whistle on them. So the latest ransom bit had to be another ploy, just like the first one had to have been a testing of the waters. Fully aware that Lorna posed a terrible threat, why hadn't they killed her? Maybe they already had but I didn't think so; if they were kids, as I suspected, they were also amateurs to boot so I think they were afraid to go that far. Even for a scumbag it takes a lot to kill a human being. When, in desperation, they had first grabbed her it had seemed an easy solution for their laziness. Future events, especially when the hacking job to change their grades had boomeranged and shown how wrong their solution was, had allowed a skunk freedom to roam in the house. Today, there was no way to chouse him out without his creating an eye-watering, nose-burning stink!

Bet You Don't Know Where Lorna Is!

What had I to do now? I'd constantly reminded myself that these were smart kids while I was equally sure Dirty Chuck couldn't pound sand down a rat hole. He wasn't the ringleader. He had to be a gopher. In any event, I hoped I was about to discover just who was the boss. Then I truly planned on planting my boot up his ass!

Another worry continued to thump me on the noggin, *fog*! In one of my literature classes one time I'd been informed a guy from Chicago, name of Carl Sandburg, visiting San Francisco, wrote that fog came in on little kitty cat feet, or something like that. Not in dear old Newport. There, she comes charging in on the veld toughened pads of a ravenous cheetah! Crossing my fingers I prayed, "Please, Big Guy above, don't let there be a blinding fog!"

Abreast of the wildlife sanctuary, coming on for eight-thirty, I called my lookouts. Biff answered and reported he'd seen what he thought had been a Toyota Camry passing, but a bloody hot-footing semi had chosen just that minute to blow a tire. The driver had stopped his rig across the entrance to the sanctuary blocking the kids' view; nary a sign of the other car as yet. I sighed and my glum silence began to get on Bernie's nerves.

"Danny, will you quit squeezing hell out of the steering wheel. We have been over and over the plan—it will work. Now quit with the sighing and listen up, I'm about to cheer you up with a remarkable story."

"Why not," I moaned. "What would a day be without one of your dumb stories? Go ahead and trot it out Bernie you may as well add to my misery."

"Good, now relax, listen closely and learn."

* * *

"A few years ago a married couple, fighting a truly nasty and icy New York winter, decided on thawing out in Florida on a long weekend. They planned

on staying at the same hotel and asking for the very same room where they'd spent their honeymoon twenty years ago. Both having jobs, they found it difficult coordinating travel schedules. The husband decided he would fly to Florida on a Thursday; the wife would follow him the next day."

"Upon arriving as planned, the husband checked into the hotel. In their room he discovered a computer so he decided to send an e-mail to his wife back in New York. Regrettably, he accidentally filled in the wrong address."

"In Houston, a widow had just returned from her husband's funeral. Sadly, the widow checked her e-mail expecting messages from relatives and friends. Upon reading the first message she fainted. Her son, hearing the loud thump, rushed into the room and found his mother on the floor. Noticing that the computer was on, he glanced at the screen and read."

'To My Loving Wife,

I have arrived. I'll bet you are surprised to hear from me. They have computers here now and you are allowed to send e-mails to your loved ones. Everything is just as we expected. I am already checked in. I also see that all has been carefully prepared for your arrival tomorrow. I am sure looking forward to seeing you. Hope your journey is as uneventful as mine was.'

P.S. 'Sure is hot down here!' "

* * *

After I regained control of the wagon, and since we were now about to enter the Van Duzer Corridor, I told him if he planned on laying any more of those little gems on me to do it before we had to run the gauntlet of dumb drivers, elk and deer.

"Ah-ha, I see I have loosened you up a tad. You get the next one for free.

Keep your eyes on the road. I'll watch out for the big critters."

"This little beauty is entitled, *Getting Older*.

"*A wife and husband are preparing for bed. The wife, standing in front of a full length mirror, is taking a hard look at herself. 'You know, Love,' she says. 'I look in the mirror and I see an old woman. My face is all wrinkled, my boobs are barely above my waist and my bum is hanging out a mile. I've fat legs and my arms are all flabby.' She turns to her husband and sighs . . . , tell me something positive to make me feel better about myself.'*

"He thinks about it for a bit and then says, 'Well . . . , there's nothing wrong with your eyesight!' "

* * *

Bernie had temporarily succeeded in taking my mind off my fears. Just the same, one of these days I'm definitely going to kill him!

We made good time through the corridor and by the time we hit Depoe Bay the clock read but nine-twenty; still more than enough light. As Sam hadn't called I knew we would reach our destination in plenty of time and, I hoped, find out the answer to those nagging all important questions: What if the kidnappers, at the outset, had not planned to kill Lorna? If they were still not inclined to do so now, how were they going to get rid of her?

It was going on dusk as we crossed the Yaquina Bay Bridge at Newport. I pulled quietly into the marina, eased over and parked beside a relieved, but impatiently waiting, Sam.

"Good to see you guys," he said. "The boat we want is still there and you'll be glad to know I finally made out her name. She's the *Sally B*. You can see her out there moored at the far end of the dock. A bunch of people went aboard around nine-thirty, but nobody's been stirring around since."

Hallelujah! I do believe we've got 'em. I hauled the shotgun out of the wagon, loaded it, and then handed it to Sam. Bernie had toted his trusty thirty-eight Smith and Wesson along. He had carried that baby to South America and back before the days of airport security. I fetched the rest of the gear, set it by the wagon and went in search of Coast Guard Bill. He was aboard his boat, the *Pelican*, checking out the motors. The old beaver had tested all the electronic paraphernalia the day before and everything was working just fine. I inquired if he had brought the things I'd recommended. I received a wounded, long-suffering look for my pains.

"Since when does an old salt require lessons from a dim-witted landlubber?" he snorted, "of course it's all aboard. When do you want to shove off?"

"We have to wait until they make their move," I said. "Once full dark arrives I believe he'll start-up and edge away from the dock. I can't see any of them wanting to draw attention to themselves from folks on the land, so they will slip away quietly. We shouldn't lose them if the fog stays away."

Bill and I joined the others where I recommended everybody, including the dogs, make a quick trip to the loo and then standby for immediate orders to board from our captain.

Why is waiting so tedious? It seemed like, seated on the gunwales of Bill's boat, we fretted for hours. The time was coming up on seven bells when Sam, he of the keenest eyes, drew our attention to burbling water disturbed by the thrashing propellers from the *Sally B's* twin engines; almost soundlessly, freed from the dock, the boat turned her bow to port and headed for the causeway. My watch now read 11:30 p.m. The night staying clear, I thanked the Boss upstairs that visibility would apparently not be a problem.

Bet You Don't Know Where Lorna Is!

"Okay, troops, we give them a twenty minute head start, then follow; Bill, me old sailing expert, if you lose 'em your lovely Jan will weep copious tears at your early and unexpected funeral!"

"Who the hell is going to teach me how to trail another boat? A flatfoot who couldn't navigate his way out of a bathtub? I'll not only have that sucker on radar, I'll also track him by satellite. Climb aboard, sit down, and shut your fat face!"

Bill's boat, not large, sat low in the water. If that bunch bothered to post a lookout which I seriously doubted, running without lights as Bill was his boat would still be hard to spot. Effortlessly, our skipper kept us right on their butt. No clouds. The moon remained a friend, the lights of a ship not far away showed as the only other sign of life. We tailed the *Sally B* a long way before I judged it was time.

"Kick her up a notch, Captain, sir. Let's close on the sumbitches and scare hell out of them. Looks like they're heading for yonder ship."

The diesel motors on Bill's boat were powerful enough to tow a boat twice the size of the *Sally B* and it could move three times as fast. I asked Sam to stand by, I'd tell him what to do with the shotgun directly; then I grabbed Bill's bullhorn and prepared to switch on his spotlight. Bill moved silently up on our quarry's port side to within about ten yards and I went into my act. Switching the searchlight on, knowing it would blind the clods, I sucked in a deep breath and, in the deepest voice I could muster, hollered through the bullhorn:

"Ahoy, you people aboard the Sally B, this is the United States Coastguard. Heave to; we are about to board you!"

Startled faces turned in our direction, but the boat kept right on motoring.

Once more I yelled, "**Sally B, this is the United States Coastguard. We are going to board you. Heave to or we shall be forced to fire on you!**"

I advised Sam if they then continued to show no sign of stopping to put a shot across their bows. It wouldn't hurt if a pellet or two broke some glass in the bloody cabin in the process!

An overloud **BLAM** accompanied by the tinkle of breaking glass and Dirty Chuck slammed on the brakes! The *Sally B* hove to.

As we came alongside I dropped the fenders over, then asked Bill to keep his light focused on Chuck's boat and to hold the *Pelican* as close in as he could without endangering boat or self. Sam and his shotgun, Bernie and his thirty-eight, Mandy, Maggie—including their polished teeth—along with the harmless one, me, would board.

"Keep an eye peeled for tricks guys this is a sneaky bunch."

Now why would a flaming novice to the art of war try to teach an ex-Green Beret how to handle trouble? Will I ever learn? Observing us climbing aboard their boat the surprised occupants seemed a tad ticked at not seeing uniforms.

"Who the hell are . . .?" began a scruffy male. Two others, some years younger, jumped guiltily. The female hissed and spat!

Sam waved the shotgun around, friendly like, and that charmed them all into immediate silence.

"Well, looky here," I said. "I do believe we have run into Bo, Bart, Taffy, otherwise known as Chuck, and this young lady is Miss Jill—the boss!" How nice to make your acquaintance. Now all of you shut-up. You know who I am and what I want. I would also be ever so grateful if none of you move. Sam, Bernie, watch them. Mandy, show these nice folks your pretty,

Bet You Don't Know Where Lorna Is!

winsome, and most friendly Pepsodent smile."

Like the dear good girl she is Mandy obligingly bared her teeth.

"If you kind folks will excuse us for a minute my pal Maggie here, an almighty curious little lady, is just dying to take me on a tour of your boat."

I knew full well if I had guessed wrong trouble was on the way. Illegal stop and search, threatening with lethal weapons, and harassing of minors would be but the beginning once Doctor Dad stuck his imperious nose in. No doubt, if he were then to have his way the last thing I'd read would be my own obituary! Still, in for a penny in for a pound; nothing ventured, nothing gained; the faint-hearted die a thousand deaths, the brave but one; onward and upward; and all the rest of those lovely clichés. Showtime!

I had taken the trouble to bring along another of Lorna's scarves. I poked Maggie's nose with it and told her to go find Lorna. My little doll took off like a shot her nose twitching like a kitten rolling in catnip. After a little sniff here, a little snort there, she hopped up on the bed in the main cabin and began sniffing the wall. Then she started scratching and barking at it. I left her guarding there, went back to our hosts, borrowed Sam's shotgun, walked over to Chuck, placed the barrel against his right knee, and snarled.

"I'm only going to make this friendly request once. Show me how to open the panel by the bed in the main cabin, or from this day forth they'll be calling you, Hop-Along Taffy!"

Dirty Chuck's complexion abruptly turned a dingy shade of gray; he turned the wheel over to Bo, led the way back to the cabin, pressed a button hidden on the inside of the bed's end and, lo and behold, the wall swung down. Peering into the gloom I beheld a very narrow bunk hidden inside the wall; a female form lay on it, scrunched way down on a filthy mattress. The figure did not move but I could see it was Lorna. I shook her a few times. She remained limp. Offering up a quick but fervent prayer I lifted her wrist and felt for a pulse. Thank God, the beat was strong and regular.

"Oh Lord, I've fallen face first into a nest of vipers here and you in your infinite mercy have most kindly stayed their bite. Vipers without bite are nothing more than little old itty-bitty garden snakes. I do thank You!"

Turning quickly, I accidentally bashed Taffy's nose with my elbow. When he picked himself up dripping claret and whining over his broken nose, I ordered him to help me lift Lorna from her cubbyhole. Drugged as she was, and totally unable to walk, I had to support her. I wrapped her in a blanket and, you're damn right, carried her tenderly back to the others. Scowls from our unwilling hosts, big, relieved smiles from my guys.

"My father will put all of you in jail for illegally hi-jacking this boat," hissed the she who we'd been told was destined for great things.

White with rage, I said, "You betcha, love, somebody *is* going to jail. But don't think for one minute it will be us. Best to keep that mean little mouth of yours shut, Miss Jill, before I pick you up and throw you to the fish!"

Bernie and I tied the four together and made them sit out on the deck. Mandy and Maggie continued to smile at them. I asked Bernie to request Bill to call the Newport Sheriff and ask him to meet us at the dock with an ambulance, and then inform Jane and the Salem police they could go home; the kidnappers would not show up at the carousel that night. I also suggested they not forget to retrieve the ransom and if Sandy would phone Diddens. I'd call him later from the Newport hospital. If the croakers decided to release Lorna I'd no intention of waiting; she was going straight home to hubby where he could tenderly tuck her into her own warm bed.

21

Hoo-boy, was I flying! I don't mind adding I also felt bloody relieved.

When Bernie returned, I sent Sam out to man Bill's boat. I wanted our four, very frightened captives, to see him in his full uniform. Down the line, when the little creeps faced charges in court, I didn't want some slick lawyer to get them off on a technicality.

As soon as Bill boarded, I left Bernie and Mandy to guard while the real member of the Coastguard, Maggie, and meself, conducted a more thorough search of the *Sally B*. I didn't really expect to find anything but a legal search this time would justify the stopping of the boat on the high seas. Whenever our Coastguard folks suspect that ships in the coastal waters of the United States are engaged in illegal activities they have the right to stop them and conduct thorough searches. We even checked in the bilges.

Bill gave all four suspects the fish eye when we returned, had me point out the owner of the boat, shook his head angrily, wrote something down in his notebook, and returned to his vessel. I'd suggested he call headquarters and recommend they send a fast ship with a full crew out to the ship waiting a half-mile away and conduct another investigation. I was sure that ship had to be the *YUKIKO MARU*. Taken by surprise the captain might not be able to ditch the supply of drugs he was no doubt transporting to friend Chuck from our good neighbor, Columbia.

Sam climbed aboard the *Sally B* from the *Pelican* and took the wheel.

Casting off, Bill swung his boat wide to port and headed for shore; the *Sally B* stayed right on his butt. Moon or no, I didn't fancy getting lost in the dark amidst cresting ocean swells. Motoring back to the marina, now cruising happily and comfortably behind the *Pelican,* Sam asked me how the hell I knew Lorna would be on board.

"Guy, I didn't know for sure, but one question about this case wouldn't stop nagging me; when these three rotten little twerps found out their hacking caper had been blown, what then? They had to know the fox had doubled back on the hounds and was busy shedding fleas on the carpet. What would the entire set of moms and dads do about that? Worse, what to do with Lorna now? Changing a grade on an English test is one thing, but offing their teacher is quite another! They could not afford to turn her loose so, short of killing her, how were they going to dispose of her? Remember, while these kids are pure trash, they are not longtime practiced criminals. Thank God, *they* didn't have the stomach for killing. I'm quite sure they were not averse to someone else doing the dirty deed though!"

"Enter another player in the guise of a floating garbage scow. Unless I'm dead wrong, those lights out there have to belong to the *YUKIKO MARU* and she has been waiting for the *Sally B*. Her home port is Hong Kong. She's returning from a voyage to South America and was due off Newport today. If you take a look at the console over there behind the wheel you will notice this boat sports a ship-to-shore radio. I'll wager a Bernie gunk-covered bagel our Dirty Chuck's been in touch by radio with the captain of that old clunker. That's why he waited so long to go out tonight; he had to wait until the *YUKIKO* showed up. The captain's radio call informed him she was here. Friend Chuck has been conducting a lot of drug business with the captain of that rust bucket. He is another scumbag with a supplier in Hong Kong as well as in Columbia. That would explain the reason Chuck went to sea in bad weather. He came out to meet the *YUKIKO MARU*. It also clears up how he always had money after returning from Portland. Capable of blending into a drug dealer's background and casually querying that sort of trash, it wasn't long before he found buyers for his own rotten drugs. Sweet Miss Jill, as we now know, is not Bo's girlfriend, she's Taffy's. She is the mean-minded one and the gang's ringleader. It was her idea to snatch Lorna; she knew she had flunked the English test. That little delight is also the one who had her eye on the Air Force Academy. Bo wants West Point. Bart wants Stanford. Their final grades on the same test would not allow acceptance for any of them. Miss Jill is a real piece of work and mighty persuasive as well. She conned Bo and Bart into grabbing Lorna and bringing her over to the Coast. Then she conned Chuckie into holding Lorna captive in Newport while she figured out what to do with her."

"Early on, our aspiring actor Bo used his phony dialect in the phone message, and then they tried to mug me. When neither ploy worked, determined to keep me occupied in Salem, they concocted those silly ransom notes. Hearing from Taffy of Lorna's escape and that we were over here looking for her frightened hell out of Jill and she nearly lost it! By now things were purely heating up. Bo and Bart got scared. Chuckie Boy grew sick of holding Lorna. Even he knew that sooner or later the drugs they were using on her would most likely kill her. At the same time there was no way they could turn their victim loose. Right away she'd blow the whistle on them and it would be 'Good-bye College, hello slammer.' Miss Jill did the research, but Taffy came up with the solution. And there you have it."

"Put the pedal to the metal on this bloody barge, will you Sam, this dear lady needs to be checked over by a croaker right quick. Also, adrenaline rush just informed my stomach that I'm starving. How about you guys? Do you suppose they will have anything edible to eat at the flaming hospital?"

A mile from shore I asked the others to kindly excuse me while Mandy and I took dear Taffy (Chuck) out on the deck for a brief chat.

"Chuck, me old son, I don't like you one little bit. In my expert opinion the world loses nothing when a scuzzball like you goes missing. I am going to ask you once only for the name of the drug you've been using on Lorna. Fail to supply it and I truly promise I'm going to chain your legs together and accidentally drop you overboard. Now GIVE!"

He couldn't get it out fast enough and even volunteered to produce the remainder from his cabin. Thank God it was Chloral Hydrate. Taken with alcohol it is known as a Mickey Finn. To begin, they'd slipped it to her in a cup of tea. After that they regularly injected her. She had escaped the one time because they had forgotten to administer her next dose. Unless they'd gotten really careless with a dirty needle that drug should not cause any lasting effects on Lorna. Coming out of it she may be jittery, nauseous, inclined to vomit, or suffer diarrhea. From my knowledge of the drug, upon her entering the hospital, it would simply be a case of waiting until she woke up. Before I changed my mind and kicked Chucky into the drink anyway I shoved the puke back inside to join his mates. The callousness of those people actually made my hands shake. It had been a long time since I had felt such a boiling anger.

My arm had gone to sleep while holding her so Bernie and I had laid her carefully on a bunk wrapped in her blanket and one of us constantly checked her pulse as we headed for shore. Though her breathing still seemed thready, last time I'd checked I was sure she'd moved just the tiniest bit. I'd have given a lot to hear a lovely loud snore.

* * *

Bill guided us to dock moorage where the police and ambulance awaited. We turned the four weasels over to the cops, and then Lorna over to the medics. I informed them of the drug that'd been used and watched them head off for the hospital with her. Next, I had a brief chat with the police lieutenant. I wasn't about to suggest their duties to them, but I did think I should mention what the Coastguard was doing at present. I also suggested sweating the kids might call forth a confession to the whole sordid crime and that a body search might turn up a little cocaine, especially on the person of Taffy. I had pegged that bum as always in need of artificial courage.

We all gave our statements to Newport's finest and then hurried to the hospital. The doctors were confident Lorna would be fine but wanted to keep her for a couple of days to be sure. I called Diddens and found out from his answering machine he and his daughters were already on the way to Newport. Looked like I wouldn't be escorting a fine lady up the steps to her house after all. Not to fret, upon Frank's arrival I caught the smile of gratitude on his face along with the tears of joy in his eyes as he hurried on past us eager to get to Lorna's room.

The Coastguard caught the *YUKIKO MARU* asleep on the deep, so to speak, boarded, searched and found a large amount of Colombian cocaine in the captain's cabin. They brought the rusty old wreck into Newport Bay where captain and crew would be detained for extensive questioning. I held out little hope they would squeeze anything out of that scruffy bunch. Still, I figured if the four we had nailed were shown the rusting relic dirtying up a pier in the Yaquina Bay, somebody might be looking to cut a deal.

By the time all that had come to pass it was burning daylight. We'd none of us eaten so I volunteered to pick up the tab for breakfast at Georgies.

Between the serving of coffee and the awaiting of our orders, Bernie, most disappointed bagels were not on the menu, decided there were more unanswered questions.

"So okay, Mr. Sleuth, you've spilled it all except the rotten kids' solution. What were they going to do with Lorna?"

"Ah, yes. I believe one would call it an even swap. The captain of the *YUKIKO MARU* planned to take the lady off Taffy's hands in exchange for an extra package of drugs. I don't believe our courts will be able to charge the S. O. B. with attempted murder or even complicity in a kidnapping, as we freed Lorna first. I suspect you guys are not aware that the third world countries still do a thriving business in 'white slavery' but not for the usual reason. Lorna was headed for either China or India. Lovely she is—a youngster she isn't. I suspect a Maharajah would tire of her pretty quick. She might not have even made it as far as a harem. Human organs, my friends, there's where scum do big business today: heart, liver, kidneys, eyes, you name it do not fetch mere peanuts in both those aforementioned countries. Nossir, those organs are worth huge amounts of money across the pond, as the Limeys would say. Doctors are excellent in both places and the corrupt ones are able to keep a human captive alive for quite some time. Sadly, our Lorna, though deeply mourned, would have disappeared forever."

"Our four first class citizens desired just that. They would then have fessed up to their switching of grades, thrown themselves upon the mercy of their parents' court, studied like mad over the summer, and taken the English test over again in the fall. No harm, no foul. Taffy's new supply of drugs would have come gratis, probably forever if he could round up more victims for that scuzzbuckets's captain. Who could gather convincing evidence that those kids had kidnapped Lorna? Despite staging the waltzing around nonsense with the ransom notes, no one showed up either time to collect the loot! While Lorna's prints were in Chuck's dump, she wouldn't have been found there. He knows a lot of bums in town and had no trouble shipping her around from dive to dive. I bet she had been gone from Chuck's hovel for quite some time the night I paid him a visit. I suspect the DNA found on the ransom envelope was Jill's, but without a kidnapped body, alive or dead, so what, a mere slap on the wrist might ensue. Everything would have been circumstantial and damn skimpy at that. No, once a drugged Lorna sailed away, there would have been no dire results for them; they'd have been completely in the clear. And there, my good young friends, you have it."

"So okay, I buy all of what you've told us," said Sam, "but what I wanna know is how come baby Jill was elected leader?"

"That little viper wasn't involved in any election, she flat claimed the position. You have but to take a gander at the other three losers to understand the why—she's always ordered and they've always followed. I surmise Doctor Dad and Country Club Mom have been so busy with their own affairs they never bothered to cast a concerned eye on their daughter. Money has a loud voice. Let the cook or the chauffeur do the parenting for them, they haven't time! Besides, she comes from quality stock and will be fine, it is ordained. Still, you are asking how come one that young, and certainly well to do, is so twisted? Friend Bernie can furnish the answer."

"Ah yes, my friends, what really decides who and what we humans are? I submit there are three important factors. As to their order, controversy intrudes here: inherited gene structure and or the environment. To those, I also add desire; the desire for money, power, recognition, parental approval, peer acceptance, you name it. List them in your own order of importance if you so desire; however, exclude none. And do not overlook plain greed!"

"So where should the blame for creature Jill fall? First and foremost, nail Doctor Dad and Country Club Mom; not for their biological combination of genes, rather for their lack of parental interest. Dad is way too busy to truly notice his daughter's needs, nor outlook; except, he convinced her she was destined for great things. He never bothered to inform his Jill she would have to *earn* them. Mom is only interested in another rubber of Bridge along with Country Club gossip and her next martoonie."

"Jill, in the final analysis however, is to blame for herself. Of the temperament inclined to run everybody off, she then bitches when they fail to return and dance for her. She also refuses to engage in any such thing as a touch of introspection; therefore, as she is very angry, she is also dangerous and will make everyone within her sphere of influence suffer. Jill will be offered psychological help in jail. I rather suspect though, like the dedicated alcoholic, she will be the last to admit she is in need of any help."

"For the young among us here, you will find that it's lots of fun when a twosome wrestles on the corncobs. But, never refuse, if by chance the stork brings you the gift of a new life as payment for all that fun to accept your share of the responsibility. Welcome, guide, nurture; give much of your time and—above all—love the new life you have created. Many won't be as lucky. I know what you're thinking, what if the stork drops off one with two heads? In that case, give it a few years and one day you'll be able to hold two different conversations with your kid at the same time, doesn't get better than that. Never forget, every life is precious."

"Uh-huh," said Sam. "Okay, teacher sir, what about the kids in class who constantly create problems, constantly disrupt, constantly make teaching a real pain in the arse. Are they precious, too?"

"Absolutely," replied Bernie, "*but they are precious few*!"

"We've got one more question for Danny," they all shouted. "What made you suspect the *YUKIKO MARU* would be the ship that Lorna would be taking an all expenses paid cruise on?"

Looking wise, I replied, "Ah, me bucko's, sure now and if I were to inform of all me secrets, how could I be sure you'd hire me when trouble she comes a-soft-knocking on your own doors?"

Would you have told them it was nothing more than an out and out flaming hunch? Not bloody likely!

With that, I called for the check, paid the tab, and eased my weary carcass homeward. Once we three were ensconced within doors I informed M & M not to bother me as I was flaming well going to sleep for a week. Happily slipping between clean sheets I bid them both goodnight and settled my head onto one of my limited perks, ye olde down-filled pillow. Soon I found myself chasing over warm sands in pursuit of a nubile young thing clad in a diaphanous gown, one such as those the angels are often pictured wearing. A soft laugh, floating back over the shoulder of the fleeing one, tantalized as the enthralling call of the Desert Song beckoned. I knew 'twould be but a short time before capture would be followed by ecstasy! I stretched forth my arms to happily clasp and enfold soft, pliant curves; those filling my nostrils with the sweet aroma of jasmine. Ah, well-earned bliss!

Distantly, I could hear the constant banging of rifle fire. Must be the Nomads of the desert are knocking one another off again, I thought. Although I was finding it harder to breathe I figured I was just a tad winded from chasing my lovely elusive peach up and down sand dunes. I redoubled my efforts to claim my prize. Finally, stretching to the utmost my eager arms captured a soft, compliant, furry body. *Furry body?*

Suddenly, and strangely, those warm welcoming sands, along with soft curves and bliss, disappeared. Semi-awakened from the disappointment and most rudely interrupted from such a grand dream, I discerned I was now afloat on an angry heaving sea and I could feel the wet. Blast, the craft carrying me must be leaking. There was warm moisture on my feet and I could hardly move. The constant loud banging followed by an increasing keening roar threatened my ears and signaled dire danger. An especially loud thump jolted me totally awake and I found I was completely entangled in the bloody bed clothes. Maggie was lying on my face and Mandy was licking my exposed toes. I hate a lickin' dog! The window blind was slapping itself silly repeatedly slamming against the window frame. Another lousy winter Oregon storm was blowing freely through the open window, happily soaking the end of the bed and my Navajo rug. Aw, the hell with it!

* * *

So that ended case number twenty-two. The lovely Lorna, fully recuperated, really dropped the hammer on those four losers. Bo, Bart, Jill and Taffy are all in the slammer. Filthy Taffy labors in the laundry. At least his clothes should be clean. Our superb Military academies won't be disgraced by the presence of two of them, nor will Stanford by the one. Dear Doctor Dad and

Momsie are no longer welcome in the Country Club. So much for long-standing patrons!

When Lorna came to visit, she brought a lamb pot pie for Mandy, a chicken pot pie for Maggie and a big hug for me. I figured I was well paid.

I charged Diddens a hundred clams for my services, plus *all my expenses* of course. He was so happy to have his Lorna back I had a hard time working up the nerve to present him with that minor tab for Eric's little shindig. You have any idea how much a tinted windshield, including charge for installation, costs for a Chevy Blazer? The judge let my Norwegian pal off with a warning and told him to stay the hell away from Newport.

* * *

Well, here we are, and already almost a year to the day has slipped on by since we brought Lorna home. She is fine and back to teaching; the only change that she's made to her record keeping is to insist on hand delivering her grades. From time to time during her current days of instruction her whole body shudders uncontrollably. Her class does not know why, but we do, don't we? You will be happy to know that as the year has progressed the shudders have become less frequent. However, the Almighty Himself couldn't get her to drink a cup of tea! I understand Jane exchanged the robin and the worm for an eagle and a snake. I think it is her way of kicking butt!

Bernie, as always, is in the pink. Are you ready for his latest?

"*Two Mexican detectives were investigating the murder of Juan Gonzalez. 'How was he killed?' asked one of the detectives. His partner replied, 'He was killed with a golf gun.' 'Ay, caramba,' said Jorge, 'joo know what is a golf gun?' 'No, amigo,' answered Esteban, 'but it sure made a hole in Juan!'*"

He is still acting as my consultant. As usual, we munch bagels at Bad Bascomb's most days. No, I won't tell you what he punished his last one with, I don't believe it myself. But I will tell about the advice he presented me on my latest case, no charge of course!

A young woman came tearing into the office yesterday in a hell of a big lather to hire me, she was positive her dearest pet tortoise had swallowed her engagement ring. She was in such a tearing sweat because her wedding is slated to take place in three days! Unfortunately, she had not discovered her calamitous loss until way too late and, in the interim, she had sold her pet to a guy has a tortoise farm.

"How the hell am I going to find the right tortoise among thousands?" I moaned to my pal.

"Easy," he chortled, "when you walk out among 'em, just keep calling for the mock turtle."

I am going to kill him. I swear, one of these days I will definitely figure out a way to do him in!

* * *

Bill J. is wowing them on the gridiron at Annapolis. Ernesto made the dean's list at Stanford. Sam is selling cars for Diddens and whenever Jane comes to Salem to give me a bad time about some little infraction of federal law, he makes goo-goo eyes at her. I can never figure how he knows she is coming! He keeps asking if I will apprentice him in the PI trade. I believe it's in his blood. Greg and Bo's ex are a steady duo. He is even working on improving academics at Sagen, and he only checks for mail now at the post office. Biff and Burt are making their parents proud in college.

Mandy and Maggie are fine. They spend more time watching out for my

Bet You Don't Know Where Lorna Is! 271

Sandy than they do me, which actually suits me fine. My lady has been getting a little misty-eyed lately when I mention marriage. I do believe I'm wearing her resistance down.

Recently, too, I've noticed this old bod is informing of middle age. Taking short walks have been cramping my legs a tad. I asked Bernie if he thought I was over the hill. As always he was ready for me.

"Being over the hill is much better than being under it!"

You'll be interested to know the one who was slated for great things is still putting the pedal to the medal. She isn't doing it in her Porsche though; now when she slams the pedal down on the machine damned if the sucker doesn't stamp out license plates. Think of all the good leg muscle she is developing as well. As I always say, if a job is worth doing it purely ought to be worth doing over and over and over again! Bo and Bart are also learning a valuable trade. Bo is heavy into weaving baskets; they go over great with the Mexican tourist crowd. Bart has been occupied lately with replacing heels on his fellow cons' boots. He only tacked his thumb to a size fourteen, once. They say his wail of hurt was heard in downtown Salem! You already know where dirty Chuck ended up! He gets to wash all his colleagues' dirty socks. Not to worry, they also help him bathe often. Fortunately, the lye in prison laundry soap used today only leaves a burn on the poor fellow for three or four days.

Diddens century note gathered dust in my thin wallet all year. I had been hanging on to it waiting for just the right investment and finally it came. Friend, if you follow the broomtails then you will remember this was the year that Funny Cide was a shoo-in to take the Triple Crown. The fleet-footed fellow had already won the Kentucky Derby and Pimlico. Thus, yon

Belmont just naturally had to belong to him as well. Bernie was determined to watch him win. So was I. It was the seventh of June, the day for the big race. 'Beat the Odds' Clyde had advised against my wagering on the darlin' horse and I knew he would soon bellyache for a week, but did I care a whit? After much careful thought I had decided to put Diddens' C-note on Funny Cide's nose to win going away. After the race, I figured a leisurely trip over to Dick's Sporting Goods to buy a new golf cart with my winnings had to be a most appropriate idea. After all, getting in and out of the cart would be good exercise for my aging bones and I would then have a handy shelf to carry the beer. Slugging a six-pack along in the bag the way I'd been doing had lately begun to put a permanent slope in my right shoulder. I knew that had to be why I was constantly slicing my drives!

Reader friend, I am reluctant to do this but I suppose it is only fair to leave you with one final Bernie gem:

"A three year old toddler, shedding silent tears, sat on a log in the middle of a southwestern desert state park. On the ground in front of her, coiled and ready to strike, there reposed a huge rattlesnake."

"Suddenly the toddler leaned forward toward the menacing snake and yelled, 'I wanna banana!' So okay Sir Sleuth, had death flown in on doomsday wings?"

"Doubtless, you will opine the kid got zapped right between the eyes! Didn't happen. A Mexican rattler, and not bi-lingual, he was not of thee knowing meaning of English word—banana! Hissing angrily, he slithered off to the next log where a muchacho sat munching on an enchilada."

I heard that, pal, and I am in complete accord!

BET YOU DON'T KNOW WHERE LORNA IS!

JACK JUDGE

Other books of his are also available

Ordering information

Shipping and handling $4.00

Mojac Books

P. O. Box 68, Lincoln City, Oregon 97367

Phone: 541-994-3472

E-mail: jjudge@charter.net